"As in the four previous books in the series, Bowen's great strength is her endearing Welsh characters, from the modest Evan to such amusing locals as the saucy barmaid and the rival chapel preachers. This mystery is sure to appeal to those who prefer old-fashioned, heartwarming stories." —*Publishers Weekly*

Praise for
EVAN AND ELLE:

"A light confection of a mystery, sweetened with the author's obvious affection for her characters, as well as for all things Welsh." —*Publishers Weekly*

"A sweet and sunny read."
—*San Francisco Sunday Examiner & Chronicle*

"Eva⋯ ⋯ontinue to charm and ⋯ —*Kirkus Reviews*

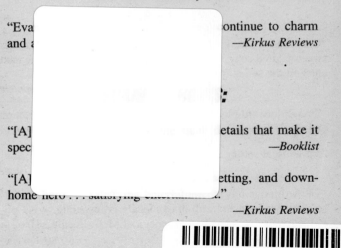

"[A] ⋯ ⋯etails that make it spec⋯ —*Booklist*

"[A] ⋯ ⋯etting, and down-home hero . . . satisfying entertainment."
—*Kirkus Reviews*

continued on next page . . .

EVAN CAN WAIT

Rhys Bowen

BERKLEY PRIME CRIME, NEW YORK

EVAN CAN WAIT

A Berkley Prime Crime Book / published by arrangement with
St. Martin's Press, LLC

PRINTING HISTORY
St. Martin's Press hardcover edition / February 2001
Berkley Prime Crime mass-market edition / December 2001

Visit our website at
www.penguinputnam.com

ISBN: 0-425-18276-2

Berkley Prime Crime Books are published
by The Berkley Publishing Group,
a division of Penguin Putnam Inc.,
375 Hudson Street, New York, New York 10014.
The name BERKLEY PRIME CRIME and the BERKLEY PRIME CRIME
design are trademarks belonging to Penguin Putnam Inc.

PRINTED IN THE UNITED STATES OF AMERICA

10 9 8 7 6 5 4 3 2 1

THIS BOOK IS dedicated to my two newest readers, Sam and Elizabeth, by their adoring grandmother.

I'd like to thank forensic specialist Mike Bowers for his advice on decomposing bodies. Thanks to Susan Davies and Megan Owen, who are my eyes and ears on the spot in North Wales. Also thanks, as always, to my faithful team of advance readers and merciless critics—John, Clare, Jane, and Tom.

Llanfair and its inhabitants exist only in my imagination. The rest of North Wales is real, as are the background stories about World War II. A German bomber really did vanish without a trace and the contents of the National Gallery really were stored in a slate mine.

Glossary of Welsh Words

Bach/fach — small. Used as a term of endearment much as the English say "love" and "dear." *Bach* for a male, *fach* for a female.

Ble ryt ti? — Where are you? (pronounced *blay root tea*)

Cariad — darling, honey (term of endearment) (pronounced *car-ee-ad*)

Cigydd — butcher (from *cig*—meat) (pronounced *kigeth*)

Diolch yn fawr — Thank you very much (pronounced *diolch in vower*)

Escob Annwyl — literally "Dear Bishop" (similar to "Good Heavens") (pronounced *escobe an-wheel*)

Fron Heulog — Sunny Hillside (name of farm) (pronounced *vron high-log*)

Gloch las — blue bell (pronounced like Scottish *loch*); (*las* — pronounced *lass*)

Iechyd da — Cheers, good health (pronounced *yacky dah*)

Mam — mother (pronounced as it looks)

Nain — Grandma (pronounced *nine*)

Noswaith dda — Good evening (pronounced *nos-why-th thah*)

Or gore — all right, okay (pronounced *or gor-ay*)

Pobl y Cwm — *People of the Valley* (a popular Welsh soap opera) (pronounced *Pobble a Cum*)

Tad — father (pronounced as it looks)

Ty Gwyn — White House (pronounced *tee gwin*)

Yr Wyddfa — Welsh name for Snowdon (pronounced *Er Withva*)

EVAN CAN WAIT

ONE

Do I remember anything of those days? It's as clear as if it was yesterday. I remember the first time she noticed me. It was at Johnny Morgan's going-away party. He'd just joined the Royal Welch Fusiliers and he was being sent to France. I thought he looked the cat's whisker in that uniform. All the girls did, too. They were all clustering around him, giving him their addresses and promising to write to him. Then She came into the room. I didn't recognize her at first. Then someone said, "Mwfanwy? It's never Mwfanwy Davies."

And she laughed and said, "You're right. It's not Mwfanwy Davies. The name's Ginger from now on, honey. Ginger, like Ginger Rogers." She did a pretty good American accent, too.

The girls all crowded around her. "Your mam's going to kill you," Gwynneth Morgan said.

"She's already tried, but there's not much she can do about it, is there?" She put her hand to her platinum blond hair. "I can't unbleach it. She'll have to wait until it grows out. And anyway I like it and she can't tell me what to do with my own hair." She pushed through the

*circle of girls and went over to the punch bowl. "Just
wait until I get to Hollywood, then she'll be sorry, won't
she?"*

*"So how are you getting to Hollywood, then?" one of
the boys asked. "I don't think the train from Blenau goes
there."*

*Some of the other kids laughed, but Ginger looked at
him coldly. "I'll get there," she said. "Some way or other.
I don't know how yet, but I'll get there."*

*Then she looked at me. She had the clearest blue eyes
and they sparkled when she smiled. "Find me a cigarette,
will you, Trefor love?"*

*I was too young to smoke, but I ran all the way to the
corner shop and bought a packet of Woodbines with all
that was left of my weekly wage packet. I'd just started
as an apprentice at the mine and it was only a few shil-
lings a week. I only kept enough for the cinema and a
beer or two for myself. The rest went straight to my mam.*

*Then I ran all the way back from the shop. By the time
I got back, Mwfanwy was sitting on the sofa with Johnny
Morgan, smoking one of his cigarettes, and she had for-
gotten all about me.*

*That's the way it was with Ginger. I knew I should stay
well clear, but it was too late. I was already in love with
her.*

Trefor Thomas, memories of World War II, recorded.

"Is this it?" Grantley Smith roused himself from the backseat and peered between the two occupants of the front
seats as the Land Rover slowed. Rain was peppering the
windscreen too fiercely for the wipers to handle, but the
frantic swishing allowed brief glimpses of a steep, narrow
road lined with gray stone cottages. A couple of bedrag-
gled sheep cropped the grass beside the stream as the
Land Rover went over a stone humpbacked bridge. It was
early evening and the light was fading fast, yet no wel-
coming lights shone out from windows. In fact, the village
gave the appearance of having shut down for the winter.

"This is it," the driver said without looking around. "The sign said 'Llanfair.' "

"Surely you jest," scoffed Grantley Smith in a voice that had been compared to that of the young Larry Olivier. He swung around to the girl beside him in the backseat. "You must have given us wrong directions, Sandie. I thought I told you to get a printout from the Internet. This can't be right."

"I did get a printout, honestly, I did, Grantley," the girl said, gazing at him with large, pleading eyes. "This has to be the right place. We've been doing exactly what it told us to, all the time you've been asleep."

"You must have taken a wrong turn somewhere," Grantley insisted. "I mean, really, I know we have to get the feel of the place because we're going to be shooting up here, but that doesn't mean that I actually crave a bath in front of the kitchen fire with the slate miners. . . ."

If he expected a laugh, he didn't get one. The other occupants of the vehicle had taken turns at the wheel all the way from London in driving rain while Grantley slept, sprawled in the back.

"If the site is up here, then it makes sense to stay somewhere close," the driver said in a clipped voice. In contrast to Grantley, who worked at looking sleek and mercurial like a young Lord Byron, Edward Ferrers was pink and solid, like an overgrown cherub. "The only big hotels are on the coast and you wouldn't want to commute up this pass every day, would you? I have to be on the spot to keep an eye on the salvage crew. I don't want anything touched when I'm not around."

"Edward and his precious plane," Grantley muttered. "Nobody's touching my toys!" He took out a packet of Gitanes and lit one, filling the car with pungent, herby fumes. Edward looked back in annoyance as the smoke wafted over him.

"Jesus, Grantley, so it's not exactly Beverly Hills up here," the passenger in the other front seat drawled in a voice that betrayed transatlantic origins. "I just don't think you'd have found any better accommodation even if we'd stayed in one of those hotels on the coast." He was an older man, dressed in a checked shirt, old jeans, suede waistcoat, and a faded black French beret. If the words "Movie Director" had been printed across his back, his profession could not have been more obvious. "This place is supposed to be okay."

"Howard, we all know that you are the intrepid one." Grantley rested his elbows on the two front seats so that his face was now between them. "Your definition of quite good is sleeping in a tent on the African veldt when the hyenas aren't biting your toes. Your idea of luxury is probably an outhouse with running water."

"It will be fine, Grantley. Just shut up," Edward said tersely. "I've made the reservation and if you don't like it, you can find somewhere else in the morning, okay?"

"Keep your hair on, Edward," Grantley said. "If you two have discovered this little gem, then I'm sure it is just perfect. My only question is, where the devil is it? We're almost out of the village again." He moved across to the side window and cleared a circle of condensation with his hand. "This really doesn't look like the kind of place anyone in his right mind would build a luxury hotel. Wait—there's some kind of sign on the left. In front of that big white building . . ."

The sign was swinging wildly in the wind and it took them a while to make out the red dragon on it.

"It's only the local pub," Edward said.

"Thank God. It looked positively dismal." Grantley gave a long, dramatic sigh. "In fact, everything about this place looks dismal. Look at those shops over there. R. Evans. G. Evans—you obviously have to be called Evans to live in this place, and what the devil is *'Cigydd'*?"

"It has a window full of meat, Grantley. I think even you can figure that one out," Howard muttered, but Grantley went on, "It's a bloody foreign country! Whose crazy idea was it to come to Wales in the middle of winter anyway?"

"You were excited when I told you about it," Edward said. "You were the one who thought it would make a great documentary."

Howard put his hand on Edward's arm. "Let's stop and ask someone."

Edward laughed. "Any suggestions? The place isn't exactly pulsing with life."

As if on cue a door opened, light shone out, and a young man in uniform appeared. He was wearing a navy raincoat and when he noticed the severity of the rain, he stood in the doorway, turning up his collar, before heading out into the street.

Grantley gave a delighted laugh. "Incredible. They even have policemen in this godforsaken place. Don't let him get away, Edward," as the policeman was clearly about to sprint for cover. "Now let's just pray he speaks English. People do speak English here, don't they, Edward?"

"It's not Kazakhstan, Grantley. It's Wales," Edward said. "I expect they'll understand you if you wave your arms a lot, like you do in France."

"My French is bloody good," Grantley said. "Go on, catch up with him."

They pulled to a halt beside the policeman, who stopped obediently, rain plastering dark hair to his face. He was a young man, broad shouldered, with a pleasant boyish smile. "Can I help you gentlemen?" he asked. His voice betrayed just a trace of a Welsh lilt.

"We're trying to find a hotel called the Everest Inn." Howard leaned across Edward. "It's supposed to be around here but I guess we must have missed it somehow."

The policeman gestured to his left. "It's just up the road past the village. You'll come to the big stone gateposts. Turn in there and you'll see it off to the right. In fact, you can't miss it."

"Is it all right? A decent sort of place?" Grantley leaned forward from the backseat.

"I haven't stayed there myself, look you, but it's very

posh," the constable said. "I understand it's got five stars."

"Well, thanks a lot, Officer," Edward said. "We mustn't keep you. You're getting very wet."

"Oh, we're used to that kind of thing around here, sir," the constable said. "It rains quite often."

He gave them a friendly grin, then crossed the street behind the car.

"There you are. All that panic for nothing," Edward said as they drove on.

"Panic? Who was panicking? It was just concern born from exhaustion." Grantley sank back into his seat and took another draw on his cigarette.

"I like that. You've slept all the way here." Howard gave a dry chuckle.

"Ah, but we don't all have your stamina, Howard," Grantley said smoothly. "All that endurance built up tramping through jungles at night, avoiding *E. coli* and cholera and not getting hacked to death with machetes by gangs of child soldiers."

"One of these days you'll go too far, Grantley," Howard said.

"Oh, I don't think so," Grantley said. "I don't think so for a moment." He leaned forward again, grabbing their shoulders as he peered out of the windscreen. "Oh look, there it is!"

To their right the shape of a large building loomed through the rain, lights twinkling on the wet tarmac of the car park.

"Christ, Edward," Grantley exclaimed as they swung off the road up to the car park. "You see, I was right. You did take a wrong turn somewhere. You've landed us in bloody Switzerland!"

The building revealed itself as an overgrown rock and timber chalet, complete with carved wooden balconies adorned with boxes of late geraniums.

"Either Switzerland or Disneyland, I'm not sure which," he went on, giggling like an overgrown schoolboy. "It's delightfully monstrous, isn't it? You know, I think this is going to be fun after all."

Howard Bauer and Edward Ferrers exchanged a quick glance that Grantley, still gazing up at the building, didn't notice.

TWO

CONSTABLE EVAN EVANS often regretted that the one window in his little sub-police station faced toward the mountains and not onto the street. Firstly, he couldn't see what was going on in the village from his desk—an oversight he had reported to his superiors more than once—and secondly because he found it a constant distraction to be able to look up at his beloved mountains when he was bogged down in paperwork, as he was today.

It was time for his quarterly expense report. He knew in advance that he was going to receive a rebuke for turning the heating on in mid-October, but his superiors down in Caernarfon and at HQ in Colwyn Bay had no idea how cold it could be, a thousand feet higher on the flanks of Mount Snowdon. He glanced out of the window at the mountain slopes and sighed. It was a sparkling day, after almost a week of rain. New rivers were cascading down the steep slopes in bright parallel ribbons. The lower slopes glowed with emerald green grass on which raindrops still sparkled like diamonds. The sheep looked like advertisements for laundry bleach. Even the rockfaces glowed warmly in the soft November light.

A perfect day for walking or climbing, and he was stuck in an office. It had rained all weekend so that he had been trapped indoors, watching rugby on the telly and playing Scrabble with Bronwen. The latter hadn't been a good experience; she was too well-read to make it a fair game.

The moment Bronwen came into his thoughts, his gaze went to the shell of the ruined cottage, perched high above the village. An English couple had owned it until arsonists burned it down. Was it an impractical dream to think that he might be able to rebuild it, finally giving him a place of his own? He was sure that the English owners would have claimed on their insurance and wouldn't be likely to return. They'd probably be only too glad to sell it for a song, but he'd still have to get permission to rebuild from the National Park Service. They were very sticky about issuing building permits, but it was worth a try. He doodled the shape of a cottage, with solid walls and smoke coming out of its chimney, on the edge of his notepad until the sound of the telephone made him jump.

"Constable Evans?" A woman's voice. "It's P. C. Jones from HQ. Chief Inspector Meredith would like to see you right away."

"Damn," Evan muttered as he got up. It was never good news if the old man wanted to see him right away. As he got into his car and drove through the village of Llanfair and down the pass toward Caernarfon, he tried to think of what he might have done wrong this time. He couldn't come up with anything, though. The only things his chief had cause to complain about were the times he'd poked his nose into murder investigations. And even then he hadn't been able to make too much fuss, since Evan had been instrumental in solving several major cases.

There had been times when his superiors had suggested that he might want to apply for a transfer to the plainclothes branch. But when he'd finally taken the plunge and sent in his application, they'd turned him down. Oh, they'd been very nice about it. Nothing to do with his ability or lack of it, they'd told him. But the directive had come from Colwyn Bay to appoint more women detectives before hiring any more men.

He swung the car into the Caernarfon police station car park and took a deep breath. Better get it over with as quickly as possible. Just as he neared the door, a slight, sandy-haired man in a fawn raincoat was just coming out.

"Hello there, boyo, fancy seeing you," Sergeant Watkins called to Evan. "Don't tell me you've found another body—I've been enjoying a quiet life for the past few weeks."

Evan grinned. "No body, Sarge. My chief wants to see me."

"Been a bad boy, have you? Cheating on your expense report?"

"Not that I know of," Evan said. "I'd better get in there and find out. The suspense is killing me."

"And I've got to get back to my thrilling stakeout at Tesco's."

"Tesco's? Is someone planning to rob superstores then?"

"Nothing so glamorous. Someone's been nicking Christmas puddings and wrapping paper—non-perishables that have been turning up on market stalls a week later. We think it's a local gang but they're quite good at it. The security cameras haven't managed to catch them yet." He rolled his eyes. "Sometimes I think a quiet life is overrated."

Evan went into the building and was surprised by the pleasant warmth. They certainly had their heating on high enough. So they couldn't begrudge him his humble gas fire.

Chief Inspector Meredith was a large, florid man

with sagging jowls and rolled up shirtsleeves. He looked up as Evan came into his office. "Ah, Evans. Good man. Glad you got here so quickly." He pointed to a chair. "Take a pew."

"Is something wrong, sir?" Evan couldn't help asking.

"Nothing. I called you down here because I've got a little assignment for you, strictly hush-hush at the moment." He leaned confidentially forward, although they were alone in the room. "I've had a request for police assistance from the Ministry of Defense."

"Oh, yes, sir?" Evan's brain was racing. IRA terrorists or Libyans might be infiltrating through the mountains at this very moment and he was being called in to help catch them. . . .

"As I understand it, it's something to do with raising a German bomber from Llyn Llydaw."

"A German bomber, sir?" Evan wasn't sure he'd heard right. "A plane, you mean?"

"Of course I mean a plane. A German bomber that crashed into the lake during the Second World War. They're attempting to raise it, so I understand. Don't ask me why after all this time. Another bloody waste of government money, I expect. Oh, and a crew is going to be filming the whole thing, so naturally they don't want local people getting in the way." He paused again. "Your job will be to keep the gawkers away and make sure everything goes smoothly for them. Got it?"

"Yes, sir." Evan felt deflated. From terrorist fighter to security guard in one fell swoop.

"They're staying up at the Everest Inn," the chief inspector went on. "They'd like you to make contact with them."

"Actually, I've already met them, sir," Evan said.

"How the devil did you manage that? I understand they wanted to sneak in with no fanfare. The damned Llanfair bush telegraph again, I suppose."

"No, just pure chance," Evan said. "They stopped to

ask me for directions a couple of days ago. They looked like film people. One was actually wearing a beret."

"Very observant of you, Constable." The chief inspector gave Evan a patronizing smile. Evan smiled back, through clenched teeth.

He got to his feet. "Will that be all, sir?"

"Yes, I think so. Go and introduce yourself to them and offer them any assistance they need. I've told them you know the area like the back of your hand. You might want to show them the best way up to the lake, to transport their heavy equipment."

"I hope they're fit, sir," Evan said dryly. "It's a stiffish climb."

"I imagine they'll be driving up there—Land Rovers, that kind of thing. I suppose there is some kind of track you can get a vehicle up, isn't there?"

"I wouldn't want to drive it myself," Evan said. "But I suppose it might be possible."

The chief inspector smiled at Evan. "Do your best, Constable. We don't want any complaints. I understand they're pretty high-powered types and these film people can be temperamental."

"Very good, sir," Evan said. "Will you be sending a replacement to cover for me in the village, if I'm stuck on the mountain all day?"

"I'll put it on a squad car route, and have them cruise by from time to time," the inspector said. "I don't think there's enough crime in Llanfair to warrant an extra man up there full-time." He looked down at his papers again. "Off you go then."

Dismissed—like a schoolboy from the headmaster's office. "Very observant of you, Constable." The words echoed through his head.

He strode down the hallway, intent only on getting to his car and driving as fast as he could back to Llanfair.

"Aren't you speaking to me now, Constable Evans?"

Evan turned at the sound of her voice. "Oh, hello, Glynis, or should I say Detective Constable Davies?" She even looked different. Her red hair had been cut into a sleek bob and she was wearing a very masculine, gray pin-striped pantsuit, which somehow managed to look feminine on her. "What are you doing here? I thought you were still in training at HQ."

"Oh, I am," she gave him a happy smile. "I'm shadowing D.I. Johnson this week and he has a case he wants to discuss with our D.I. Hughes. It's nice being back on my old stomping ground. I hope they assign me here when I finish training."

"So you're having a good time then?" he asked.

"Brilliant." Another big smile. "I was worried that they might resent my being a woman, but everyone has been very supportive so far. They're all really nice to me."

Maybe that has something to do with your dating the chief constable's nephew, Evan thought.

"Well, nice seeing you again, Glynis," he added. "I have to get back to work."

"This detective stuff is a lot of fun, Evan," she called after him. "You should apply. You'd be good at it."

He had the grace to turn back with a little smile as he pushed open the door. Her words echoed through his head as he drove back up the pass. And she had called him Constable Evans. To think that he had once thought she fancied him. He was too bloody naive, that was his problem.

It wasn't her fault, he told himself as he calmed down. She was too good to stay a glorified office girl for long. She was brainy, wasn't she? She had a university education and she was very savvy when it came to computers. She'd probably make a bloody good detective, too. And it wasn't her fault that she was a smashing looker.

The road began to climb as it left the town of Llanberis with its long, glistening lake dropping away to

his left. He wound down the window and crisp mountain air rushed in to meet him. It smelled of green and
growing things. A flight of seagulls dipped to land on
the lake. On the breeze came the distant bleating of
sheep.

He had Bronwen, he reminded himself. He was a
lucky man. She, too, was smart and good-looking.
What more could a bloke want? He knew the answer
right away—something more to offer her than being a
humble bobby on the beat. Oh well, there was no point
in dwelling on it. He'd had his chances and he'd turned
them down. He'd just better make sure that he did his
job and did it damned well.

───── THREE ─────

EVAN FOUND THE filmmakers alone in the paneled oak bar of the Everest Inn. They were seated at a table close to the fire, which blazed away in a huge river rock fireplace. There was a pot of tea and a half-eaten plate of scones in front of them. The rest of the table was covered in papers and maps, plus an ashtray full of cigarette stubs. The two armchairs by the fire were occupied by two young men, one dark, one fair. Evan recognized the fair, chubby one as the driver who had asked him for directions. He was dressed in jeans and a denim shirt and looked very much at home in this setting of paneled walls and hunting trophies.

The other armchair was occupied by a slim, dark-haired young man. He lay sprawled across the chair with one leg thrown over the arm and a cigarette dangling from his fingers.

They were direct contrasts, Evan decided, figures from an allegorical romantic painting of good and evil, Cain and Abel, day and night.

The older man who had worn a beret was sitting on an upright red leather chair, with a notepad in one hand

and a half-empty glass of whisky in the other. Evan could now see why he wore a beret. Thin strands of hair were combed across a pronounced bald spot.

The fourth member of the party, whom Evan hadn't seen before, was a pale, slender girl who perched on the edge of a straight-backed chair, a pen poised over a clipboard. She was too thin, Evan thought, eyeing her more closely. Not unattractive but definitely too thin. He didn't care for chubby girls, but this one looked as if a good breeze would blow her away.

They all looked up as his footsteps clattered on the slate-tiled floor.

"Oh, it's our helpful policeman," said the dark young man. His voice was languidly upper-class. He gave Evan a charming smile and motioned toward the table. "Grab a chair and help yourself to tea. I don't think it's too stewed. There should be a clean cup because Howard's already started on the scotch. I'm Grantley Smith, by the way." He held out his hand. "I'm producing our little epic. Howard here needs no introduction, of course. World-famous Hollywood, Oscarwinning director . . ."

He let the words hang in the air. Evan nodded to the older man. "I'm afraid I'm not too well up on films," he said.

"I doubt you'd have heard of me anyway," the older man said. "I got an Oscar in the documentary category."

"*The Heart of Darkness.* About genocide in a civil war in Africa. Very dramatic stuff. He's very respected within the profession, aren't you, Howard?" Grantley Smith gave him an admiring smile.

Evan sensed an undercurrent of tension. He pulled over another upright chair and sat. "I'm Constable Evans, sir," he said. "My chief inspector has assigned me to help you. I understand you're planning to make a film about a German plane?"

The fair-haired man leaned forward. "Actually, the

primary object of the expedition is to raise the plane," he said in an accent that might have originated in Yorkshire but had been polished by contact with the South. "I'm Edward Ferrers, by the way."

"He's our expert expedition leader—the World War Two plane buff," Grantley chimed in. "Some men go trainspotting. Edward drools over old planes. *Chacqu'un à son gout,* I suppose."

Edward shot him a momentary glance of annoyance. "I'm overseeing the whole business," he said. "It's a very delicate operation. That's why we need you around, Constable—to make sure nobody tampers with the equipment or generally gets in the way."

"Nobody has any desire to tamper with your equipment, Edward." Grantley Smith stubbed out his cigarette fiercely in the ashtray and took another from the packet. "And you make it sound as if the filmmaking is merely incidental."

"Well, it is. I could get the plane raised with or without you. It's just nice to have it documented for the museum. And must you smoke those filthy things, Grantley?"

"Don't suggest I give up my Gitanes, Edward. One has so few pleasures in life, don't you think?"

Evan detected a distinct chill. He cleared his throat.

"So I understand the plane is in Llyn Llydaw," he said. "You know that for a fact, do you? I've been past that lake a hundred times and I've never seen anything looking like a plane in it."

Edward Ferrers's smile was patronizing. "It's a deep lake, Constable. You couldn't actually see the plane from the surface. We sent down underwater cameras and located it last summer. Maybe you noticed our camera team."

Evan returned the smile. "Not especially, sir. We have all kinds of strange people on the mountain during the summer—most of them with cameras."

Edward cleared his throat. "This would have been a

little larger than your average Sony and luckily it confirmed what I had suspected. I've been writing a history of wartime plane crashes in Snowdonia. As you probably know, an awful lot of planes were lost up here during the war, both RAF and enemy bombers. The mountains and the cloud proved a lethal combination. This particular Dornier-17 is shown on German lists as missing. We know it took part in a bombing raid on October 11, 1940. It was attacked by Spitfires and caught fire. But then it disappeared. Judging by the flight path it must have taken, and the fact that no debris was ever spotted, I assumed it had to have slid into one of the deep lakes up here. Finally we located it, a couple of hundred feet down and pretty much intact. So we're hoping to raise it in one piece, maybe with its flyers still inside it."

"You mean, men might still be in there?"

"Oh yes, I hope so. She carried a crew of three. I'm hoping their uniforms are still identifiable."

"I think it's creepy." The girl spoke for the first time. A well-bred little voice. "I don't want to watch when you fish out bodies."

"You are just too sensitive for words, Sandie, my love." Grantley leaned over and patted her knee. She gave him a shy smile.

"Anyway, they won't be bodies," Edward went on. "They will be skeletons. If they are still sitting in their correct seats, we'll be able to identify them."

"That could be a touching moment if the brother gets here." Grantley turned to Howard.

"The brother?" Evan asked.

Grantley roused himself slightly from his recumbent position. "We're trying to get some human interest into this," he said. "A fifty-year-old plane coming up from the depths might be exciting to some people like Edward, but it won't sell to the BBC. When Edward came to me about the project, I decided we needed to expand the idea to sell it. I'm calling my documentary *Wales*

at War. We've located a woman who was evacuated
here as a young girl and we're bringing in the brother
of Gerhart Eichner, who was the pilot of the plane."

Howard Bauer looked up from the list he had been
studying. "And you might be able to help us here, Constable. Can you ask around the village for us?"

"Great idea, Howard," Grantley added. "We can get
some old biddies to share their wartime memories—
you know, 'I can remember when we had to queue up
three days to get a cod's head to boil and it had to feed
a family of ten and we were grateful,' that kind of
thing. The public laps up other people's hardships,
doesn't it?"

"I haven't lived in the village very long." Evan hesitated. Usually he was more than willing to be helpful—Bronwen described him as an overgrown Boy
Scout—but he hadn't exactly warmed to these people.
He had the feeling that he could easily be turned into
their general dog's body if he wasn't careful, "I could
ask around for you," he said slowly. "Better still, why
don't you come down to the pub one evening? Some
of the older men like Charlie Hopkins know everything
there is to know about the local people."

"I don't think we want it generally known that we're
up here filming." Grantley Smith lowered his voice.
"I'd rather not broadcast our presence in the pub. In
fact, I'd much prefer that you asked around discreetly
and let us know who might be worth interviewing. If
everyone knows, we'll have sightseers traipsing across
the set and spoiling our shots."

"I don't think you'll be able to keep the locals from
finding out what you're doing," Evan said. "Everyone
knows everyone else's business in a village like this."

"Then your job is to make sure they stay away, Constable," Grantley said, a pleasant smile still on his face.
"Time is money when you're filming."

"In which case we don't want to waste too much
footage on interviewing old biddies and local color,

Grantley," Edward warned. "It's only a sixty-minute documentary, not a six-part series."

"Now there's a thought." Grantley turned to Howard again. "We could always stretch it to a six-parter if we get enough material. *Wales at War*—the mini-series."

"We'll be lucky to get enough material to fill a sixty-minute slot," Howard said dryly. "I'm not sure how hot anyone is on the old days anymore. We need up-to-date stuff—"

"Like children being hacked to pieces in Africa," Grantley finished for him. "Well, you'd know all about that, wouldn't you, Howard?"

"So when exactly do you want to start?" Evan asked, feeling uncomfortable with vibes he didn't understand.

"Right away," Edward said. "We have the salvage equipment and operators standing by. If we could go up to the lake tomorrow, we'll be able to assess whether we can get our equipment in by vehicle or whether we'll have to have it helicoptered in."

A well-funded expedition, Evan thought. Where was the money coming from? And which of these men controlled the purse strings?

As he walked back down the pass from the Everest Inn and drew level with the two chapels, he saw that new texts had been posted on the billboards outside each. Capel Bethel on his left today had chosen as its text "I to the hills will lift mine eyes." Psalm 121. Capel Beulah, on his right, had replied with "Every valley shall be exalted and every hill made low." Isaiah. Thus did Reverends Parry Davies and Powell-Jones wage polite but ongoing warfare.

As he paused to smile at the billboards, the side door of Capel Beulah opened and a group of schoolchildren came running out. They grinned at Evan as they ran past.

" 'Ello, Mr. Evans. Are you looking for Miss Price?" Terry Jenkins called to him. "She's just coming out, I think."

"She's wearing ever such a pretty dress today, Mr. Evans," young Megan Hopkins added slyly. "I think she looks lovely."

Evan was well aware that the schoolchildren were determined to get him married off to their teacher and thought that he was being painfully slow about it. Sometimes he thought he was being slow as well. It was just that he was enjoying things as they were at the moment—his needs taken care of by motherly Mrs. Williams, free time for hiking and climbing at the weekends, and Bronwen living just up the street in the little house attached to the school.

As he stood there, Bronwen came out of the chapel door. The stiff breeze caught wisps of ash-blond hair and blew them around her face like a halo. She was wearing that blue denim dress again—the one that matched her eyes—with her Little Red Riding Hood red cape over it. The cape swirled in the wind as if it was alive. Evan had no problem agreeing that she did look very pretty.

"Hello, what are you doing?" he called as she hurried toward him. "I didn't know you'd joined the rival chapel. Teaching Sunday School now, is it?"

"No, thank you." She wrinkled her nose. "I like my Sundays free and childless. Mrs. Powell-Jones bullied me into helping her with the Christmas pageant this year. You know what it's like trying to say no to her."

Evan nodded. He knew very well. "So how's it going so far?"

"We've just had our first meeting and already there are big problems. Mrs. Powell-Jones is insisting that the Angel Gabriel was male and none of my top-class boys will volunteer to wear a white nightie."

Evan laughed. "Mrs. P.-J is directing, of course."

"Directing, making costumes, painting scenery, and probably making the sandwiches for tea afterward. I'm there to hold the clipboard and say, 'Yes, ma'am.' "

"Sounds like the people I've just met up at the Everest Inn," Evan said.

"Oh, the film crew? Then the kids were right. They are shooting a film in the area."

"How the devil do they know so quickly?" Evan asked. "I really think that inhabitants of Llanfair could hire themselves out to the Secret Service."

"Glynis Rees's cousin works as bellboy at the Inn. He carried up their bags and he saw cameras and rolls of film. And the old man was wearing a beret. And they asked how far it was to Llyn Llydaw. Are they going to make a new King Arthur epic? Wasn't Excalibur supposed to have come from the middle of Llyn Llydaw?"

"Nothing so exciting, I'm afraid. They're shooting a documentary about raising a World War Two plane from the lake—only please don't spread it around. They want it kept hush-hush."

"Fat chance around here." Bronwen laughed. "They'll have every child in the village showing up at the weekend offering to help them."

Evan frowned. "I've been assigned to keep sightseers away. And I'm not looking forward to it, I can tell you. They seem like a temperamental bunch."

"It's a shame I'm not still married," Bronwen said.

Evan swung around to glare at her.

She smiled. "I didn't mean it like that. It's wonderful that I'm not still married. What I meant was that my ex-husband would have been in heaven if they'd been raising a World War Two plane nearby. He'd have been up there, volunteering to hold their bags and make their tea. He was obsessed with old planes, especially World War Two planes."

They started to walk together down the deserted street. The wind blew hard into their faces.

"Very boring," she said and shuddered. "I can't believe I ever married him."

They walked on in uneasy silence. Evan had questions he wanted to ask, but didn't. They had respected each other's privacy for so long. He knew she'd tell him when she was good and ready.

"My, but it's been a grand day," Evan said. "Pity it's a weekday. Last weekend was so wet and dismal."

"Only dismal for you because you lost at Scrabble twice." She gave him a challenging smile.

"Don't rub it in. I'm aware of my intellectual inadequacy."

"Don't be silly. I had to read a lot of boring books at University and I picked up a lot of useless knowledge." They had reached the gate to the school playground. There was smoke coming out of the schoolhouse chimney. "Shall we do something this weekend if the fine weather lasts?" she asked.

"I don't think I'm likely to have the weekend free," Evan said. "I suspect the film crew will work whenever the weather is fine."

"It's not fair," Bronwen said. "They're always making you work weekends."

"It's the same for all policemen. When there's work to be done, we work. You don't find detectives taking days off when they're on a murder case, do you?"

"Supervising old planes is hardly the same as chasing a murder suspect," Bronwen said. "Never mind. You'll have your evenings free, won't you? Maybe I can try another of those French recipes I learned."

"Maybe you could teach me," Evan said.

She looked surprised.

"I've got to learn to cook if I want to live on my own sometime."

"Now that's a very good sign," she said.

"Sign of what?" he prodded.

"That you're finally growing up," she shot back. Then she rested her fingers lightly on his arm. "Are you still thinking about old Rhodri's cottage?"

He nodded. "I haven't had the time to find out what channels I'd have to go through to get hold of it. I'd imagine those English people would be only too willing to sell it, but it's on National Park land, isn't it? Any plans to rebuild would have to go through them. And I understand nothing is easy with them. But I'm still thinking about it."

"I think it's a lovely idea." Bronwen smiled up at him. "And it's plenty big enough, isn't it?"

Big enough for two, Evan thought as he walked home alone. Is that what Bronwen was thinking? And Bronwen liked the idea. He was amazed how happy that made him. He planned to marry someday, of course. And he was pretty sure that he wanted to spend the rest of his life with Bronwen. So get on with it, boyo, he told himself. You can't go through life suffering from a major case of cold feet.

FOUR

A PLEASANT HUM of conversation greeted Evan as he pushed open the heavy oak door to the Red Dragon pub that evening. For once, he wasn't looking forward to an evening of beer and good company. It wasn't going to be easy, steering a middle course between the locals' curiosity about the new project and his instructions to keep it hush-hush. He suspected that every man in that bar knew almost as much about the newly arrived filmmakers as he did and was waiting to pump him for more details.

"Here he is now!" Charlie Hopkins looked up as he lifted a full glass from the bar. "Young Betsy was wondering what was keeping you, Evan *bach*. She was scared you were hobnobbing with all those movie starlets!"

Betsy the barmaid turned her wide blue eyes on him. Her hair was bright red this week and the effect was alarmingly Little Orphan Annie. Ever since she'd almost been seduced by a great opera singer who had suggested she change her hair color, she had been experimenting. Lately, she seemed to have settled on varieties of red.

"I don't see what movie starlets have got that I haven't," Betsy said, her gaze holding Evan's. "I've got plenty of everything in all the right places, haven't I, Evan *bach*?"

Evan had noticed that Betsy was wearing what should have been a demure sweater. It was white and fuzzy, with a high turtleneck. Unfortunately, it was also about three sizes too small for her and emphasized every curve. Evan also suspected that she was wearing some kind of padded bra. He hadn't remembered her breasts as quite so big before. As his eyes went down, he was disconcerted to find that the fuzzy sweater stopped about three inches below her breasts, revealing a tantalizing glimpse of smooth white flesh around her middle.

He swallowed hard. "You look as good as any movie star, Betsy," he said.

"You see." Betsy leaned forward to the group of men around the bar. "I told you he really fancies me, didn't I? That Bronwen Price might be all right for hiking up mountains with, but in the end it's only one thing that makes men happy, isn't it? And it's not hiking up mountains, either!"

Her gaze didn't leave his face as she spoke. He found the room was suddenly very warm indeed.

"What this man wants right now is a pint of Guinness, please, Betsy," he said.

"And there's some of us been waiting for a refill so long we're dying of thirst," Barry-the-Bucket complained. "I don't know why you waste your time waiting for Evan Evans to come around when there are plenty of good-looking, strong blokes here who'd know how to give you a good time."

Betsy turned to face the young bulldozer driver. "I'd be happy if you'd introduce me to one of them then, Barry," she said sweetly.

The other men in the bar broke into noisy laughter.

"You can't outsmart her, boyo," Charlie Hopkins chuckled. "Sharp as a wagonload of monkeys is our Betsy, right, Betsy *fach*?"

Barry's face flushed red. "If she knew what was good for her, she'd take what was offered and be happy," he said. "Not too many chances for a girl in a dump like this, are there now?"

Betsy ran her hands through her bright red curls. "And who says I intend to stay in a dump like this? I'm just biding my time, look you, waiting for fate to take a hand." Her wide, innocent gaze moved on to Evan, "And who knows—maybe fate has just knocked on my door."

"That was me, thumping on the bar for another pint," Evans-the-Meat growled. "Stop mooning around and get on with it, Betsy. Men are dying of thirst around here."

Betsy smiled serenely as she pulled the pint and placed the foaming glass in front of the butcher. "You'd better appreciate me while I'm here, Mr. Evans. Maybe I won't need to be doing this much longer."

"Why, where are you going then?" Evans-the-Milk asked.

Betsy smiled mysteriously in Evan's direction. "I was hoping that Evan Evans would introduce me to the movie directors. They must be needing extras in their film and maybe I'll be discovered and go to Hollywood."

"Hold on a minute, Betsy," Evan said hastily. "You've got it all wrong. They're not from Hollywood. . . ."

"I don't care. British movies are just as good. I wouldn't mind starring opposite Hugh Grant—I think he's lovely just. And what about Ieuan Griffith? I wouldn't mind doing a love scene with him either— and we could do it in Welsh, too."

"Betsy!" Evan raised his voice more than he meant to. There was a sudden hush in the bar. "They are not here to shoot a movie."

"Then what is all that stuff for?" demanded Roberts-the-Pump, the local petrol station owner. "Mrs. Rees-Number-Twenty-three was telling me that her nephew, Johnny, who works at the Inn, had to carry the luggage upstairs for them. He said they had all these strong-boxes full of film and big heavy cameras, too. And they only gave him a lousy one-pound tip—"

"Bloody foreigners," Evans-the-Meat muttered.

"And they were talking about location and shoot-ing," Roberts-the-Pump went on. "If that's not shooting a movie, I'd like to know what is." He leaned closer to Betsy at the bar. "I bet they want to keep quiet about it because they're bringing some big star in who doesn't want to be mobbed."

"Ooh, I hope it's Mel Gibson," Betsy said. "He gives me the shivers all up and down my spine. He reminds me of you a little, Evan *bach*!"

"Oh yeah. Same great body, is it?" Barry chuckled.

Evan laughed to hide his discomfort. "You say the daftest things sometimes, Betsy."

The other men were laughing too. "Maybe you could offer to be his stand-in, boyo. If he has to fall off the top of Yr Wyddfa, you can do it for him."

"Hang on." Evan held up his hand. "You people have got it all wrong. It's not a movie they're shooting at all. It's just a group of people who've come to pull an old German plane out of Llyn Llydaw and these blokes are going to film them doing it for some mu-seum or other. That's all."

"Is that it?" Betsy asked, the disappointment show-ing on her face. "No Hollywood stars then?"

"No stars at all. Just one old plane."

"Out of Llyn Llydaw, you say?" Charlie Hopkins put down his glass and was suddenly attentive.

"That's right. A German bomber from World War Two."

Charlie let out a whoop of delight. "Then we were right all along. The plane did go down after all."

"You know about it, Charlie?"

"Of course I do. My old dad and I saw it. I was a young lad at the time, just left school and apprenticed at the slate quarry. We were in the living room one evening, listening to the radio, when we heard this plane. We knew it was one of theirs right away—well, you did in those days, didn't you? We rushed outside and we saw it coming up the valley, very low overhead. The engine sounded like it might be in trouble.

"My old dad, he starts rolling up his sleeves. 'They better not think of landing here or they'll have me to deal with,' he says. Oh we did laugh, to think of my old dad taking on German military men with his bare fists. Although, come to think of it, I reckon he might have shown them a thing or two. Fit as a fiddle, he was. You built up good muscles working with slate, didn't you, boys?"

Several heads nodded.

"I wish I'd been there to show those Germans a thing or two," Betsy's father, Sam Edwards, muttered from his usual corner table, where he slumped with his whisky chaser.

"You'd never have been able to see straight enough to hit them, Sam," Charlie commented.

Betsy's father accepted this affably. "Bloody Germans. No good's ever come since we started making friends with them, has it? We join the bloody Common Market and what happens? They close the slate mine and we lose our jobs. Germans don't want slate on their roofs, do they?"

"Oh stop talking so daft, Tad. The Germans didn't make you lose your job." Betsy dismissed him with a wave of her hand. "Go on with the story, Charlie. What happened to the plane? Did it crash?"

"No, it kept on flying until it reached the top of the pass. Then it swung off to the right. If he'd only kept on down Nant Gwynant, I reckon he'd have been okay. He'd have made it out to sea and probably back to a French airport. But he kept on turning until he was heading up the mountain. The cloud had come down, see. He probably didn't know there was a bloody great mountain there.

" 'He'll never make it over the mountain, the way he's going,' my father says. Anyway, he disappears out of sight and we hear a couple of popping noises like an engine sputtering and cutting out, and then nothing more. No explosion, no fire, nothing.

"Of course, we run to the police station to call the local RAF, and they sent up people to look when it got light, but they never found anything. They thought we were making it up. But we were right all along. So it went to the bottom of Llyn Llydaw. Fancy that!"

Evan had been listening to Charlie's animated account with growing interest. "Charlie, how would you like to tell your story to the film crew, just like you told it to us? They're wanting to get firsthand accounts of the war for their film."

"Firsthand accounts, is it? Well, how about that." Charlie looked pleased. "Tell the gentlemen I'll be happy to be in their film."

Evan decided there was no point in being discreet any longer. "Anyone else who was in the village during the war and might have a story to tell?" he asked.

"I'll see what my wife Mair remembers," Charlie said. "She was here. And there's Owens-the-Sheep up at Ty Gwyn. He was a young boy at the time."

"And there's Mrs. Powell-Jones, of course." Evans-the-Meat lowered his voice and looked around as if he expected her to be eavesdropping, although the minister and his wife never came near the pub. "She was living up at the big house, wasn't she? I think they had evacuees billeted on them."

Harry, the pub landlord, had come to listen in on this conversation. He threw back his head and laughed. "She won't want to admit that she's that age. She goes around telling everyone she's forty!"

"She's sixty if ever she's a day," Charlie Hopkins said. "I remember when I was a lad, she was a snooty little thing who sat in the front row at chapel and gave herself airs and graces. And she got us in trouble for stealing conkers from their tree."

"Did anyone else around here have evacuees?" Evan asked.

"I think all the farmers did," Charlie said, nodding to himself. "There wasn't much room in the cottages. We were sleeping two to a bed as it was in our place. Went in for big families in those days."

"Well, they didn't know any better, did they?" Barry chimed in. "All those long dark winter nights and no telly."

"You be quiet, Barry." Betsy reached across and slapped his hand. "It's a pity that Granny died last year. She had lots of good stories, didn't she, Tad?"

"Indeed, she did," Betsy's father answered. "Wonderful woman. Saintly. I really miss her." He gave a big sigh as he stared down at his now empty glass.

"When she was alive, he called her the old hag, remember?" Evans-the-Meat dug Roberts-the-Pump in the side.

Betsy saw her father begin to stir from his seat.

"So it's only old people who get to be in the film, is it?" she demanded loudly. "Well, I don't think that's fair."

"They only want to add some human interest, Betsy," Evan said.

"What about young humans? They're interesting too, you know—and nicer to look at."

A sudden thought had struck Evan. "Hey, what about Mrs. Williams? She might have some good stories for them." Nobody had mentioned his landlady so far.

"But she's not from around here," Charlie Hopkins said.

"She's not?" Mrs. Williams seemed like such a fixture in the Llanfair landscape that he couldn't imagine the village without her.

"No. She only came here as a bride when she married Gwillum Williams after the war. He'd been away in the services and we all thought he'd marry a local girl—in fact, Mair's sister Sioned was sweet on him, but then he shows up with her one day. But she fitted in soon enough. Didn't bring too many foreign ways with her."

"I'd no idea she was a foreigner," Evan commented.

Charlie Hopkins chuckled. "You ask her about it, boyo."

"And tell that film director he needs someone young and sexy in his film if he wants people to pay to watch it," Betsy added.

"So will they be needing a bulldozer, do you think?" Barry-the-Bucket demanded. "How are they going to get their stuff up the mountain otherwise?"

"It sounded like they had the whole thing planned," Evan said. "They were talking about bringing in supplies by helicopter."

"By helicopter! Fancy that! I'd like to see that."

"Just a minute, folks." Evan held up his hand. "They asked me to tell you—They don't want anybody around when they're filming. I've been assigned to keep sightseers away, so please cooperate and make my job easy, all right?"

"You don't need to worry about us, Evan *bach*," Betsy said sweetly. "As if we'd give you any trouble!"

Evan shot her a glance but she was calmly pouring another pint.

"Is that you, Mr. Evans?" Mrs. Williams called as he let himself in later that evening. She always called the same thing and he was always tempted to give her a facetious answer.

"Yes, it's me, Mrs. Williams," he called back.

"Home early from the pub, aren't you? Would you like a cup of cocoa? I'm just making one," she called out.

Evan came through to the kitchen. "No cocoa for me, thanks. I've drunk enough for one evening."

"How were things at the Dragon—lively, was it?"

"Lively enough," he said. "I've been hearing things about you."

"Me? They were never gossiping about me in the pub. *Escob Annwyl!* What were they saying?"

Evan smiled. "Slander, I think. Charlie Hopkins said you were a foreigner."

Mrs. Williams put a hand to her ample bosom. "A foreigner indeed. You tell that man that I haven't one drop of foreign blood in my veins. Welsh through and through, I am. What on earth made him say that?"

"Maybe because you don't come from Llanfair."

"Ah—so that's what he was getting at!" She started to laugh. "Silly old fool. That goes back to when I first came here after the war. My Gwillum's friends used to tease him that he'd married a foreign girl."

"So where did you come from?" Evan asked.

"Blenau Ffestiniog," she said. "That's where I was born and grew up. Gwillum was in the army with my brothers. He came to visit when they were demobbed and . . . and we started courting." She looked down shyly. "My family thought I'd never like it in Llanfair. They thought it was like moving to the end of the earth. But I've been happy enough here. I just wish my daughter and granddaughter hadn't moved away. And speaking of my granddaughter, she was telling me about this dance they're having at the Pavilion in Rhyl. She'd love to go but she wants the right escort, of course. So of course I thought that possibly you might . . ."

"Oh, I'm sorry, Mrs. Williams," Evan said, "but no doubt you've heard there's a film crew here. I've been assigned to be on duty night and day until they're finished. I had to make a solemn promise to my chief that nothing would happen to them, so it looks as if I'm stuck here for a while."

Mrs. Williams made tutting noises. "They work you too hard, Mr. Evans," she said, but then her eyes lit up. "So it's true what they're saying about shooting a film up here?"

"Only a documentary, Mrs. Williams. They're going to pull an old German plane out of the lake and take a film of it."

"Oh, is that all? Then I don't see what all the fuss is about."

"But they are going to interview people who have memories of the war," Evan said. "I don't know if you'll count, coming from so far away."

He went up the stairs chuckling. Blenau Ffestiniog was all of fifteen miles from Llanfair.

FIVE

THE NEXT MORNING, Evan took the filmmakers up to the lake. Clouds hid the mountain peaks and a misty rain swirled down the pass as they set off. Hardly the right conditions to be driving Land Rovers up mountains.

"Maybe it would be better if we walked from the car park," Evan suggested. "It's less than a mile and not too steep."

"Walked? In this weather?" Grantley exclaimed. "Nonsense. Land Rovers are built to go anywhere. And we have to see where we can get the equipment up. Get in."

Edward took the driver's seat, Howard sat in the front seat beside him. Sandie was left behind for lack of space. She stood at the Inn doorway, staring wistfully, like a child being left out of a game.

"She'll die of a broken heart before you return, Grantley," Edward muttered.

"Poor child. Can I help it if she's mad about me? Everyone is."

"You shouldn't encourage her, Grantley. It's not fair."

Grantley smiled. "Do you think she'd make my tea and give me back rubs and stay late typing up scripts if she didn't adore me? I can't help being irresistible, Edward. You should know that."

He maneuvered his long legs into the backseat, where Evan was already perched.

"God, it's like a sardine tin in here. I think we need to rent another vehicle, Edward," Grantley complained. "An occasion might arise when we need to go our separate ways."

"The foundation has lent us a Land Rover," Edward said, without turning to look at him. "I think we have to make do with it for now. We have to keep within budget and that salvage equipment doesn't come cheap." He turned out of the Everest Inn car park onto the bleak road heading up the pass. "If the operation takes more than a week, I'm not sure what we'll do. I've got my own money sunk into this, remember."

"Then we get a loan from the bank on the strength of the future documentary," Grantley said in an exasperated voice. "Tell them we've got Howard Bauer directing and BBC2 have more or less promised to buy it. This whole thing is a guaranteed moneymaker, I tell you."

"It better be, Grantley," Edward said coldly. "A couple of weeks ago you said that BBC2 had made an offer. Then it was a promise. Now it's almost promised. I've risked a lot on the strength of this bloody film doing well."

"Turn right here." Evan tapped Edward Ferrers on the back.

"Here?" Edward sounded startled as he looked at the mountain rising before them into cloud. A track, just wide enough for two people to walk side by side, led up and over a ridge.

"Holy cow," Howard muttered. "You're not going to try and take a car up that?"

"What's the matter, Howard?" Grantley asked. "You're supposed to be the intrepid one."

"Knock it off, Grantley. I've never been suicidal."

"This was the way they used to bring copper out of the old mine," Evan said.

"You see, Howard. A well-used vehicular route," Grantley said.

"Actually, it was donkeys," Evan pointed out. "They brought all the copper out on donkeys."

"Well, that's bloody reassuring," Edward muttered. "I can't see where I'm going. We'll be in the cloud in a minute."

The Land Rover lurched and bumped its way up the path. Evan was glad that the mist concealed the drop that he knew was on their left. They reached the top of the ridge without incident, then bumped and slithered down a short drop to the lakeshore. Nobody spoke until they stopped beside the black, still expanse of water.

"It's over here," Edward said, as they clambered out, uncoiling stiff limbs. "Right below that big rock."

"I think you'll need to have the equipment helicoptered in, Edward," Grantley said.

"It's not very large," Edward said. "I think it will make it up that track all right."

"How are you going to lift the plane? Won't it take a large crane to do it?" Evan asked.

Edward's face lit up. "No, actually, that's the beauty of it. We're trying something that has worked in other deepwater salvage expeditions. You get divers to place an inflatable collar around the plane, then you pump in compressed air to inflate it. When it's full of air, hopefully it will float to the surface."

"That's very good," Evan agreed.

"Yes, isn't it?" Edward was still beaming. "Of course the Dornier-17 wasn't very big compared to modern planes. We're not dealing with a jumbo jet here. It should float easily enough."

"Unless it's caught on a rock or somehow trapped in the mud," Grantley said sweetly.

"It will work. Trust me."

"I always do, Edward. It's just that you don't always trust me."

Evan looked from one to the other. He hadn't figured this one out yet. Howard Bauer was supposed to be the director, therefore in charge of the project, yet he hardly ever said a word and stayed clear of the other two. Grantley Smith was the producer, but apparently Edward had the money for the project. So why did the other two let Grantley Smith act as if he was God?

"We can't film in conditions like this," Howard muttered. "You'd better pray that the clouds lift sometime soon."

"The weather will clear," Edward said.

"Edward the eternal optimist." Grantley went to stand at the edge of the lake. Cold mist swirled around his knees, drifting in strands over the surface of the water. There was no sound except for the sigh of the wind through dead bracken. Grantley bent to pick up a rock and threw it into the lake. The plop was unnaturally loud. Perfect, round ripples spread across the black surface.

"God, it looks like something out of a horror movie," Howard commented. "Let's hope you haven't woken the beast that lives in the lake, Grantley."

"Is there a beast that lives in this lake, Constable?" Grantley asked with a smile.

"Not that I've heard of," Evan said. "But they say that the Lady of the Lake lived up here and gave Excalibur to King Arthur from this very lake."

"Grantley would accept Excalibur like a shot if it's offered him. He's always wanted to be king," Edward chuckled.

"I can't think why any lady of the lake would choose

to live up here. I've never seen a more dreary place."
Grantley threw a second rock into the lake. "Nothing
lives up here. The whole place is godforsaken."

"Oh, it's quite nice up here when the sun comes
out," Evan said. "The lake is very blue and you can
see the mountains reflected in it. It's especially dramatic when they've got snow on them."

"Snow?" Grantley shot him a horrified look. "Now
that's all we need. Grantley Smith lost in a snowdrift.
Dog teams mushing to my rescue."

"Stop being so bloody dramatic, Grantley, and let's
get to work. We need to decide where a helicopter
could land, where we can set up the generator," Edward
said.

They walked off together. Evan remained standing
beside Howard Bauer. The American stared out across
the bleak valley, lost in thought. His hands were thrust
deep into the pockets of a down parka. His beret was
jammed down onto his head.

"Damned cold, isn't it?" he muttered.

"I don't suppose you're used to the cold if you've
spent a lot of time in Africa," Evan said with sympathy.

"I went there to make one goddamned picture,"
Howard snapped, "but it seems that nobody's ever going to let me forget it."

Edward and Grantley were returning.

"She definitely moved up here, didn't she?" Grantley's voice echoed from unseen rocks. "You should
look her up for old times' sake."

"Oh, I don't know. . . ."

"Of course you should. I'm dying to see her living
at one with nature and a pet sheep."

"You're very cruel, Grantley. So she has slightly
green inclinations."

"Slightly? I bet you'll find she's growing her own
bread and spinning her own underwear by now."

"Anyway, I don't have her address, I only heard it
was a village in Snowdonia."

"Ask the constable. I'm sure he knows everyone up

here. I'll ask him." Grantley strode through the tall
grass toward Evan and Howard. "We're wondering if
you know a young woman who moved here recently.
Her name's Bronwen Ferrers—"

"I think she went back to her maiden name," Edward
interrupted. "Price. Bronwen Price."

Evan stared at him in disbelief. He remembered
Bronwen telling him her ex-husband was crazy about
old planes. But he couldn't believe that she had ever
been married to this pink, chubby, pompous prig.

Tell him you've never heard of her, a voice whispered in his head.

He fought to remain calm and relaxed. "I do know
her, actually," he managed to say. "She's our local
schoolteacher." And she's my girl now, he wanted to
add but didn't.

"A schoolteacher in a village school. How charm-
ingly quaint." Grantley smiled at Edward. "See, I told
you there was something definitely wrong with that
girl, and you wouldn't believe me. We must go and
say hello, Edward."

"I'm not sure that it's such a good idea."

"Of course it is. To bring closure, as they say in all
the self-help books these days. You need to reassure
yourself that she's not pining over you."

Evan felt his fingers curl into a tight fist. "If you
gentlemen have finished up here, maybe we should go
down before the mist gets any thicker," he said. "You
wouldn't want to miss the track and land a thousand
feet below, would you now?"

"Yes, there really isn't much more we can do up
here now, is there?" Grantley Smith walked over to the
Land Rover. "Bloody godforsaken place. If I'm going
to shoot a film about salvaging something, I should
have chosen a treasure ship in the Caribbean."

"Yes, but nobody funded you for that one, did they,
Grantley?" Edward commented sweetly. "And people
were only interested in this little venture because you

dragged Howard on board—and how you managed to do that is a mystery to me."

"Everything's a mystery to you, Edward." Grantley climbed, with catlike grace, into the backseat of the Land Rover.

They made it back to the village in silence and without incident.

"You run along and contact your equipment people, Edward," Grantley said. "Maybe the helicopter is the way to go, based on the state of the track. And in the meantime," he turned to Evan, "there's no sense in hanging around doing nothing. Let's do some local color, Constable. Who have you found for us to interview?"

"Oh sorry, were you talking to me?" Evan's mind was still trying to digest Bronwen having been married to Edward Ferrers. It took a lot of digesting.

"Yes, we want people to interview, Constable. Local color, you know. Quaint village types with stories to tell."

Evan tried not to show his dislike for Grantley Smith. "We could see if Charlie Hopkins is at home," he said after a moment's thought. "He's semi-retired these days and he has a good story about your bomber."

"Excellent. Howard, I'll grab a camera." He rushed ahead of them as they pulled up outside the Everest Inn.

Howard Bauer turned to Evan. "Now he's taking over as cameraman, too. He thinks he can do the whole goddamned thing single-handed. We've got my professional crew arriving tomorrow, but he thinks he can do better."

"Why don't you tell him to wait? You're the director," Evan said.

Howard shot him a glance he couldn't interpret. "It's not as simple as that," he said. "You don't exactly direct Grantley."

Grantley rejoined them, triumphantly waving a video camera. "Lead on, Macduff!" he shouted.

Howard winced. "Isn't it unlucky to quote from that play?"

"Only if you're an actor, Howard. And I have moved onward and upward from my thespian days."

The clouds were beginning to lift as they walked down the hill to the village. Slanted shafts of sunlight hit the slopes then moved on again, as if a giant searchlight was at work.

They were just drawing level with the chapels when a piercing voice yelled, "I say, yoohoo! Wait a minute!"

Evan's heart sank as he saw Mrs. Powell-Jones running toward them. She was dressed in pea green tweeds, wellies, and a gardening apron. A large pair of pruning shears was in her hand.

"I presume you gentlemen are the filmmakers we've all heard about," she said, looking quite flustered. "I am the minister's wife, Powell-Jones is the name, and if you want to know anything about this village during wartime, you only have to come to me. I will give you all the information you need. My family, you see, owned the slate mine at that time. The fine, distinguished-looking house you see behind our chapel was our family seat . . . and Mummy directed the entire war effort."

She paused to beam at them. "I, of course, was only a very small child at the time, but I remember Mummy putting all the village women to work knitting scarves for the soldiers. She organized concert parties for the local air force base, and she was the local billeting officer for evacuees—Mummy was a wonderful organizer. I take after her, of course. My husband always says he doesn't know what he would do without me."

"Have a good time, I expect," Evan heard Howard Bauer mutter.

"I see you have your camera," she went on, "so if

you'd like to conduct an interview shortly, over tea and some of my homemade jam, I can tell you all you need to know about the village during the war."

Evan was enjoying watching Grantley and Howard's faces as Mrs. Powell-Jones leaned toward them, brandishing her pruning shears. For once, even Grantley was almost speechless. "So kind. Most grateful. Must run. Urgent appointment," he mumbled and broke into a trot on down the street.

"A rather rude young man, I'm afraid," Mrs. Powell-Jones said. "I suppose it's the artistic temperament. I'll expect you later, then."

"Geez, what an awful woman," Howard muttered to Evan as they hurried to catch up with Grantley. "Reminds me of my ex-wife!"

Grantley had come to a halt outside the school playground, where children were noisily at play.

"Don't tell me—this is the school where Edward's former spouse teaches!" he exclaimed. "How incredibly quaint. Let's go in and surprise her!"

"You knew her too?" Evan asked.

"Of course. We were all at Cambridge together. One big happy family," Grantley said. "Oh look, there she is now! Oh my God, she really has gone all green and ethnic. Hey, Bronwen, over here. Guess who?"

Evan watched in speechless torment as Bronwen focused on them, then crossed the playground, followed by fascinated children. She was wearing her long red cape over a long woven skirt and did look very much like a character from an old fairy tale. As she came closer, she looked inquiringly from Evan to the others and her eyes suddenly registered recognition. "Grantley? My goodness, what are you doing here?"

"Filming an old plane, my sweet. And you'll never guess who's our expert consultant?"

The color drained from her face. "Edward's here with you? I wondered when Evan said a World War Two plane buff was organizing the project."

"And dying to see you, my sweet. We're staying up at the Chalet from Hell. Why don't you come up and have drinks with us later—for old times' sake?"

Bronwen hesitated and looked swiftly at Evan before she said, "All right. Why not?"

"At around five-thirty? Are you free of your little charges by then?"

She nodded.

One of the children tapped her on the arm. "Miss Price, should I ring the bell for you? Playtime's over."

Bronwen reacted like a person coming out of a trance. "What? Oh yes, Aled. Ring the bell. Thank you."

She swept the children back toward the school building while Evan stood there watching her go.

Evan had just returned home and was changing out of his uniform when Mrs. Williams tapped on his door. "Miss Price is downstairs for you, Mr. Evans. I've shown her into the front parlor."

Evan pulled on a sweater over his T-shirt and cords and hurried downstairs.

"Are you ready?" Bronwen asked. Evan noticed she was dressed in very un-Bronwen fashion, in dark slacks and a blue silky blouse with a gray knitted stole around her shoulders. She'd even put her long braid up into a twist and was wearing a hint of makeup.

"Ready?" Evan asked.

"We promised to go for drinks up at the Inn."

"You want me to go with you?" Evan tried not to show the flush of satisfaction he felt.

"Of course I want you to go with me." She looked suddenly vulnerable. "If that's all right with you . . . you don't want me to face the lions alone, do you?"

"I'll come if you want me to," he said. "I thought you might want a private chat."

"Oh God, no." She made a face. "I don't really want to go at all. I was just too startled to say no."

"We don't have to stay long," Evan said.

She smiled up at him. "No. Just to let them see I'm wonderfully happy and well-adjusted and adore my life, then I don't have to see them ever again."

Evan opened the front door for her. "Is this going to be hard for you?" he asked. "I always had the feeling it was an amicable split-up—because you'd both changed so much."

It was getting dark. The sky was silver, streaked with lines of navy blue cloud. Street lamps shone pools of light onto wet pavement. Evans-the-Meat was pulling down the roller blind on his shop window. *"Noswaith dda!"* he called as they passed.

Bronwen waited until they were well past the butcher. "I didn't exactly go into details with you," she said. "Mainly because I didn't want to face the truth myself. I haven't seen Edward since he announced he was leaving me for someone else."

"Oh, I see."

"It was a big blow, as you can imagine," she said. "That's why I came here, to a little village where nobody knew me."

"I'm glad you did," Evan said.

She reached out and took out his hand. "I'm glad I did, too."

There was a big fire roaring in the river rock fireplace as they entered the lobby of the Everest Inn. A harpist was playing in the corner and an elderly couple in hiking gear was having tea by the window. Grantley's group was again seated around the fire.

"Here she is now." Grantley leaped up, although Edward remained sitting. "With our faithful policeman escorting her in case she was attacked by bandits along the way. I must say, the police give wonderful service up here. Far better than the Met!"

Evan took Bronwen's arm as they crossed the expanse of lobby. Edward now rose to his feet. "Hello, Bronwen. How are you?"

"Very well, thank you, Edward. And you?"

"Oh fine, thank you. I must say, you're looking lovely."

"Thank you."

"Let me get you a chair." He ran to drag one across from the nearest table.

"And Evan will need one too," Bronwen said.

"It's okay. I can get my own." Evan reached for a chair before anyone else could move. He sat slightly behind Bronwen.

"There's no need to wait, Constable," Grantley said. "We'll make sure she gets home safely and no wolves eat her."

"Evan's with me," Bronwen said evenly. "We don't go anywhere without each other."

"Oh, I see." Edward's pink face turned even pinker. "Oh, right."

"I don't think you've met our director, Howard Bauer," Grantley said.

"I've heard of you, of course." Bronwen exchanged a smile with Howard. "I've been very impressed with your work."

"And my secretary, Sandie. Sandie, Bronwen is an old friend from our Cambridge days."

"Oh, how lovely." Sandie smiled shyly. "I've heard a lot about your time in Cambridge. It must have been such fun."

"It was," Grantley said. "Oh, it was. We belonged to this radical theater group. . . . Remember that play we took to the Edinburgh fringe?"

"It was a ridiculous play," Bronwen said, laughing. "You made me spend the entire second act with my head in a birdcage, spouting the sayings of Chairman Mao."

"And the audience couldn't understand what it was about." Edward laughed too.

"They didn't even know when it had finished or whether they should applaud."

"We thought we were out-Ionescoing Ionesco, didn't we?" Grantley demanded loudly.

As the noise level rose and the conversation flowed around the table, Evan sat in the shadows behind Bronwen, watching uneasily. This was a new Bronwen, one he had never seen before—witty, animated, laughing easily, discussing things that were outside his world and experience. He had hoped that seeing him and Edward together would make her realize what good choices she had made. Now he felt that exactly the opposite was happening. She was back with her own crowd, on her own intellectual level, and she must realize how very much was lacking in her quiet village life.

SIX

As a matter of fact, I was quite looking forward to the war. I'd turned fourteen in 1939, see, and that meant leaving school and going down the slate mine like my father and all the other men. There wasn't a choice. If you lived in Blenau, you were a slate miner, unless you were a preacher—we had more than our share of chapels in those days, although I don't know why we needed them. Anyone who worked down a slate mine knew all about hell. In the winter months, we went all week without seeing the light of day—down the mine before it was light in the morning and back in the evening after the sun had already set. That kind of thing gets to you, especially a lad like me who loved the open air. When I was still in school, I was out on the moor, any spare moment, with my paintbox and my sketchbook, drawing and painting anything I saw. The schoolmaster, Mr. Hughes, told me I had real talent. He encouraged me and he even bought me paints once. Never make do with cheap colors, Trefor, he told me. He also said he'd write a letter to a chap at an art college in London. They'd give me a scholarship, he said. But of course they only laughed at home when I

*told them. What's the good of art down a mine—too dark
to see much to draw, down the mine, my dad said.*

*I hated it down there from the beginning—well, quite
scary for a fourteen-year-old, I can tell you. Down and
down, all those hundreds of steps, almost no light at all,
and then that huge cavern, dotted with pinpoints of light
where the miners had hung their lamps. All day long in
the darkness with the echo of the hammers and the ghostly
murmur of voices. Yes, it was pretty much like hell all
right.*

*War was declared in the summer of '39. That summer I
turned fourteen, left school, and went down the mine.
Some of the older boys in the village went straight off to
join the services. I thought they looked pretty good in their
uniforms. I was too young, of course, and I just prayed
the war would last long enough for me to turn seventeen.
Johnny Morgan was sent to France. I would have given
anything to trade places with him. France—the country
of painters. I'd seen the pictures in the books Mr. Hughes
had lent me.*

*Of course I didn't envy Johnny so much when the tele-
gram came. He never saw much of France. He was killed
on the beaches of Dunkirk.*

*There were many times after when I wished that had
been me.*

The next morning, the inhabitants of Llanfair rushed out
of doors at the sound of an approaching helicopter. It appeared, laboring slowly up the pass, dangling below it a
large piece of cargo that wasn't immediately identifiable.

"It's the army doing exercises again," Evans-the-Milk
called to Evans-the-Meat.

"No it's not. It's those foreigners and their bloody
German plane. We won't have a moment's peace until
they go. You wait and see—it will be helicopters up and
down the pass, day and night...." His last words were
drowned out by the throb of the helicopter motor. He

glared up at the mountains. "I think I'll go up there and tell them what I think of them. This is a quiet place. We don't want to be disturbed."

"For once I'm with you, Gareth," Evans-the-Milk agreed. "I don't mind the tourists, but helicopters coming and going up and down the pass all day—that's too much."

"Mr. Owens-the-Farm won't be too happy either, I'll warrant. That thing will panic the sheep."

"And Mr. Howell's dairy cows might be too unsettled to give milk, and then where would I be?"

"We should make an official complaint and get all the villagers to sign it," Evans-the-Meat said. "They never asked us if we wanted a film crew here, did they?"

"We should go and see Reverend Parry Davies. He'd know how to make an official complaint."

"He would, only Reverend Powell-Jones would do it better."

"He would not!"

"He most certainly would. Being the senior minister, who preaches better sermons, and in Welsh, too."

For a moment they faced each other, fists raised. Then Evans-the-Milk laughed.

"Or the ministers' wives. They're even better. Nobody stands up to Mrs. Powell-Jones, do they?"

Evans-the-Meat started laughing also. "No time like the present, is there? What do you say we both go up there now—as representatives of the village."

"I'm with you, Gareth *bach*."

For one brief moment the two men were in complete agreement and harmony. They joined other curious villagers, young and old, who were hurrying after the helicopter.

They hadn't reached the two chapels when a Land Rover, laden with equipment, pulled up beside them.

"We're supposed to be going up to some lake to film a helicopter arriving." A young man with a ginger beard stuck his head out of the window and called to the two

Evans. "Llyn Llydaw—any idea where that would be?"

"The helicopter has already passed over," Evans-the-Milk called back. "Frightening all the bloody sheep and disturbing the peace."

"Damn. I knew we were running late," the man muttered. "So where is it now?"

Evans-the-Milk looked at the crowd now working its way up the pass. "Follow them. You can't miss it."

The young man muttered "Damn" again, and roared off up the street.

Meanwhile, up at the lake, Evan stared dismally across the bleak waters, while he played the scene from last night over and over in his head. Bronwen was reassuring as they walked home together, but Evan had not been comforted. It had been a shock to see this new, witty, laughing Bronwen. Why had she never mentioned that she'd been to Cambridge before? Maybe because he'd never asked. He knew she'd been to University, but Cambridge—well, only the very brightest went there, didn't they? Would it only be a matter of time before she decided that village life didn't have enough to offer her?

As he watched, the helicopter appeared and lowered its cargo to the lakeshore. Grantley was filming the helicopter's arrival, not in the best of tempers since the camera crew hadn't shown up in time. Howard was standing beside him, watching silently.

Then Evan's gaze was suddenly riveted to the top of the pass, where several heads were now appearing. It seemed that the entire population of Llanfair was coming to see the helicopter. He clambered up the slope and intercepted the front-runners.

"They don't want people up here, I'm afraid, boys," he said.

"What do you mean—it's a perfectly good public path up the mountain, isn't it?" one of the young men demanded. "You can't keep people off public paths."

"I've been instructed to keep everyone away—my chief inspector's orders—so that they can get on with their filming with no mishaps. So be good lads and go back home."

The two boys turned back reluctantly, but Evan found that more people were sneaking in on either side. He ran back and forth, feeling like a sheepdog.

"I thought I asked you to keep everyone away," Grantley yelled. "That's another sequence ruined by grinning faces popping up from behind rocks."

The camera crew arrived, bumping and lurching along the track, and soon a large camera and lighting were set up on the shore.

Grantley came over to Evan, who waited for more complaints.

"Everything's working smoothly now, Constable. I can leave the directing to Howard and the crew. I want you to come with me on another little venture. We'll take the vehicle."

Evan climbed into the Land Rover beside him and they set off. "I've got a woman arriving from Manchester in about an hour," Grantley confided. "We're meeting her from the train in Bangor and then taking her to a farm called Fron Heulog. It's supposed to be around here—do you know where it is?"

"Fron Heulog?" Evan deciphered the name from Grantley's butchered pronunciation and tried to remember which farm was called what. "I know it's one of the farms around here. Do you know the name of the owners?"

"James," Grantley said.

"Oh, then I do know it. Old couple, aren't they? I don't think they farm actively any more. Down the valley toward Llanberis—little white house."

"Splendid. I'm arranging a sentimental meeting." Grantley smiled mischievously. "I'm bringing their old evacuee back to visit them. She hasn't seen them since the war ended. Should make great cinema."

Evan didn't take to Pauline Hardcastle when they met her at Bangor station. She had a hard, pinched look to her face and her little, deep-set eyes darted around nervously.

"I'm not sure I want to do this—wake old memories," she said, "but you say it will be good for both of us, so I'll give it a try. Both alive, are they? I thought they would have kicked the bucket years ago. Is the son still living with them? Nasty little bugger he were."

Evan glanced across at Grantley. There was still a smile on his face.

The Jameses came to their cottage door at the sound of the approaching car. Two elderly border collies stood at their feet, tails wagging tentatively.

"Well, well, look you, Father," Mrs. James came forward, holding out her arms. "If it isn't little Pauline from the war, come back to see us after all this time."

"Little Pauline," the old man muttered.

The gaunt, bony woman stood there and allowed herself to be hugged.

"Come inside now, for goodness sakes, and let's all have a cup of tea," Mrs. James said in lilting English. "Put the kettle on, Father."

She led them through to a spotless, scrubbed kitchen with its well-polished Welsh dresser and high-backed settle. The old black stove stood unused in the corner while Mr. James plugged in a modern electric jug. There were radiators along the walls and the kitchen was delightfully warm.

"A bit different from when you were here last, is it?" Mrs. James asked shyly. "My, but I remember that day like it was yesterday. What a poor little mite you were, standing there shivering. Nothing but a bag of bones. Not an ounce of spare flesh on you. Clothes all ragged and dirty and I don't think you'd had a bath in weeks. I had to take you out and scrub you under the pump so you didn't bring fleas into the house."

Evan noticed that Grantley had the camera going.

"I remember it too," Pauline said. "I nearly froze to death when you scrubbed me at that pump. It took all my skin off. I cried but you didn't care."

"Oh, but we had to do it, love," Mrs. James went on in her soft voice.

Pauline cut in. "Had to do it. You treated me like shit and you know it. Talk about child abuse. If this were today, you'd be up in court for the way you treated me."

"Here, hang on a minute," Mr. James interrupted. "There's no need to go yelling at my wife. It was good of us to take you in. . . ."

"Good of you?" Pauline was yelling now. "All you wanted was an extra slave. You wouldn't feed me if I didn't work—remember that? I went to bed hungry in a bedroom with no heating in it. I cried myself to sleep every night."

She turned to Grantley. "I did, you know. I begged them to send me home, but they wanted a slave to help on their farm. I had to get up at the crack of dawn and feed their bloody hens—I were scared to death of those hens. And you made me peel potatoes and do the washing. I were eight years old and you treated me like a bloody slave. And you took the strap to me if I back answered you and you made me go to that bleedin' chapel every Sunday."

There was a pause during which the only sound came from the rhythmic ticking of the clock on the mantelpiece.

Pauline looked from one face to the next. "I've waited all these years to tell you to your face, and now it feels bloody marvelous!" She got to her feet. "We can go now. I've got nothing left to say to these people."

The Jameses looked stunned. "It wasn't like that at all, Pauline, love," Mrs. James said. "We treated you just like our own children. Everyone has to work hard on a farm or the chores don't get done. We only gave you the lightest things to do and you made a terrible fuss about those. I don't think you'd ever lifted a finger at home, had you? Didn't know how to cook or sew or mend . . ."

"I were eight years bleedin' old," Pauline yelled. "I were a little kid, for Christ's sake! I was away from my mum for the first time in my life. And you let him abuse me."

"What do you mean?" Mr. James demanded.

"You know what I mean, you dirty old man." She turned to the wife. "He couldn't keep his hands off me, and you turned the other way."

She started toward the door. "I've had my say. This is too painful to talk about. Get me out of here."

Grantley had been filming. He got up, camera still rolling, and followed Pauline out of the house. Evan stood awkwardly, not quite knowing what to say to the old couple.

"It wasn't like that at all, Constable Evans," Mrs. James said at last. "I don't know where she got those ideas, but we treated her like our own child. Why would she want to come here and say those things?"

"Wicked, that's what it is," Mr. James said. "Someone's been putting ideas into her head. Like as not one of these therapists you read about." He looked as the boiling water jug clicked off. "You'll not be wanting that tea now, I'm thinking."

"I'm sorry, Mr. James," Evan said. "I'm sure Mr. Smith didn't think it was going to be like this, or he'd never have suggested meeting up with Pauline again."

Grantley was subdued until they had dropped Pauline back at the station. Then he let out a great whoop of delight. "How about that, eh? Brilliant stuff. That will make them sit up in their seats, won't it?"

Evan stared at him. "You knew she was going to say those things?"

"My dear chap, that was the whole point. I put out feelers for evacuees who had had bad experiences in North Wales. She was the only one who fitted the bill."

"But she really upset those old people," Evan said.

"I'm sure they deserved it." Grantley was still smiling. "Don't worry, Constable. I'll send them a check to cover their contribution to the documentary. Money has charms to sooth the savage breast, doesn't it?"

•   •   •

"Sit you down, Mr. Evans. You look worn to a frazzle just," Mrs. Williams greeted him that evening. "Hard work looking after a film crew, is it?"

"You have no idea, Mrs. Williams." Evan collapsed into his seat. "I had to work harder than any sheepdog, keeping people away from the set, and then I had to witness a most unpleasant encounter between the Jameses up at Fron Heulog and their wartime evacuee. Then I had to listen to that obnoxious creep, Grantley Smith, telling me how brilliant he was and how he was going to win awards with this film."

"Get that down you and you'll feel better." Mrs. Williams opened the oven and took out a plate on which three slices of lamb's liver and several rashers of bacon lay smothered in fried onions and rich brown gravy. She added a generous mound of fluffy mashed potato and then runner beans and cauliflower in a parsley sauce. It was times like this that Evan knew why he was being so reluctant about moving into a place of his own.

He had barely taken a mouthful when the phone rang.

"Now who can that be, disturbing your dinner?" Mrs. Williams demanded angrily. "Always so inconsiderate, aren't they? Never think that you might need to eat your dinner in peace for once . . ."

She bustled to the phone. "He's having his dinner, just," Evan heard her saying. "Oh, very well. I'll get him then." She came hurrying back into the kitchen. "I'm sorry to disturb you now, Mr. Evans, but it seems there's something nasty going on at the Everest Inn. Major Anderson wants you up there right away."

Evan grabbed his jacket as he ran out of the front door.

All was quiet as he entered the Everest Inn, but he saw a tense group of people sitting at the table by the fire. Behind them the hotel manager—Major Anderson—and one of the hotel employees were holding a struggling man between them.

"Here's the police now. Over here, Constable." Major

Anderson beckoned. "I'm afraid we've had a bit of a fra-
cas. I witnessed most of it myself. This person came in
and started shouting at these gentlemen, then he grabbed
Mr. Smith around the throat. It took two of us to prise his
hands away."

Grantley looked paler than usual and smiled wanly.
"Bit of a shock, I can tell you," he said, "and unfortunately we didn't have a camera handy. Now that would
have made great cinema."

"Great cinema?" Sandie demanded. "Grantley—he
nearly killed you!"

"All right, sir. You can let go of him," Evan said, turning to face the prisoner, a middle-aged man with the
weatherbeaten face, aged tweed jacket, and tall boots of
a farmer. He looked vaguely familiar to Evan. As soon as
they released him, he swung his arms and Evan half expected to be on the receiving end of a punch.

"Easy now, boyo," he said. "Now what's been going
on here?"

"You should be ashamed of yourselves," the man said,
with venom in his voice. "You especially, Constable
Evans, for bringing that . . . that disgusting creature to my
parents' house. Do you know what it did to them? We
had to get the doctor for my dad's heart condition. What
did you think you were doing, bringing back that . . . Pauline person . . . to my parents' house after all this time?
What was supposed to be the good of it?"

"You must be the Jameses' son then?" Evan asked.

"I am. And my parents are decent, hardworking people.
Worked their fingers to the bone every day of their lives.
They didn't deserve to be put through that unpleasantness
this morning. He set it up, didn't he?" He made to step
toward Grantley again. Major Anderson put out a restrain-
ing arm. "Easy now, fellow," he said. "This isn't going
to help your case at all."

"If you're not careful, I'm going to have to book you
on a charge of disturbing the peace, Mr. James," Evan
said.

"And what about him? Hasn't he disturbed the peace—our peace?" the man roared. "Bringing that Pauline back to our house. I remember her right enough. I was only a little child at the time, but I remember clearly enough. She was a proper little madam, Constable. She whined all the time, wouldn't lift a finger to help, stole food. Our parents treated her the same as they treated the rest of us. And this is how they are rewarded." He spun to face Grantley again. "Men like you—muckrakers like that filth in the tabloids—you don't deserve to live. Let me catch you anywhere near my parents again and I'll kill you, understand?"

"So what was it all about, Mr. Evans?" Mrs. Williams greeted him as he arrived home much later. "Nothing too serious, I hope."

Mrs. Williams shook her head in disbelief as Evan told her what had happened. "The Jameses-Fron-Heulog? I know them well enough. Decent God-fearing chapel people, that's what they are. No good ever comes from stirring up the past, Mr. Evans."

She produced a rather dryer, older version of his dinner from the oven. "I kept it hot for you," she said.

Evan sat down, but his appetite had gone. Mrs. Williams pulled up a chair opposite so he was forced to eat rather more dried-out liver than he would otherwise have done, while making small appreciative noises from time to time.

"Funny, talking about the past," she said. "I hadn't thought about my girlhood and the wartime for years, but after you asked me, it all started coming back. I can see it clear as yesterday. Oh, it was an exciting time, Mr. Evans. I was just a young girl, going into my teens, but my, did we have fun."

Her whole face lit up and the years seemed to have fallen away.

"Fun—in wartime?" Evan asked.

A dreamy look spread across her face. "There was this

boy called Trefor Thomas—ooh, he was lovely just. Handsome like a young Clark Gable, and talented, too, Trefor was. I've never seen anyone draw pictures the way he could. He wanted to be an artist, but of course he had to go down the slate mine, like his dad. Everyone did up there. All the girls had crushes on him, but he only had eyes for Ginger."

"Ginger?"

"That wasn't her real name, look you. She was really plain old Mwfanwy, but she called herself Ginger after Ginger Rogers. She was mad about film stars and Hollywood. She bleached her hair and piled it up like Ginger Rogers. Her old *mam* was fit to be tied, but there wasn't much she could do about it, was there?"

Mrs. Williams chuckled. "I was younger than the rest—just a hanger-on, like, but I was happy to be included, I suppose. And then later I met Mr. Williams, and well . . . that was that. I came here and I've been here ever since."

"So did Trefor marry Ginger?" Evan asked.

"No! She ran away with an American—a G. I. who came up here to recuperate. Just upped and left one night and sent Trefor a note saying she'd gone to Hollywood. Poor old Trefor. Broke his heart, it did. He changed after that. He got quite bitter and shut himself away. I heard he did marry and have a son, but he was never his bright, fun-loving self again. He'd had so many hopes, you see—what with the National Gallery coming to Blenau. He thought he'd be able to help with the paintings."

Evan had been listening politely while he ate, but not paying too much attention. Suddenly he stopped, liver poised on his fork. "The National Gallery? The art gallery in London, you mean?"

"I do. They took out all the pictures and stored them in a slate mine in Blenau during the war. Didn't you know that?"

"No. I'd never heard that before."

"Oh 'deed to goodness yes. They brought all the pictures from London in big lorries. Trevor had just started working in the mine. He hoped they'd let him handle the pictures, but of course they all came in wooden crates, didn't they? All he helped build was the sheds to put them in."

"Sheds?"

"That's right. They built sheds in one of the caverns, seven floors down it was—centrally heated and everything so that the pictures didn't spoil. It's my belief if the Germans had ever invaded, they'd never have found where we'd put all the good paintings. They might have been there still."

"This is very interesting," Evan said. "I wonder if the film crew knows. Is Trefor Thomas still alive?"

"Last I heard he was."

"I think they should get you to tell your story for the film," Evan said. "I'll mention it tomorrow."

"Me? In a film? *Escob Annwyl!* Whatever next." Mrs. Williams put her hand to her vast bosom, but she looked pleased all the same.

SEVEN

WHEN EVAN ARRIVED at the Everest Inn the next morning, Edward was sitting alone with a pot of coffee, Howard was pacing around, now dressed in a leather flight jacket with fur collar, and there was no sign of Grantley or Sandie. Evan was just about to ask where they were when Sandie came running down the stairs, followed by Grantley.

"Sandie, darling, be reasonable," he called after her.

"Don't you Sandie darling me," she snapped. "I hate you. I never want to see you again as long as I live. I'll never forgive what you've done. Never!"

"Sandie," he caught up with her as she reached the reception desk.

"Would you please phone for a taxi," Sandie said, her voice quivering. "I'm leaving."

Grantley came over to Edward and grabbed his arm. "Say something. Make her stay, for God's sake. Tell her it was all a joke. Tell her anything, only don't let her go!"

"You tell her, Grantley." Edward shrugged him off.

But it appeared that Sandie was not to be persuaded.

A bellboy came downstairs with her luggage and she disappeared in a taxi.

"And then there were three," Edward commented. "I don't care what hysterics are going on, my salvage crew is waiting for me. And if you want to shoot this operation, you'd better get up to the lake with me."

A glowering Grantley climbed into the car. Howard was humming to himself as if the incident had lightened his spirits. Evan sat next to Grantley, feeling very uncomfortable.

The lakeshore was bustling with activity. A floating platform was now on the lake above the sunken plane. Two divers were working and another man was directing a robot camera. A large generator was running and lights and camera were in place.

"Any chance that they'll raise it today?" Howard asked.

"That's probably a trifle optimistic," Edward said. "The divers can't work for long at those depths and those temperatures. It's very murky down there, you know. Still, I'm hopeful a couple more days will do it."

"That's the spirit—the one optimist in the group." Howard slapped him on the back.

Cameras started rolling. Divers went down. Suddenly Grantley yelled, "Cut! What the hell is that over there?"

Evan looked where he was pointing. "Oh no," he groaned.

Betsy had just emerged from behind a large rock. She was wearing a tiny purple and white polka dot bikini that barely covered the interesting parts of her body. As the men watched, enthralled, she walked down to the shore, spread out a towel, and lay on it.

"What the hell is she doing here?" Grantley yelled. "Constable, I told you to keep people away! For God's sake, do your job."

Evan walked over to Betsy.

"What are you doing?" he demanded.

She smiled up at him. "I'm sunbathing. I always come up here to sunbathe, away from it all, in the middle of nature."

"Betsy, it's the middle of November and I told you to stay away. These gentlemen are busy trying to shoot their film."

Betsy got to her feet, giving a good imitation of a surprised Marilyn Monroe. "Oh, are they shooting a film up here? I hadn't noticed. Ooh, I'm sorry. I hope I didn't get in your way."

The young camera crew were grinning. The man operating the robot camera wasn't paying attention to his screen. Betsy looked at Evan's angry face. "I'm sorry, but it was worth a try, wasn't it? Po-faced lot, aren't they? All right, I'm going now. 'Bye." She blew a kiss in the direction of the camera.

"Sorry about that," Evan muttered. "She likes sunbathing—comes up here all the time, even in winter. It won't happen again."

Shooting continued. The underwater remote camera brought up dramatic shots of the plane, half-hidden in silt. Then Grantley stiffened. "Oh no, not again!"

Evan half expected to see Betsy reappearing, but instead a lone man, dressed in knee britches and hiking boots, a hat with a feather on one side and carrying a stick, came up the trail.

"It's only a hiker," Evan said, "and this is one of the major routes to the summit of Snowdon. We should just wait until he's gone."

"I suppose so," Grantley snapped. "Break, everybody."

Instead of continuing up the trail, the hiker veered off and came toward them.

"You are the Mr. Grantley Smith?" he demanded in a heavily accented voice. "I am Gerhart Eichner. You have found my brozzer's plane?"

Grantley leaped forward, his hand extended. "My

dear Herr Eichner. So good of you to come." He turned
to the others. "The brother of the pilot. I told you I'd
located him. Start the cameras rolling, Will. This
should be good—human interest. Emotion." He es-
corted the German toward the monitor. "Yes, we've
located the plane and they've got a remote camera on
it now. See, on the screen? That's one wing sticking
up to the left. It won't be long before we raise it."

"My brozzer's body—it is still in the plane?"

"We can't see yet. We'll have to wait until we bring
it up."

"And what do you do wiz zis plane ven you bring
it up?" There was an edge to the German's voice now.

"Oh, actually it's going in a new museum." Edward
bounded across like an eager puppy. " 'War in the
Skies.' It's being created in a hangar at a disused RAF
base. This plane will be a centerpiece."

"No!" The German let out a roar. "Zis I do not like.
Zat plane vas my brozzer's coffin. He is not a centerpiece."

"Oh, don't worry—you'll be able to take home the
remains for burial, if that's what you want," Grantley
said. "If we can sort out who is who at this stage."

"I vant him left in peace where he lies. He was a
shy man. He would not vant to be part of zis spectacle."

"Sorry, old chap," Grantley said. "We've got permission to raise the plane and we're going to raise it."

"I am his brozzer. I forbid it!" Herr Eichner yelled.

"Nothing you can do to stop us, I'm afraid. It's Ministry of Defense property." He patted the German on
the shoulder. "Now please go away, we're very busy."

The German's face had turned puce. He waved his
walking stick at Grantley. "I stop you!" he shouted. "I
find a way to stop you. You have no right!"

"I have every right," Grantley said. "Your side lost,
remember? Spoils of war and all that!" He faced the
German, an insolent smile on his face. "Now please
leave before I have Constable Evans throw you out."

"I come back!" The German waved his stick again. "I find a way to stop you, I promise!"

He stomped off down the track.

"Our Grantley has quite a way with people, doesn't he?" Howard muttered to Evan. "Proper little diplomat. Thank heavens he didn't decide to be secretary-general of the United Nations or we'd have had World War Three by now."

"I heard that," Grantley said. He looked amused. "And of course I'd never have been secretary-general of the U.N. My name's too ordinary. You need to be called Boutros Boutros Ghali or Perez de Queyar before they'll even consider you."

He's enjoying this, Evan suddenly realized. Grantley was one of those people who fed on conflict.

"You're right," Howard added. "Your name is too ordinary."

For some reason, Grantley shot him a venomous glance. "Let's stop chattering and get back to work, eh?"

At that moment the rain began—not a gentle mist but a drenching downpour.

"So far today hasn't been exactly scintillating," Grantley said as they scrambled into the vehicles and negotiated the track down to the village. "Somebody say something to cheer me up. I'm about to sink into depression."

"It's your own fault, Grantley," Edward said, "you've behaved like a complete prat."

"Me? I was defending myself against a Hunnish invasion." He turned to Evan. "Now, our honest village constable, say something to cheer me up. Tell me you've unearthed a brilliant war story for us that will bring our dreary little epic to life."

He was being so obviously sarcastic and patronizing that Evan was tempted not even to mention Mrs. Williams's story. But then he decided that the story would be a definite coup.

"I do have one woman I'd like you to meet," he said.

"Oh God, please say it's not that awful preacher's wife!" Grantley wailed.

"No, actually she comes from a village about fifteen miles away. She can put us onto somebody who helped to store all the paintings from the National Gallery in a slate mine during the war."

"The paintings from the National Gallery? Are you serious?"

"Oh." It was Evan's turn to smile. "Didn't you know about that? The whole lot, seven stories down in a cavern, for safekeeping."

Grantley wriggled around in his seat. "What an incredible story. Take us to her right away!"

An hour later Evan was at the wheel of the Land Rover, driving Grantley Smith up the winding road to the slate town of Blenau Ffestiniog.

"God, what a dismal-looking place," Grantley exclaimed as the settlement came into view ahead of them, two lines of gray cottages, surrounded by slag heaps of slate, nestled under gray slate quarries. "I'd go mad if I had to live here." He waved his cigarette dramatically, sending pungent smoke into Evan's face.

"Don't say that to the locals. They think it's the best place on earth." Evan grinned. "Ever so proud of their choir and their chapels, they are here." He slowed as they turned into the village high street. "I'll just stop at the pub. I'm sure they'll know where Trefor Thomas lives."

The cottage was perched outside the village at the edge of a high, bleak moor. A slim, good-looking man in his forties or fifties opened the door. "Can I help you?" he asked warily in Welsh.

"Yes, we're looking for Trefor Thomas. Have we got the right house?"

The man reacted to Evan's uniform. "You have. I'm his son, Tudur Thomas. Is something wrong?"

"No, nothing. This gentleman is from England and

he's making a film about Wales in the war. We understand that your dad was working in the mine when they stored all the paintings down there. Mr. Smith would like to interview him."

Grantley Smith's eyes had been darting from one face to the other as they spoke in Welsh. He stepped between the men with his hand extended. "Grantley Smith," he said. "I expect he's told you we're making a film. We'd like to feature your father in it."

"Oh, I see." Tudur Thomas glanced back into the house. "You better come inside and we'll see. I'm not sure how much you'll get out of him." He leaned closer to them and lowered his voice. "His mind's going, see. Some days he's quite clear and lucid, other days he doesn't even know me. He had a stroke last summer and I came back here to look after him. He's recovered pretty well physically—he always was as strong as an ox. All those old slate miners were, weren't they? But his mind's definitely rambling. That's why I've stayed on—so that he doesn't set fire to the place."

"Are you his only relative?" Evan asked.

Tudur nodded. "My mother died when I was young. Dad more or less raised me by himself. He's never been an easy man—a bit of a hermit, I suppose you could say. But he's been good to me. I want to do right by him. I've taken leave of absence from my school— I'm the art master at a comprehensive in Wrexham."

"Following in your father's footsteps, eh?" Evan smiled at him. "We heard your dad was something of an artist."

"A really talented artist," Tudur Thomas said. "Unlike me. He paid to send me to art school, but I never was much good, unfortunately. Good enough to teach. Come on in then, I'll see if he's awake."

Tudur Thomas went ahead of them. Evan and Grantley Smith followed, ducking their heads under the low doorway into a dark entrance hall.

"Tad? Ble ryt ti?" he called out. "We've got visitors.

Gentlemen come to see you." There was an exchange of rapid Welsh conversation, too low for Evan to catch.

"Come on in. He'll see you." Tudur ushered them into a gloomy, cold living room. A coal fire was burning in the fireplace but it didn't seem to give off much heat and the room had a chill, dampish feel to it.

It was clear that Trefor Thomas had once been the handsome man Mrs. Williams had sighed over. Even at seventy, he had a shock of white curly hair and a strong, angular face. In some ways he looked like a bigger, more vital version of his son. He stared at the visitors warily.

"Have you come to arrest me?" he asked, looking at Evan's uniform collar peeping out from under his jacket.

"Why, what have you done?" Evan asked good-naturedly.

The old man shot a glance at his son. "He knows, don't you?"

Tudur laughed. "Oh, he means the time he took a Cadbury's Fruit and Nut bar from Tesco's. I made him put it back."

He motioned them to sit on the sofa.

"I'll make us a cup of tea, all right, *Tad*?" Tudur said in English. He disappeared into a kitchen. Evan looked around the room. The furniture was threadbare and faded but the walls were covered with paintings. There were several cheap reproductions of masterpieces, plus a couple of local landscapes Evan guessed had been done by Mr. Thomas the elder. Evan thought they were quite good.

Grantley leaned forward in his seat. "Mr. Thomas. We've just been talking to Mrs. Williams in Llanfair. You remember her?"

Trefor Thomas shook his head.

"She wasn't Williams then. She was Gwynneth Morgan. She said you used to play with her brothers."

A smile of recognition spread across Trefor's face.

"Gywnneth Morgan? A skinny little thing, wasn't she? I wonder what happened to her?"

Evan thought that Trefor couldn't have seen Mrs. Williams lately.

"She lives in Llanfair, Mr. Thomas," he said. "She married Gwillum Williams and she has a daughter and a granddaughter."

"A granddaughter? Little Gwynneth Morgan? No!" He shook his head in disbelief.

Grantley got up and switched on his camera. "Mr. Thomas, Mrs. Williams told us you had helped build the sheds where they stored all the paintings during the war. Can you tell us about that?"

"Paintings?" Mr. Thomas looked around. "I like nice paintings. Always have. Always keep a few good ones around to look at. Got some of the best here, haven't I? *The Laughing Cavalier*—one of my favorites, and a Constable and that Rembrandt. Always did have good taste in art. Mr. Hughes at school, he taught me." He pointed at the painting over the fireplace. "Those old artists knew how to paint. None of this modern splashing and daubing."

"Not these paintings, Mr. Thomas," Grantley said patiently. "I'm talking about the paintings they put in the slate mine, during the war."

A troubled look spread across his face. "They came all wrapped up, didn't they? I was hoping I'd be able to look after them, seeing as how I worked there, but they wouldn't let us see them." A faraway look came over his face.

"So can you tell us what you remember about that time—about building the sheds down in the mine . . . ?"

"You can't paint skin tones like that with modern paints," he said, pointing at the Rembrandt print. "I don't know what he used back then, but they had different paints in those days. I've tried but . . ."

"They don't want to know about your painting, Dad." Tudur came in with a tray with four mugs on it and a plate of Cadbury's chocolate finger biscuits.

"I was pretty good when I was younger, wasn't I, boy?" the old man said, holding out huge gnarled hands to them. "But I haven't painted in many years. Sort of lost interest. Not much to paint when you're down a slate mine every day of your life." He pointed up at the wall. "That's one of my paintings. Not bad for an amateur, eh? Better than that great lump can do, anyhow." He glanced at his son. "I paid for him to go to school, but he hadn't got my talent."

Tudur put the tray down on a low table and handed his father a mug. "They want you to tell them what you remember about the war."

"A long time ago that was," Trefor said. "I was young then. Not like you see now. Strong. Handsome. All the girls liked me. I could have had any one I wanted." He chuckled, then the smile faded. "A long time ago, that was." He took a noisy slurp of tea, then picked up a biscuit from the plate. They waited patiently but his head sank down onto his chest.

"It's not easy," Tudur apologized. "He comes and goes. Some days he can be quite lucid and talkative. Other days—well, like now."

"I tell you what," Grantley said. "I've got a portable recorder with me. Why don't I leave that with your dad and he can talk into it when he feels like it." He brought the small tape recorder out of his bag. "How about it, Mr. Thomas?"

"What's that?" Trefor Thomas looked at the small machine with suspicion.

"A tape machine," Grantley said, holding it out to him. "You don't have to talk in front of us. Why don't you take your time and let the memories come back to you? Then, when you're ready, you just press that red button there and talk into the machine. Anything you can remember about the war, the slate mine, any good stories about when they brought in all the pictures . . . anything you can think of that might be interesting."

"How about that, Dad?" Tudur took the machine for him. "See, you just push the red button and talk. You can take it to your room. That might be fun, to remember when you were a lad, mightn't it?"

The old man took the machine and sat staring at it. Then he put it down and took another noisy slurp of tea.

EIGHT

GRANTLEY SMITH WAS bubbling with excitement as they drove back down the High Street.

"Who knows what we'll get out of him? Complete gobbledygook, I'm afraid. But never mind. I suppose the old mine is around here somewhere. We should ask. I'd like to meet the former mine manager, and other men that worked there . . . and maybe we can get in touch with the National Gallery. They must have documented all this on film." He turned to beam at Evan. "This is going to be good stuff, Constable. Bloody brilliant of you to find this!" He fumbled with his packet of Gitanes. Evan sighed as he lit another cigarette.

They were just leaving Blenau Ffestiniog when there was a violent shriek from a whistle and a little train crossed the street ahead of them, a small antique steam engine pulling a line of scaled-down carriages. Grantley let out a whoop of delight. "A little train! Look at it, Constable—it's a real little train."

"That's right," Evan said. "It used to carry slate down from the mine to the port at Porthmadog. Now it's been resurrected to carry tourists."

"What fun. We have to get the little train into the film somehow. I can't wait to show it to Edward and Howard!"

Evan looked at him almost with affection. Grantley's problem was that he had just never grown up. He sat beside Evan with a big, satisfied smile on his face. Then, without warning, he asked, "So, tell me, Constable—is it true that you're bonking the lovely Bronwen?"

"I don't think that's any of your business." Evan continued to stare at the road ahead.

"No need to be defensive about it. She must be delighted. I'm sure Edward wasn't up to scratch in that department. A big, burly policeman is probably just what she needs."

Evan wondered how he could have thought Grantley childlike. His first assessment had been closer to the mark. Grantley was a man who got a delight out of pressing other people's buttons.

"She's having dinner with us tonight, at the Inn," Grantley went on. "Maybe you'd like to join us."

Evan didn't want to admit that Bronwen hadn't mentioned this dinner date. "Oh no thank you," he said easily. "I'm sure you have a lot of catching up to do. I'd just be superfluous."

"As you wish, only . . ."

He sensed that Grantley was annoyed he hadn't risen to the bait.

When they arrived back in Llanfair, Grantley wanted to be driven straight back up to the lakeside. "Edward's probably going to be in a complete tizzy because I've been away so long," he commented with a wicked grin.

This was confirmed as Edward came hurrying over to meet them. "Where the hell have you two been? It's been farcical up here. We've had a bulldozer show up, loaded with lager louts. We've had that red-headed girl back with snacks for everybody and then she wouldn't leave. I thought we were assigned a policeman to help deal with things like this, not to go driving all over the countryside on one of your whims!"

"Keep your hair on," Grantley said. "You wait until you hear what we've found. Not only have we got ourselves a great slate mine story, with a firsthand account and a promised tour of the mine, but we've discovered a wonderful little train as well. We're all going to take a ride tomorrow up from the coast to the slate town."

"And exactly how does a little train, however cute and appealing it may be, fit into a film about raising an aeroplane?" Edward asked in a clipped voice.

"I have to agree, Grantley," Howard said. "We do have a budget and we're only shooting a sixty-minute feature. It's not a travelogue on the beauties of North Wales."

"We'll find a way to fit it in," Grantley said impatiently. "Maybe an intro sequence to set the scene. Anyway, at least say you'll ride it up with me tomorrow. Then we can tour the slate mine and you can see for yourselves that we'll have an absolute scoop with our wartime art story."

Edward sighed. "I know him too well. He won't shut up until we ride his bloody train with him. All right, Grantley. We'll ride the train tomorrow. Satisfied?"

"Thank you, Edward. Okay. Where have we got to with our filming?"

He was suddenly all business again.

My chance came when all the older boys were called up and left. Then I was the pick of the younger crop—head and shoulders taller than the rest of the fifteen-year-olds and well built too, even in those days. Ginger liked them well built.

I remembered that summer day when we walked up onto the moor together. It was hot and sunny and she made me take my shirt off. "My but you've got lovely muscles," she said, and she ran her hands down my back as we sat together on a rock. The feel of her hands turned me to jelly. I was on fire, my head was a jumble of confused thoughts. Was she egging me on? Did she want me to go all the way? I knew about her reputation, of course. She'd done it with several boys in the village. I hadn't done it at all yet, but it was about bloody time. I turned and reached out for her, but she jumped up onto a flat rock and hitched up her skirt. "How about this then, Tref?" She started to sing, "Heaven . . . I'm in heaven," and she danced, gliding over the flat rock just like we'd seen in the movies. Then she grabbed my hand and dragged me up there with her. "Hold me around the waist, Tref. That's right. Now, off we go . . . 'when we're out together dancing cheek to cheek.' " I wasn't even conscious of my feet touching the ground. She was spinning me around, the sky and the moor were flashing past as she twirled me, and somehow I kept up with her crazy dance until we both collapsed, panting and laughing.

"You know what, Trefor—I bet you could get work in Hollywood too, with that body." She grabbed my shoulders. "We don't belong in a dump like this, either of us. Let's run away together."

"Don't be daft," I said. "There's a war on. How are you going to get to Hollywood with a war on?"

"It can't last forever."

"Yes, but I'm bound to be called up before it's over. And what if Herr Hitler lands here, eh? How are you going to get to Hollywood then?"

She ran her hands through that blond, wavy hair. "I have a feeling that my type appeals to German officers."

"You wouldn't!"

"I'd do what it takes, my darling. Whatever it takes to get me there." She squeezed my shoulders. "You've got to believe that good things will happen, Tref. We've got to make them happen."

"How?" I asked bleakly. "I've only got two years until I'm called up and then I don't know if I'll ever come back, do I?"

"Don't talk daft." She let go of my shoulders and hugged her arms to herself.

"I'm not talking daft. Look what happened to Johnny Morgan at Dunkirk. And Will Jones's ship got torpedoed. You don't live long in a war."

"Then we've got to make sure we come out okay," she said. *"If you get called up, show them your drawings. You could go into the army as an artist."*

"Now you're talking daft again."

"No, I'm not. They have army magazines and posters and things. Someone has to draw them. Why not you?"

She snuggled close to me, her sweet, blond hair tickling my cheek. *"You have to take your chances in this world, Trefor. There are those people who sit back and let things happen to them, and those that reach out and grab what they want. We're getting out of here, you and me, Tref. We're going to Hollywood and we're going to be stars."*

Cautiously, I put my arm around her. *"It's all dreams, Ginger. It can't ever happen."*

She shrugged me off and jumped to her feet. *"I'm going to make it happen. I don't know how yet. I know there's a war on, but I'm not going to stop believing. One day my chance is going to come, and when it does, I'm going to be ready for it!"*

Evan didn't sleep well that night. He couldn't help thinking about Bronwen spending an evening with her former husband and friends. He told himself he had nothing to worry about. Bronwen hadn't exactly been pining for her ex-husband. But why had she kept quiet about her dinner date last night, unless she didn't want him to know? Was it still possible that she had feelings for Edward Ferrers? Was she missing the intellectual stimulus of her former life? Bloody film crew, he thought. They've been nothing but trouble since they came here.

Then he remembered something that lifted his spirits instantly. This morning his charges were going to take their ride on the little train. He wasn't needed. He could spend a quiet morning in his office catching up on paperwork in blissful silence!

He worked until midday, went home for a satisfying lunch of shepherd's pie and cabbage, and then went back to the Everest Inn to wait for the Land Rover. By two-thirty, there was still no sign of it. Evan walked up the trail until he could overlook the lake. The diving team was working but there was no sign of any filming taking place. He walked down again to wait. Obviously, Grantley had got his way yet again. He'd probably taken them all down the slate mine and found other miners for them to interview. Evan was sure he'd taken his portable video camera with him.

Evan asked the hotel receptionist to call him when they returned, then headed back to his office. School was just over and noisy, laughing children were fighting to be first out of the playground.

"Hello, Evan." Bronwen appeared behind the children. "How's my favorite sheepdog then? Should I start calling you Mot or Gel?" Most of the farmers in the area had a border collie called Mot or Gel.

Evan didn't smile. "So how was your evening?"

"My evening? All right, I suppose."

"Did you have fun?"

"If you can call marking twenty-five history tests fun. You'd think I'd never taught those children spelling or history. Tommy Howell said that the Magna Carta was a kind of racing car."

Was she bluffing, Evan wondered, not telling him because she didn't want to hurt his feelings?

"So you didn't go out at all?"

"Evan." She tossed back her braid over her shoulder. "When do I ever go out on a school night? There's always too much work."

"Of course not. Well, I'd best be getting back to the station. I'm waiting for a message about the film people. They haven't shown up all day."

He went on his way, leaving her standing at the school

gate. Had she just lied to him? She hadn't seemed agitated, but some women were good at telling you lies while
they looked right into your eyes. He had known one once.
Not Bronwen, he told himself. He could definitely trust
Bronwen. If she had been to dinner with Edward last
night, she would have told him.

It was after five and he was about to close up the station
and go home when the phone rang.

"Constable Evans—you asked us to call you when the
film people came back. They're just pulling up outside
the Inn now."

Evan hurried into his jacket and up the street. Maybe
it was nothing to do with him and he should be minding
his own business, but they had kept him waiting up at the
lake. They did owe him an explanation at least.

As he came into the Inn, the filmmakers were just picking up their keys at the front desk.

"Yes, terrible accident," Evan heard Howard Bauer say.

"What happened?" Evan hurried over to them. "Is
something wrong?"

"Grantley fell out of the train," Edward said with a big
smile on his face.

NINE

EVAN STARED AT Edward Ferrers in disbelief. "He fell out of the train? Is he—all right?"

"You know Grantley," Edward said. "Charmed life. He fell onto thick bracken, he rolled, and his fall was stopped by a friendly oak tree. Two more inches to the right and he'd have tumbled all the way down into the gorge a thousand feet below. They're keeping him in hospital in Dolgellau overnight for observation, but all he seems to have are scrapes and bruises. The camera is a goner, though."

Edward didn't seem at all horrified over the incident, in contrast to Howard, who looked ashen.

"I think we all need a drink," he muttered. "You too, Constable. Drinks on me." He led them through to the bar.

"Geez, that's better," he muttered as he drained the glass of Scotch in one gulp. "I needed that. Look, my hands are still shaking."

"What exactly happened?" Evan asked. "How can someone fall out of a train?"

"You know Grantley," Edward said again. He still

sounded animated and almost amused. "He insisted on leaning out of the carriage to film the whole way up. They are antiques, those carriages. The door handle can't have worked too well. It came flying open and Grantley made a spectacular exit."

"He came flying right out," Howard said. "I was in the next carriage. I saw the whole thing."

"He had a very lucky escape," Evan said. "There are places on that route where a fall would mean certain death."

"Exactly," Edward said. "But we all know that Grantley has sold his soul to the devil and will live for ever and ever."

"You shouldn't joke about things like that, Edward," Howard said. "Very bad taste."

"Oh, come on, Howard. Just a way to steady the nerves, that's all. It's my way when I've had a shock. I have to joke about it. Sorry."

He picked up his own glass and drained it.

"Will this put filming on hold?" Evan asked.

"No, we have to press on tomorrow," Edward said. "If they let Grantley out of hospital, he said he'd get a taxi back. We can't keep the diving crew on too much longer—they're costing a fortune. That plane has to come up in the next day or so."

"Why's it taking so long?" Evan asked.

"They're having problems attaching the damned inflatable collar. A plane isn't exactly an easy shape to work with. We might have to resort to attaching grapples and wynching it up instead—but then we'll need a floating crane and there's more chance of the plane breaking apart."

"Relax, Edward, its going to be fine," Howard said. "Things usually have a way of sorting themselves out."

"Thanks, Howard, you're a pillar of strength," Edward said.

"No, I'm a fatalist." Howard held out his glass for a refill.

• • •

It was around ten o'clock the next morning when Grantley stepped out of a taxi in front of the Everest Inn, moving a little stiffly, a large sticking plaster across his temple, but otherwise fine and bursting with energy. "I lay in that awful, hard bed in that dreary hospital and you know what I was thinking all night?"

He looked around his audience. "I kept thinking, damn—why didn't we bring a second camera? If Howard had been filming me, just think what a sequence that would have made!" He started to laugh. "Oh well, back to work. Edward, you and Howard go up to your plane. I've got phone calls to make, a slate mine to tour . . . busy, busy, busy."

"You see, I told you," Edward muttered to Evan. "Unstoppable. Nothing fazes him. You have to admire him for it, I suppose."

Grantley took off again. Work continued without incident at the site and it seemed to Evan that they were getting close now. The collar was almost in place. With any luck the plane would float to the surface very soon, the filming would finish, and he could go back to his normal life. And the sooner Edward disappeared from Bronwen's life, the better.

He hoped that they might take the weekend off, so that he and Bronwen could get away together. But the weather forecast was for a fine, dry Saturday, so Edward decided they ought to press on, and not push their luck.

"It's a shame they're making you work on your Saturday morning, Mr. Evans," Mrs. Williams said. "Still, I've made you your weekend breakfast. Get that inside of you and you won't do too badly."

She put down a plate laden with an egg, two rashers of bacon, a sausage, mushrooms, tomatoes, baked beans, and fried bread in front of Evan. Evan felt his belt tightening just through looking at it, but he didn't turn it down either. He was walking up and down the track to the lake every day, he rationalized. Although he suspected he'd have to trot up and down Snowdon a few times before he burned off these calories.

He was feeling full, fortified, and ready to face the emotional electricity of working with Grantley Smith, when the phone rang. He picked it up, hoping against hope that they were canceling work today. But it wasn't one of the film crew.

"Constable Evans? This is Robert James—you know, son of the Jameses-Fron-Heulog? Where can I find that Mr. Smith who brought Pauline to see my parents?"

"I should think he's at the Inn, but I don't think . . ." Evan began but Robert James interrupted. "No, he's not. I already called there. They said he'd left early this morning."

"Then I expect he already went up to the lake where they're filming." Evan reached for his jacket. "But I don't want you going up there. Why don't you let me pass on a message if you have one. We don't want any more trouble, do we?"

"You give him a message from me then, Mr. Evans," Robert James spat the words. "You tell that self-satisfied little prat that they rushed my father into hospital last night with a heart attack. They don't know whether he's going to make it—all thanks to your Mr. Smith and his little games."

"I'm very sorry to hear that, Mr. James," Evan said. "I do hope he makes a speedy recovery."

"They don't know if my father's going to make it." Robert James's voice cracked. "He'd had heart trouble last year, but he was doing fine until that Smith fellow showed up and upset him like that. That bastard has no right to muck about with other people's lives. You tell him he's going to get what's coming to him, Mr. Evans. I'll stop him from finishing this stupid film, you see if I don't."

The line went dead. Evan shook his head, then put

on his jacket and hurried out of the door.

There was no sign of the Land Rover in the car park at the Inn, so he headed straight for the lake. As he looked up the trail, he saw a solitary person ahead of him. He realized with surprise that it was an old woman, wearing a long black dress, a black head scarf and shawl; what's more she was hobbling up the path, doing her knitting as she went. Evan had no idea who she might be or where she might be going. He hurried to catch up with her.

"Can I help you, ma'am?" he asked. Then his jaw gaped in disbelief. The face might have been given some wrinkles with makeup and she might be wearing a gray wig, but none of the above disguised who she really was. "Betsy, what do you think you're doing?"

She looked at him defiantly. "You said yourself that they were only interested in interviewing old people for the film. All right. I'm an old person—Granny Jones who knitted scarves for the soldiers during the war."

Evan laughed. "Betsy *cariad,* you couldn't fool anyone."

"I might. I'm a good actress, you know. Anyway, you can't stop me. It's a public path up the mountain."

"I've been told by my chief to keep people away from the site. So I can arrest you for disturbing the peace if you're not careful."

"You wouldn't dare!" She glared up at him, her face looking so comical with its fake wrinkles that he had to laugh again. He grabbed her arm and firmly turned her around. "Go on, Betsy *cariad,* go home and wash that lot off your face before anyone sees you."

She shook herself free. "Don't you *cariad* me, Evan Evans. I'm not your darling. If you really cared about me, you'd want me to be a famous star. You're thwarting my Hollywood career, Evan Evans, that's what you're doing."

She turned and stomped angrily down the track again. Evan smiled as he watched her go.

When he reached the lake, he saw several men sitting on rocks smoking, but no sign of Edward, Grantley, or Howard.

"What happened? Where are they?" he asked the cameraman.

"You tell me, mate." The man took an impatient puff on his cigarette. "Last thing yesterday they told us to be here, nine o'clock sharp. We're here. They aren't. Still, it's their money. . . ."

Evan stared at the path back to the village. He supposed he ought to go back down again, to see what was keeping the filmmakers. But the big breakfast was still sitting heavy on his stomach and he didn't relish repeating that climb in a hurry. Then he decided that it was none of his business. He'd been assigned to provide protection. Well, he was here and he was protecting. If they'd wanted him somewhere else, they could have called him. He sat on a rock next to the cameraman.

"We'll just have to wait until they show up, then."

"Cigarette, mate?" The cameraman offered his packet.

"Thanks, but I don't."

"Smart of you. Wish I could quit, but it's so bloody stressful, working with these artistic types." He grinned at Evan. "You're lucky with your job. I don't suppose anything ever happens up here, does it?"

"Not very often," Evan admitted. "We get our small doses of excitement."

"I bet this lot was an excitement you could do without!"

Evan thought of the unpleasant scenes he'd been forced to witness. "You can say that again," he agreed.

It was around noon when Edward came hurrying up the path, his face red and sweating from the exertion.

"Isn't Grantley back yet?" he asked.

"Nobody's shown up all morning," Evan said. "We wondered where you'd all got to."

"Howard wasn't feeling well and said he'd stay in his room," Edward said. "And Grantley insisted on dragging me up to that Blenny whatsit place again at crack of dawn."

"Blenau Ffestiniog?"

"That's it. He's got a new bee in his bonnet."

"Oh, what now?" Evan asked.

Edward took out a large handkerchief and mopped his forehead. "I don't exactly know. He was being bloody-minded. When he's in that kind of mood, it's better to leave him alone. Besides, I didn't want to waste a whole day tramping around slate mines. If he had his way, he'd turn this picture into a melodramatic farce."

Evan noticed that Edward was still sweating.

"So, are we going to wait for Mr. Smith to show up?" the cameraman asked. "We're all getting pretty cheesed off waiting around doing nothing. It's bloody cold up here, you know."

"No, we'll start work again this very minute," Edward said. "We have to make the most of fine weather. The cloud could come down again tomorrow and stay down for weeks." He turned to the cameraman. "Just use your judgment about how much film you shoot. If the director and the producer can't be bothered to show up, they'll have to take what they get. I'm going to get this damned plane raised if it's the last thing I do."

He stomped over to the divers and instantly the generator and winch sprang to life. Edward worked like a man possessed, rushing from one activity to the next. The longer the day dragged on, the angrier he got.

"Damn Grantley. He's never where he should be—always rushing off on some tangent of his own, trying to do something nobody else has thought of doing, and neglecting what he should be doing. Fine. Who needs him?"

The sky clouded over and by late afternoon the light was too poor to continue.

"And now we have to walk back because he's got the bloody Land Rover," Edward growled. "My bloody Land Rover. The museum lent it to me, specifically. He acts as if it's his and I'm his bloody chauffeur."

Evan said nothing as they walked down the path together. There was nothing really to say. He was only thankful that Betsy hadn't chosen this moment to spring another of her disguises on them.

As the Inn came into view, Edward paused and scanned the car park. "Look, he's not even back yet. The Land Rover's not there. Don't tell me he decided to go down to London . . ."

"London—why would he want to go there?" Evan asked.

"Oh, another of his whims. He phoned the National Gallery about those paintings. He seems to think they'll make a good story. . . ." Edward quickened his pace, leaving Evan behind.

TEN

EVAN HAD JUST turned off the TV set after the nightly news and was going up the stairs to bed when the phone rang. He rushed to answer it so that it didn't wake Mrs. Williams, who was always in bed no later than ten.

It was Edward Ferrers. "Constable Evans, sorry to disturb you, but frankly I'm worried. We've had no word from Grantley yet."

"You said you thought he might have gone to London?"

"Yes, but he would have left a message by now. And I don't think that even he would be callous enough to run off with our only means of transportation."

"Do you happen to know the Land Rover license number, Mr. Ferrers?" Evan grabbed the message pad beside the phone. "I'll call HQ and ask the patrols to keep an eye out for it. And I'll give the police at Blenau a call as well—just in case he's still up there."

"What if he's met with an accident on the way to London?"

"I'll see what I can do," Evan said.

"What about filing a missing person report?" Edward demanded.

"A little too early for that. I'm sure you'll have heard from him by morning."

"I hope so," Edward said. "God, I hope so."

Evan called headquarters to report the missing Land Rover's number, then went back upstairs. Just what was Grantley Smith up to now? Evan wondered as he climbed into bed, pulling the wool-stuffed Welsh quilt over him. Grantley's life seemed to be one ongoing drama. Was this latest disappearing act another example of his taste for the dramatic? If he'd gone to London, Evan only hoped he'd stay there!

The phone rang again at seven o'clock on Sunday morning. Evan groped for his dressing gown and peered at his watch. Seven o'clock. Bloody hell. Why did emergencies always seem to happen at weekends? He stumbled down the stairs, meeting Mrs. Williams just emerging from her room in her old chenille dressing gown and slippers.

"It's all right, Mrs. Williams. I'll get it," he said.

"Now who can that be, disturbing your sleep on a Sunday morning? It ought not to be allowed," she called down the stairs after him.

It was Edward Ferrers again. "No news yet? I haven't slept a wink all night. Where can he be, Constable Evans? He can't just have vanished." Edward sounded close to panic.

"Just keep calm." Evan resorted to his best professional manner. "If an accident had happened, we'd have heard, wouldn't we? I'll call headquarters for you and see if the latest patrols have turned up something."

"And then I want to file my missing person report. It's been almost twenty-four hours now."

"I'll come up to the Inn as soon as I get dressed," Evan said, "but don't worry too much. He strikes me as the sort of person who goes in for drama—isn't that right?"

"Yes, but . . ."

"So he'll probably come breezing in as if nothing's wrong today and act surprised that you were all so worried about him."

"That's just the sort of thing he would do. I pray to God you're right," Edward said.

Evan put down the phone. The distant ringing of church bells floated up on the breeze. Sunday morning. Supposed to be a day of rest, not a day of stress. Now it didn't even look as though he'd be getting his Sunday off. Damn that Grantley Smith, he thought. He dressed hurriedly, then put in a call to headquarters.

W.P.C. Jones was manning the switchboard. "Oh, Constable Evans, we were just about to call you. We've found your Land Rover for you."

"You have—where?"

"At Porthmadog. Down by the harbor."

"Porthmadog. What could it have been doing there?" Evan demanded. "Nobody in it, I suppose?"

"Not that I know of. Constable Roberts from Porthmadog just called it in."

"Who's on duty this morning from the plainclothes division?"

"Sergeant Watkins is supposed to be on duty today. I don't know whether he's here yet—oh, hold on a second, he just walked in. Constable Evans at Llanfair for you, sir."

"So they've got you working bloody weekends as well, boyo, have they?" Watkins sounded cheerful in spite of the early Sunday morning hour. "I've had to miss my DIY program on the telly and they were going to be doing shelves today—which the missus has been nagging me to put up for months. What's the problem?"

"Maybe it's nothing, Sarge, but I thought I'd better report it right away. One of my film crew is missing."

Watkins chuckled. "Ooh dear. How embarrassing for you, boyo. You're assigned to look after them and you bloody well go and lose one. I wouldn't want to be in your shoes, explaining that to the chief."

"It's not funny, Sarge. The stupid man's missing and his colleagues are very worried."

"Missing in the mountains, you mean? I don't know what I'm supposed to do about that. You're the mountain rescue whiz, aren't you?"

"It wasn't in the mountains, Sarge," Evan interrupted tersely. Being roused by the phone on a Sunday morning hadn't done much for his temper. "He was last seen up in Blenau Ffestiniog early yesterday morning. He didn't check in all of yesterday. He didn't get in touch all last night and this morning his Land Rover was found parked by the docks in Porthmadog."

"It was Saturday last night. What's the betting he had one too many in a pub and is quietly sleeping it off somewhere?"

"He doesn't seem like that sort of bloke and the expedition leader is very worried."

"So you don't know what would have brought him down to Porthmadog?"

"No idea. I know he was interested in the narrow-gauge railway and the depot's down there. And there's a main-line station as well."

"And you think he might have gone somewhere by train?"

"His colleague thinks he might have gone to London."

"Well then, there you are. He's a grown man, after all. He can go to London if he wants, can't he?"

"But they can't imagine why he hasn't called them. They're in the middle of shooting up here—they've got the crew standing by idle. They want me to file a missing person report."

"You can't file a missing person report just because some bloke takes it into his head to go wandering off," Watkins said. "It isn't as if he's mentally incompetent or a runaway, is it?"

"No, but . . ."

"He's a grown man, Evan, for God's sake. He might have met a bird and spent the night with her, and calling his colleagues might have been the last thing on his mind." He paused. Evan said nothing. Watkins cleared his throat and continued. "Okay. I can't do anything officially yet. They're not even next of kin, but if he hasn't shown up by tomorrow . . ." He left the words hanging. "And if I was in your shoes, boyo," he added, "if I was the one who'd lost him, I'd show willing and start looking right now. Check out the area where that car was found and where he was last seen. Ask at the railway station to see if anyone remembers selling him a ticket—well, I don't have to tell you how to go about it, do I? You know how to solve a case as well as I do; better, in fact."

"Yes." Evan wasn't in the mood to be magnanimous. "I'll start looking, then. I hope that Roberts in Porthmadog doesn't think I'm treading on his turf. He doesn't like me much."

"Tell him you're there with my blessing," Watkins said. "Call me if you get any flack. And let me know when the bugger turns up."

"Right. I will."

Evan hung up and stood frowning at the phone. "Damn Grantley Smith," he muttered and dialed Porthmadog.

"So what great case are you solving now, Evans?" Constable Roberts asked. He was an ambitious young man and seemed to have resented Evan's brief moments in the limelight. "Land Rover stolen, was it?"

"No, it belongs to a bloke who's missing—one of the film people I was assigned to. Last seen early yesterday in Blenau Ffestiniog, I understand, and hasn't checked in with his colleagues since. I suppose the Land Rover was empty?"

"Absolutely. Parked on the street in a two-hour park-

ing zone. Lucky he didn't get a ticket, but we're short-
staffed at the moment."

"So it's still there?"

"That's right. And it bloody will get a ticket if it's
not moved today."

"Mind if I come down and take a look?" Evan asked.
"And then maybe we'd better have it towed to a garage,
just in case."

"You suspect funny business, then? This bloke
hasn't just wandered off and not told anyone?" Roberts
now sounded interested.

"We don't know yet."

"You're right," Roberts agreed. "Better safe than
sorry, eh? And I'll spread the word about your bloke
down here. What did he look like?"

"Young, arty type, black curly hair, speaks with a
posh English accent," Evan said. "I think anyone would
remember him."

"Right, then. We'll do what we can."

"Thanks, mate. *Diolch yn fawr.*" Evan hung up. Roberts wasn't so bad after all.

He got dressed in a hurry and made his way up to
the Inn.

Howard and Edward were sitting in the window, a cof-
feepot and undrunk coffee on the table between them.
Evan was also surprised to see Sandie at the table with
them. She looked disheveled and white-faced, as if she
hadn't been to bed all night. She jumped up as he came
in. "Any news yet?"

"They've found his car," Evan said. "Down at the
docks in Porthmadog."

"What on earth was it doing down there?" Edward
demanded.

"You have no idea yourself? He didn't mention anything he wanted to check out in Porthmadog?"

"Never mentioned a thing," Edward said.

"Not that he wanted to redo his train trip, without

falling out of a window this time?" Evan regretted saying this as soon as the words slipped out.

"Oh my God," Sandie wailed. "You don't suppose he's fallen out of another train, do you?"

"I don't think he makes a habit of it, Sandie dear," Edward said, "and he didn't mention anything about trains."

Howard also looked ashen faced and not at all well. "So what the hell do we do now, Constable? We're more or less prisoners here—no transportation, no nothing."

"At least the Land Rover's been found," Edward said. "Maybe the constable here would be kind enough to drive one of us down to Porthmadog to pick it up."

"I don't think I'd better do that at the moment," Evan said cautiously. "Our Forensics boys might want to go over it, if . . ."

"Oh my God, something's happened to him, hasn't it?" Sandie wailed. "It's all my fault."

"What exactly do you mean by that?" Evan asked.

"I mean"—she paused, collected herself, and went on—"if only I'd been here, it wouldn't have happened. Grantley's always doing stupid things. You have to look after him." She saw Evan looking at her with interest and she blushed. "I shouldn't have let my personal feelings get the better of me. I was hired to be his production assistant. I shouldn't have left, even if he did behave like a creep."

"When did you come back?" Evan asked.

She bit her lip. "I never really left. I went down to the station at Bangor, but then I couldn't make myself get on that train. I kept on thinking that I'd got it all wrong. There had to be some mistake. . . ."

"Mistake about what?"

She shook her head. "A personal matter. So I checked into a hotel and sent him a note to say where I was. He called and apologized and told me how much he needed me. So I came back yesterday but . . . but he didn't show up." She dissolved into tears, fumbling in her jeans pocket for a packet of tissues. Then she grabbed Evan's sleeve. "You've got to help us find him. If anything has happened to him, I'll kill myself!"

"I'm sure we can do without the hysterics, Sandie sweetie," Howard said calmly. "And I'm sure we'll find him. There's a main-line station in Porthmadog, isn't there?"

Evan nodded.

"There you are then. He decided he had to go to London on the spur of the moment, just as you suspected, Edward. We'll get a call from him any moment now saying he's at the Dorchester and he's just had a scrumptious breakfast and sorry he forgot to call last night, but he was invited out to dinner by someone very important."

They all nodded as if this was what they wanted to believe. But it was obvious none of them did believe it.

"We won't just assume that he's gone to London and that he'll call," Evan said. "I'll check out the places where he was last seen." They nodded again. "If any of you wants to come with me?"

"I've already called and canceled our crew for today," Edward said. "I hope we find him soon—I can't afford to have the crew just hanging around. If Grantley really has just run off somewhere without telling us, I'll wring his bloody neck."

Evan got out his small notepad. "Maybe you could tell me exactly where and when he was last seen?" he asked. "You say he dragged you up to Blenau Ffestiniog at crack of dawn yesterday?"

"That's right. I was in the middle of breakfast and he came rushing into the dining room. 'I've just had the most brilliant thought,' he said. 'It came to me in the middle of the night. It's going to give us the drama this film was lacking.' He grabbed my arm and literally dragged me from the table.

"I told him I had more important work to do. I was needed up at the lake to help raise a plane, which was, after all, the whole purpose of the film—and the one reason we'd got any financing."

He gave a long sigh. "But you know what Grantley's like. He's like a little child when he doesn't get his own way. He whined, he pleaded. It wouldn't take long and he couldn't go on his own, could he? And when he'd proved his point, then even I would be excited."

"What point was this?" Evan asked.

"He wouldn't tell me. He said he had things he needed to check out first."

"So you drove to Blenau? What time was this?"

"We left here before eight, I know that. Got there around eight-thirty, maybe."

"And when you got there?" Evan asked.

"I don't know exactly what he planned to do. He wanted to see around a slate mine, I know that. He was going to meet the custodian."

"But you didn't go with him?"

Edward flushed. "Me? No. I had more important things to do. I was needed back here, so I took a taxi back and left him to it."

"So the last you saw of him was in Blenau, at around nine o'clock?"

"That's right."

"And you expected him to come straight back here afterward?"

"That's what I understood, yes," Edward answered. "He knew we had a film crew waiting to start work and that Howard wasn't feeling up to par. I just assumed he'd come straight back as soon as he could."

"Did he have a mobile phone with him, by any chance?" Evan asked.

"Of course. He was never without his mobile."

"So he could have called you to let you know if he was running late," Evan said. "That's odd, isn't it? I take it you've tried calling his number?"

"Of course, several times, but he must have it switched off. It doesn't ring."

Evan tucked the notebook into his pocket. "Is there any chance he might have a photo of himself in his room? It would help if I could show it around when I'm asking questions."

"I'm sure he has oodles of photos," Edward said. "Grantley is very much in love with himself. I'll come up to his room with you, if you like. Maybe he's left some kind of notebook or agenda, giving us a clue to where he might have gone."

"All right." Evan went to find Major Anderson, the hotel manager.

"Missing, you say?" the major asked, frowning. "He didn't attempt to go up a mountain alone, did he?"

"No, he left his car down on the harbor in Porthmadog," Evan said. "We've no idea where he went."

"Rather worrying, what?" The major stroked his mustache speculatively. "I hope this doesn't bring us any bad publicity like that other time when those climbers were killed. We had a lot of reservations canceled as a result."

They walked up the broad central staircase and Major Anderson unlocked a door at the end of the first hallway. Grantley's room was supremely messy, with clothes, books, and papers strewn about at random. The major stepped over discarded underwear with distaste. Edward followed Evan into the room.

"He had a briefcase. I don't think he took it with him in the Land Rover. Ah yes, this is it."

He retrieved a pigskin case from under a sweater and a pair of socks. Evan opened it. It contained the sort of things you'd expect to find in a briefcase: an agenda, a file of possible contacts with war experiences, and, tucked into a slot on the lid, a large envelope full of photos.

"There you are—what did I tell you?" Edward reached out to lift up an eight-by-ten glossy of Grantley, looking more like Lord Byron than ever.

"His head shot," Edward said, "from the days when he fancied himself as an actor. Imagine still carrying it around. There's no end to the man's vanity."

"Oh and here's one of Howard doing his great white hunter bit." Edward thrust another eight-by-ten of Howard Bauer, surrounded by heavily armed African tribesmen, into Evan's hands.

"Very impressive." Evan smiled.

"There doesn't seem to be anything in here to indicate where he went." Edward was thumbing through the other folders in the case. "Maybe we should look around the rest of the room, but I don't think we'll find anything. Most of Grantley's ideas were in his head." He closed up the case and started piling clothes from the dresser onto the bed. Evan watched him speculatively. He was almost sure that while he had been studying the picture of Howard, Edward Ferrers had pocketed a small snapshot from the pile.

ELEVEN

IT WAS NINE o'clock on a blustery Sunday morning as Evan drove down to Porthmadog. He had asked the film people if any of them wanted to accompany him, but they had rejected his offer. Howard claimed he was still feeling a little shaky, Edward didn't want to leave the Inn in case Grantley phoned or turned up, and Sandie said she was just too upset to be of any use.

Church bells were ringing as he passed through Beddgelert. Old women in hats were walking arm-in-arm to chapel or the Anglican church as he drove through Porthmadog. He found the Land Rover easily enough, parked on the street that overlooked the harbor. It was locked. There was no sign of the keys. Unfortunately, what would have been a busy street yesterday was now deserted, but Evan knocked at the nearest houses. Nobody remembered noticing the man in the picture, or when the Land Rover had arrived. He looked around the docks. A couple of men were working on sailing boats, but the harbor wall would have concealed a view of the vehicle and they hadn't seen the man in the photo.

He went on to the main-line station and showed the picture again. The girl at the booking office was sure she hadn't sold Grantley a ticket yesterday. "Ever so handsome, isn't he?" she said, smiling coyly at Evan while assessing that he wasn't bad-looking himself. "I'm sure I'd have noticed him."

The ticket collector hadn't seen him either. Not many trains ran from the station on a weekend and he was sure he'd have noticed a foreigner.

Evan wasn't feeling too hopeful when he tried the narrow-gauge train depot. In contrast to the deserted main-line station, this one was bustling with activity. Sunday was a day when volunteers came to work on the old rolling stock and have a chance to drive the small steam engines up the mountain. The photo produced instant recognition this time.

"Of course I saw him." The man was polishing an old steam engine with the name Linda emblazoned on its side. "He was the silly fool who fell out of my train, wasn't he?"

"What about yesterday? You didn't carry him back up the mountain yesterday, did you?"

The driver shook his head. "No. If I'd seen him, I would have told him to bugger off. I wouldn't want to take that chance again. Nearly scared the daylights out of me when I heard that scream and saw him come tumbling out. I was lucky to be able to stop so quickly."

"So you're sure he wasn't around here yesterday?"

The man stared out across the estuary. "Not on a train I was driving. Of course, he could have taken another train up when I was coming down. I'd ask Billy Jones over there. He drove the other engine yesterday."

But Billy Jones didn't remember seeing Grantley. Whatever Grantley had been doing in Porthmadog yesterday, he hadn't made his presence obvious.

Evan paid a brief courtesy visit to the police station and made copies of the photo.

"Strange, isn't it?" P. C. Roberts said, coming to peer over Evan's shoulder as he worked at the copying machine. "He's quite a distinctive-looking bloke. You'd think someone must have seen him. We'll ask around the local B-and-Bs and maybe you should check the buses. Either he's still here or he took some other form of transportation out of town."

"Unless someone stole his car," Evan suggested. "And dumped it here."

"Then why ditch it again? Land Rovers are pretty valuable, aren't they? And if his car was stolen, then where the devil is he?"

"Good question," Evan said. "I'm off to Blenau Ffestiniog now, where he was last known to be. Let's hope someone up there can tell us something useful."

P. C. Roberts smirked. "You say you were assigned to him—what, for protection? No wonder you're so worried, boyo. You'll be for it if he doesn't show up, won't you?" He was clearly enjoying Evan's discomfort.

"Thanks for the reassurance," Evan muttered with a half smile. He started to go.

"Don't worry," Roberts called after him. "I expect he'll come sauntering in, saying, 'Oh sorry, old chap. Were you looking for me?' Bloody English. Nothing but trouble, are they?"

Evan agreed with the sentiment in the case of this lot of bloody English. He put his foot to the floor and swung his aged car around the bends until the slate hills of Blenau Ffestiniog appeared ahead of him—great gray gashes cut out of the mountainsides around the village. A chapel was just emptying on the High Street, mostly older women, plus a couple of old men and a few children. Evan parked his car and hurried to question the worshippers.

"I saw him." An elderly woman pushed her way through to the front of the crowd. She was a tiny bag of bones with a beaky nose and black flowerpot hat perched on top of pure white hair. "You saw him too, didn't you, Gwladys?" Another elderly lady nodded. "That's him all right."

"When was this? What was he doing?"

The first woman screwed up her face in concentration. "Ooh, let's see. We were on our way to catch the bus to do our shopping yesterday. The bus goes at nine-fifteen, so it must have been before that, mustn't it, Gwladys?"

Her friend nodded again.

"Can you tell me what he was doing?"

"Shouting, that's what he was doing, wasn't he, Gwladys?"

"Shouting something shocking," Gwladys finally spoke. "The two of them, yelling at each other, right there in the street."

"Foreigners, I said to Gwladys. What can you expect?"

"Can you remember who he was shouting at?"

"Another foreigner, it had to be. They were speaking English, weren't they?"

"Big sort of chap," Gwladys cut in. "Youngish. Fair hair, I think."

"And what happened after that?"

"We don't know. They were still at it when the bus came."

"All right—what's going on here?" a male voice demanded and a uniformed policeman pushed through the crowd. He eyed Evan with suspicion. "Can I help you?"

Evan extended his hand. "P. C. Evans from Llanfair. I'm looking for a missing person who was last seen up here."

A big smile spread across the constable's face. "Evans from Llanfair. I know who you are."

Evan flushed. He hated the way his fame as a super-sleuth had spread around the force. It usually meant either resentment or teasing. "Yes, I know all about you, what kind of food you like, what kind of girls you like. . . ." The constable paused, watching Evan's confused reaction. "I'm Meirion Morgan. You're lodging with my auntie Gwynneth."

Evan laughed. "Morgan, of course. That was Mrs. Williams's maiden name. Nice to meet you, Meirion."

"Now what can I do to help?" P. C. Morgan asked.

"It's this Englishman from a film crew who are shooting near Llanfair. He came up here yesterday morning, supposedly to visit a slate mine, and hasn't been heard of since. And his Land Rover was found parked in Porthmadog."

"That's odd, isn't it?" Meirion Morgan agreed.

"And we saw him," the first elderly lady tugged on his arm, "didn't we, Gwladys?"

"These ladies saw him arguing with someone in the high street yesterday morning."

"Right down there it was, outside the fish-and-chip shop," the woman pointed down the street. "Yelling and screaming at each other something terrible."

"Foreigners," Gwladys muttered conspiratorially.

"Did anyone else happen to see this?" P. C. Morgan addressed the crowd that still hung around.

Several other women admitted hearing shouting in English. The newspaper shopowner remembered hearing the shouting and then seeing a man go running past his shop front.

Then Evan asked about the Land Rover. Some people thought they had noticed it, but one woman was definite. It had been there when she went to fetch her son home from school for lunch at twelve o'clock and it was gone when she went to meet him from school at four o'clock. She remembered because her son had commented on it. He thought Land Rovers were cool and wanted to know if they could buy one. She had told him they cost too much money.

"So, what do you think he was doing up here until early afternoon?" Meirion Morgan asked as he and

Evan moved off together and the crowd broke up. "He must have been in someone's shop, had a cup of tea somewhere surely?"

Evan nodded. "All I know is that he came up here to visit a slate mine and he had an appointment with the custodian."

"Which mine would that have been? Llechwedd or Glodfa Ganol?"

"Manod."

"That's closed now. Been closed for some time."

"Right. But it's where they kept the paintings during the war."

"Oh yes, I heard about that." Meirion Morgan nodded. "My granddad was working in that mine in those days."

"Mr. Smith wanted to include that story in the film he's making on Wales in the war. That's why he wanted a tour of the mine."

"Oh, in that case you'll want Eleri Prys. He used to work there and he has the keys. I'll come with you if you like."

"Thanks," Evan said. "You're sure I'm not keeping you from anything?"

Meirion Morgan grinned. "No, just making a quick patrol through the town before I go home to my Sunday lunch, and Megan won't have that ready until one. You're welcome to join us if you like. My Megan does a lovely roast lamb with all the trimmings."

"It does sound tempting," Evan said. "I'll see how we're going with this. I have to find some sort of clue as to where he went. There's a main-line station here, too, isn't there? It's just possible he took a train to London."

"Then who drove his vehicle down to Porthmadog?"

Evan shrugged. "I know. Nothing here makes sense." He clapped Meirion on the shoulder. "Let's go and see this Mr. Prys. Maybe he can shed some light for us."

They walked together past the row of shops and then dropped down a narrow side street until they came to a pleasant bungalow on the edge of the town. Eleri Prys was a strong, square-jawed man with a young face, although his hair was streaked with gray.

"That's right," he said. "I used to be the mine manager until they closed it. I wasn't there in the war, of course. I'm not that old, thank you very much, but I understand it must have been quite a sight with those sheds built right inside the slate cavern."

Evan produced the photo. "I believe you had an appointment with Mr. Grantley Smith yesterday. Did you show him around the mine?"

"He never turned up, did he?" Eleri Prys asked with disgust in his voice. "I told him I'd meet him outside the mine at ten o'clock, but he never came. I waited half an hour, then I said, 'Bugger this,' and went home. It was bloody cold yesterday."

"And he didn't contact you afterwards to say why he hadn't shown up?"

"I haven't heard from him since," Mr. Prys said with a sniff.

"Mr. Prys," Evan began. "Is there any way he could have gone down the mine alone?"

Eleri Prys shook his head. "I've got the key, haven't I? The entrance is padlocked."

"And you checked the actual mine entrance yesterday, did you?" Evan asked.

A fleeting look of alarm crossed the man's face. "No—no, I can't say that I did. I waited by the street, like I told him. Then I did walk up the path to see if he might have gone on ahead of me, but no one was there. I could see that."

"Would you mind going with us to take a look?" Evan asked. "Just to make sure?"

"I'm just about to have my elevenses," Mr. Prys said. "I've got the kettle on."

"The man you were supposed to meet is missing,

Mr. Prys," Meirion said. "The constable here has been searching for him. We have to check every lead at the moment."

Eleri Prys nodded. "All right. I'll just turn off the kettle and get my coat then, shall I? Bloody nuisance. I wasn't too thrilled about showing him the mine in the first place. Too many hazards down there, and the emergency lighting's not good. But he's the kind of bloke who knows how to pull strings. I got a phone call from the mine owners saying I had to be helpful."

They walked back up the steep alleyway and then continued on to the edge of town. The wind was blowing off the high moor so hard that they had to lean into it.

"Raw old day, isn't it?" Mr. Prys said.

Evan nodded. "We came up here a few days ago when I took Grantley Smith to see Trefor Thomas. You know him, of course?"

"Everybody knows old Tref," Eleri Prys said. "Poor old bloke. I don't suppose you got much out of him. His mind's gone, hasn't it? That son of his has to look after him like a baby. Wonderful with him, so I hear."

"What did you go and see him for?" Meirion asked.

"He used to work in the mine," Evan said. "He was there when they built the sheds for the pictures and Grantley thought he'd be good to talk to, because he was quite an artist himself."

"Old Tref was?" Eleri asked.

"Yes, I heard that, too." Meirion nodded. "When he was a young man, anyway. I never saw anything he painted."

They reached the mine entrance. Eleri Prys unlocked the gate and led them up a path made of crushed slate, between slag heaps of slate to a hole in the mountainside. An iron grille now blocked the opening. It was secured with a large rusty padlock. Above it a rusted sign warned: "DANGER. PRIVATE PROPERTY. Vandals and Trespassers will be prosecuted to the full extent of the law." If it had stated, "Go back. You have been warned," it could not have been more forbidding.

"There you are," Eleri Prys said. "Just as I left it."

Evan was searching the ground for signs that the padlock might have been opened recently. But he couldn't detect any flakes of rust lying on the slate.

"You're right," he said. "It doesn't look as though anyone's been here. Sorry to have bothered you."

"That's all right." Eleri Prys managed a smile. "I'm just relieved to find the door still locked. I'd be for it if anyone had got in there."

"This is definitely the only way in then?" Evan asked. "He couldn't have found another entrance?"

"No," Eleri Prys said, then he hesitated. "Well, there was an old emergency exit, in case there was a cave-in or a fire at the front of the mine, but it's round the other side of the mountain. There's no way he'd find it. I doubt that I'd even find it now." He pointed to the scarred cliff face, hidden as it curved away sharply to the right by a slag heap and a jumble of rocks. "Somewhere behind those rocks, it was. Anyway, it's locked too if it's still there."

"As you say, there's no way he could just stumble on it then," Evan said.

Eleri shook his head. "No way at all. It would take a bloodhound to find it these days."

"Well, it looks like he never came here then," Meirion Morgan commented. "Unless he was stupid enough to try his hand at a little mountain climbing on those cliffs and he fell."

Evan stared up at the cliffs, their slate ledges slickened black with recent rain. He was a pretty fair climber and there was no way he'd want to tackle those cliffs. "I can't think why," he said. "He didn't strike me as an outdoor type. And he'd have had no reason. . . ."

"Fair enough," Meirion Morgan said. "Well, that's that then. It looks as though he came here, changed his mind, and went away again." They walked back down the path with Mr. Prys and parted from him on the High Street.

Meirion turned to Evan. "Where now?"

"I've no idea." Evan stared out across the bleak landscape. "I should call the hotel, just to make sure he hasn't turned up while I've been out here and nobody has bothered to call me. I should call P. C. Roberts in Porthmadog, just to make sure he hasn't found out anything down there, and then I think I've done almost all I can for now. If he isn't found by tomorrow, I'll hand it over to the plainclothes boys. He could be anywhere by now."

"You can use the phone at the police station and then come and have some lunch," Meirion Morgan said, putting a friendly hand on his shoulder. "I always say there's nothing like a good meal to help things make sense."

Evan managed a smile. "And I think I'll just double-check at the train station and the petrol station, too, and maybe any cafés that are open today. Someone must have seen him after nine o'clock if his car was parked here until midday."

"You'd certainly have thought so," Meirion said. "The police station's down here. I'll give you the key. Just lock it after you're finished and then come on up to my place. I live in that row of cottages up there. Number Twenty-one with the red door."

"Thanks very much," Evan said. "I'll see you in a while then."

"I hope you have some good news soon," Meirion said. "These bloody Englishmen—always coming here and getting lost, aren't they?"

Evan laughed. They parted company. Evan let himself into the police station and made his calls. P. C. Roberts had asked questions at local B-and-Bs. He'd asked the worshippers coming out of a nearby chapel. Nobody recognized the photo of Grantley Smith.

Next he called the Everest Inn. Edward Ferrers sounded distraught. "No, we've heard nothing," he snapped. "Didn't anyone see him park his car? He must have gone on by train somewhere. Have you contacted the police in England? He must have met with some kind of accident."

Evan felt hopelessly inadequate as he put down the phone. There was nothing he would have liked more than to have looked good to Bronwen's ex-husband. It would have been so nice to have announced breezily that he'd located Mr. Smith without too much trouble and Mr. Smith was sorry he hadn't contacted them before. No problem, sir. All part of the job. But instead he had to admit that he was getting nowhere.

He came out of the police station and stood staring down the deserted High Street. Grantley Smith had been here until noon yesterday. Someone must have seen him. He was loud and offensive and looked so distinctive that he must have been noticed. Evan began to walk down one side of the street, showing the photo to everyone he passed. He tried the booking clerk at the train station, the man who pumped the petrol, small boys on bikes, the woman in the Gloch Las Café. The result was the same—after the morning shouting match, nobody had seen Grantley Smith.

Evan paused, watching the clouds building over the coastline. It would rain before long. He stuck his hands in his pockets and started to walk again. Based on what he knew so far, the last person to have been seen interacting with Grantley was the man with whom he quarreled—and that man, from his description, sounded awfully like Edward Ferrers.

TWELVE

EDWARD FERRERS, WHO now seemed so completely bewildered and distraught, was the last person who had seen Grantley Smith. Now it appeared that he was also the person who had had a very public fight with Grantley.

Evan continued on down the High Street. What was all this about? Edward sounded and looked genuinely worried, but then Edward had been an actor, hadn't he? They'd all gone to the Edinburgh fringe with a play when they were at Cambridge. Howard looked sick and scared, too. Sandie was hysterical. Did they all know something that they weren't telling?

Evan took this one stage further: Was someone trying to do away with Grantley Smith? He had fallen out of a train a few days previously, after all. People didn't fall out of trains that often. And if the train hadn't been going so slowly on the steep gradient and Grantley hadn't rolled into an oak tree, he'd have kept on tumbling down a thousand feet into a ravine. Was it possible that someone had repeated the process, successfully this time?

Evan glanced at his watch. He had time before lunch. He should check the train's route down the mountain for himself. He went to his car and started back down the mountain, slowing whenever the narrow-gauge railway passed over a road or river or hugged the edge of a cliff. After a while it became too frustrating. The train tracks hugged the edge of a steep slope almost the whole way down to Porthmadog. You could push someone out and possibly kill them at almost any point along the track. It would take a whole team to search the ravines and gullies for a body.

Evan pulled over to the side of the road beside a noisy mountain stream and sat thinking again. If Grantley even suspected he had been pushed, it had to have been by one of his friends. And he wouldn't be likely to give anyone a second chance by leaning out again, would he? But was that why he had chosen to disappear? Now that made more sense. Someone he knew— Edward?—had either threatened or tried to kill him. So Grantley had chosen to vanish for his own safety. In which case, nobody was likely to find him in a hurry.

You're being overdramatic, he told himself. Look at them—pink pudgy Edward, seedy inoffensive Howard, and Sandie, skinny as a rake. Could any of them be a potential killer? It was too absurd to think about. Evan turned the car around and drove back toward Blenau Ffestiniog. A good lunch might well put things in perspective.

As he glanced up at the moors, another thought came to him. It was just possible that Grantley had gone back to visit Trefor Thomas again, maybe to see how he was getting on with his tape recording. He might just have fitted in a visit there before his appointment with the mine caretaker, which would mean after he parted from Edward.

Classical music was playing loudly as Evan knocked on the cottage door. Tudur Thomas opened it, saw Evan, and scowled. "Oh, it's you," he said. "Look you,

I don't think you better see my father again. He's been quite upset since your visit. He's a sick old man, you know. He's been fretting that he'll get in trouble when the man comes back for his machine because he can't remember things properly anymore."

"I'm sorry, Mr. Thomas," Evan said, "but I've come here because Mr. Smith is missing. Did that man I brought to see your father come by yesterday? I just wondered if he came here yesterday."

"He'd have been out of luck if he had," Tudur Thomas answered. "We weren't here. I always drive my dad down to get his pension on Saturday mornings and then we do our shopping at Tesco's. We were gone all morning."

"Oh, I see. Well, thanks a lot," Evan replied.

"Missing, you said." Tudur Thomas displayed a flicker of interest. "Run off, you mean? Done a bunk?"

"We're not sure yet," Evan said. "If he does come back here, please phone me straightaway, won't you? And give my regards to your father."

"I will, although he doesn't know who I am today again. Up and down, like I said, but it's definitely getting worse. We've got an appointment with the Social Services next week—trying to get him into a home. Frankly, he's getting too much for me."

Evan nodded. "It can't be easy for you. And you've got your own life."

Tudur Thomas stared out across the bleak moors. "That's right. I had quite a nice little life." He looked up at Evan. "When this Mr. Smith turns up again, tell him he can come and get his tape machine. The old man's displayed no interest in it whatsoever."

A mouthwatering smell of roasting leg of lamb greeted Evan as he was shown into Meirion Morgan's cottage and seated at a white-clothed table.

"A drop of red wine with it?" Meirion asked as Megan passed the gravy boat. "I brought a whole case back with me from our last holiday to France. It's plonk but it's not bad. Keep me company." He pulled the cork with a satisfying *plop*. "Megan won't. She was raised chapel."

"So were you," Megan retorted with a smile. "Only you've slipped."

"I better not, thanks. I'm on duty," Evan said.

"Go ahead. A little glass won't hurt you. And it's supposed to be your day off."

Evan smiled. "You're right, and I think I've done just about everything I can for now anyway. If Mr. Smith has chosen to vanish for any reason, I'm not likely to find him. I'll hand it over to the CID, and let them worry about it."

"Quite right. They're paid to have the headaches." Meirion grinned as he poured two glasses of wine. "There you are. Good for the arteries."

They had finished second helpings of lamb and Megan had just brought in a jam roly-poly and custard when there was a knock at the front door. Meirion got up. "Is it like this for you?" he asked. "Whenever we're eating, that's when people always come looking for me."

"It's always the same," Megan muttered to Evan as her husband went to the door. "They never think he deserves any time to himself. It's like he's village property."

They both stopped talking and looked up as Meirion came back into the room with another man. "It's Mr. Prys," he said, ushering him in. "He wants a word, Constable Evans."

"I thought I better come straight away," Eleri Prys said. He had been wearing a tweed cap. Now he held it in both hands, twisting it nervously. "It might be nothing at all, but . . ." He paused and looked from Meirion's face to Evan's. "After I left you, I started thinking about that back entrance to the mine and whether anyone could have stumbled on it by mistake.

So I went there, just to reassure myself, and I found it without any trouble. In fact, it looks as though the path has been used lately. The brambles have been trodden down. And there used to be a big wooden door across it, all nailed shut. But the wood's pretty rotten and I tried it—you can force it open now if you really use a little strength. So I wondered if you wanted to come and take a look for yourselves because it's just possible that your man did find his way in after all."

Evan looked at Meirion with a sigh and got to his feet. Without a word, Megan swept away their plates to the oven. They hurried to the mine without speaking, then followed Eleri Prys as he picked his way between rocks and slag heaps. If it had once been a path, Evan wouldn't have known it. It was overgrown with a tangle of dead brambles and stinging nettles.

"See here." Eleri Prys pointed at the ground. A large foot had recently crushed some dying nettles.

The rockface loomed ahead of them—a wall of gray slate rising sheer above them. "This way," Eleri Prys said. "Mind your heads."

He led them under an overhang where a passage was cut into the hillside. A few feet inside, the passage was barred by a heavy wooden door. "See what I mean." Eleri Prys went up to the door frame and shook it. It wobbled. "You can push this enough for a skinny bloke to squeeze through," he said, glancing at Evan's rugby player build. "He'd have to be strong, though. But it's all right for us. I've got the key, if the lock isn't too rusted."

He fitted a key into the rusty padlock. It opened with a squeak and the heavy door swung inward at his touch, revealing a square tunnel, a little higher than a man and about as wide. A few feet into the dark passageway, it plunged downward. Eleri Prys switched on the big torch he was carrying and shone it down into the darkness. "If anyone went down here, he couldn't have gone more than a couple of yards without a torch," he said. "Did your bloke have a torch with him?"

"I very much doubt it," Evan said.

"Then he couldn't have gone far. It's pitch black after a few yards and those old steps are treacherous. He'd have broken his neck if he tried to go down without light—" He realized what he had just said and looked up at them with a horrified face. "You don't think that's what might have happened, do you? He wouldn't have been daft enough?"

Evan shrugged. "It doesn't make sense to me. If he was about to meet you and get a proper tour of the mine, why go ahead on his own like that? What would it achieve?"

"And why risk this dangerous back entrance when the main entrance still has the electricity working?" Eleri Prys stared down into the darkness. "So, do you think we ought to go down and take a look?"

Evan was fighting back the rising dread he felt, looking down into that blackness. He swallowed hard to master himself. "Yes," he heard himself saying. "I think we probably should."

"Righto, then. If you gentlemen will wait here, I'll just pop around to the front entrance and turn on the electricity. They still keep an emergency system with a few lights working—just in case. No sense in risking our bloody necks in the dark, is there?"

He hurried back down the path, leaving Evan and Meirion standing together. Evan tried desperately to think of small talk but nothing would come.

"I can't say I'm looking forward to this much," Meirion confided. "I never did like mines. I'm glad I wasn't born in my father's time, or I'd have been down there with the rest of them."

"I don't like them either," Evan confessed. "I remember when my school class visited a coal mine. I got in such a panic they had to bring me back to the surface."

"You don't really think he went down there, do

you?" Meirion peered into the blackness. "Christ, he'd have needed his head examined."

"He has to be somewhere," Evan said. "And this is the last place he was seen."

"In which case how did his car get down to Porthmadog?"

"Good question," Evan agreed. "Nothing about this makes sense."

They turned around as they heard the sound of heavy feet trampling the dry undergrowth. "We're in luck. It's still working," Eleri Prys called as he came toward them. "Come on then, let's go. Unfortunately, there's no light until we get close to the bottom of this stair, so watch your step please."

He started downward, his torch lighting a few steps before them. Evan put his hand on the wall to steady himself as he descended. The rock was cold and damp. He forced his feet downward.

The stairway went on and on. One hundred steps. Two hundred steps. Darkness all around, so thick he could feel it pressing on him. Their feet, echoing in that narrow tunnel, and the light bobbing further and further ahead as Eleri Prys strode confidently down. Evan wished he hadn't gone last. He was glad that the steps were broken and uneven so that he had to concentrate on where he put his feet.

Then at last a glimmer of light and one anemic bulb lit the final steps before the passageway opened into a black cavern.

"Well, he didn't fall down the stairs, look you." Eleri Prys shone the torch around the rocky floor ahead of them. "So either he didn't come down here or he went on." His voice now echoed from a high invisible ceiling. "This way leads to the main caverns. There should be some lights working, but watch your heads. It's low in places."

They left the echoing space for another square passageway. Evan walked at a crouch as the ceiling was less than five feet high in places.

"They must have been small men in those days," Meirion commented after he banged his head.

"They didn't care about the men," Eleri said. "As long as the passages were big enough to get the slate through. That's all that mattered, wasn't it? They had little railcarts going through here. Ah, here we are now."

They stepped out into what was clearly a vast space. Even though the one light lit only a small area around it, they could sense the openness. When Eleri pointed his torch upward, the beam melted into darkness without hitting the ceiling.

"This was the chamber where they kept the pictures," he said. "They had it filled with sheds in those days. All gone now, of course."

"How did they get everything down here?" Evan imagined staggering down those steps with large crates.

"The lift was working in those days, of course," Eleri said. "How do you think they got the slate to the surface then?"

In the silence even their breathing echoed. Evan's heart was hammering so loudly he was sure that the other men must hear it. He forced himself to walk away and inspect the area. All around the walls were piles of slate, jagged outcrops, small dark pools—but no indication that anyone had been here recently.

"Looks like I've brought you down here for nothing," Eleri Prys said. "This would have been what he wanted to see. Not that there's anything to see these days. I told him that, but he was very insistent. He'd already called the mine owners and made a fuss, so I had to agree, didn't I?"

Evan came upon other dark openings in the walls. "What if he got confused and took one of these tunnels instead?"

"Ah well, he'd be in trouble then, wouldn't he?"

Eleri Prys sucked through his teeth. "That one leads to the main exit, but he would have found it barred, so he'd have had to come back down. But that one over there leads to older chambers that haven't been used for a hundred years. A whole network of passages in that direction. It's easy enough to lose your way in a mine."

"Then perhaps he's still down here and he's lost," Meirion suggested. "Try calling for him, boyo."

"Grantley? Mr. Smith? It's Constable Evans—are you down here?" Evan's voice boomed around the cavern and echoed back from high rock walls, so that it sounded as if ten men were shouting. As the echoes died away, they waited, listening hopefully. Silence except for the distant dripping of water.

Evan stood at the entrance to the tunnel, straining his ears for any sound. As Eleri came toward him with the torch, its light picked out something on the soft carpet of damp slate. "Just a minute." Evan bent to pick up the object. He held it up carefully in the torchlight. It was a cigarette butt. As Evan brought it closer to the light, he could read the words *Gitane Internationale* written around the top of the filter in dark blue letters. "Grantley Smith smoked these," he said.

"Bloody hell," Eleri Prys muttered. "So it looks like we'd better go on. But I'm not going too far. There's no light down here and these old passages run for miles. It won't help anyone if we end up getting lost too."

They started forward again, wet slate crunching under their feet. Eleri thrust the torch into Evan's hands. "Here, you take it, Constable Evans. You've got good eyes. You might spot another clue."

Evan could hardly say that he'd rather follow, or better still, wait for them at the surface. He took the offered torch and shone it around ahead of them. This passage was smaller and wetter. Instead of running straight and even like the last one, it wound away from the large cavern. Small chambers opened on either side, some piled high with slate debris, some filled with dark pools. The ceiling got lower and lower until Evan was bent over, feeling the cold wet rock brushing against his hair and icy drips running down his neck.

Suddenly, the passage curved sharply again. Evan had been concentrating so completely on not banging his head that he didn't notice the turn until almost too late. Ahead of him was dark water. As he reacted, he went to stand up and banged his head on the rock. Sparks shot across his eyes and the torch went flying from his grasp. He grabbed for it, but it bounced off a rock and rolled into the water.

Evan's heart was racing as he anticipated the total darkness. Instead, miraculously, the torch stayed alight, turning the water from black to beautiful shades of gold and highlighting the rocky depths. It also illuminated the figure of a man, sprawled on the bottom.

THIRTEEN

Ginger. It seems strange to say that word out loud now, after so long. Funny that I haven't got a single photo of her. Well, cameras were a luxury in those days. We only borrowed them to take pictures at weddings and funerals. It doesn't matter though because I can see her right now, clear as if she was standing here in front of me. Lovely, truly lovely. That platinum blond hair piled up on her head like Ginger Rogers. Those long Betty Grable legs. She was as good as any film star. I was sure she would make it in films if she could just get to Hollywood somehow. And she'd promised to take me with her.

I dreamed about it all day down in the mine. I pictured myself as the new Tarzan, Ginger as Jane, both of us swimming together in a blue Hollywood swimming pool with the palm trees swaying. When I was with her, it all seemed so possible, if we could just get through the bloody war in one piece.

To tell you the truth, I was itching for a little excitement that first year after war was declared. Nothing was happening at all in Wales—you wouldn't even have known there was a war on, except that the young men put on uniforms and went away and everything was on ration. But I was already bored with working down the mine. All the older boys had already been called up and gone. I couldn't wait to turn seventeen. Not that I wanted to be killed, but I wanted excitement. I wanted to get out of the mine and I wanted a uniform. Well, I was young and stupid in those days, wasn't I?

And I was getting really tired of being heckled whenever army blokes came through. Every time a convoy of troops drove past, they'd yell at me: "What are you, a bleedin' conchie? You should join up and do your part, son."

Then they were gone before I could tell them that I was only fifteen and the army wouldn't take me for another two years. It wasn't my fault that I looked like a grown man.

I didn't see so much of Ginger anymore in those days. She'd got a job working in one of the big hotels in Llandudno that they'd turned into convalescent homes for wounded servicemen. It used to drive me wild with jealousy thinking that she was around all those blokes all day.

"You do get yourself into a state about nothing, don't you, Tref," she said, and she ruffled my hair the way she always did. "I told you. They're only a lot of cripples with half of their limbs blown away. What would I want with them when I've got a big strong bloke of my own, and every part of him is working just fine." She reached out and demonstrated what she meant, letting her hand rest until I was excited.

She had finally let me do it with her. I was too keen and completely inexperienced but she seemed to like it all right—well enough to want to do it again next time we had a chance to be alone, and again the next time after that. But now she could only get off work every couple of weeks and I was going crazy working on my own in the dark every day, and my mind wandering into all kinds of worries about her.

And then it happened. My cousin Mostyn came looking

for me in the mine one day. "The foreman wants you, Trefor bach. What you been doing, eh? Not disgracing the family name, I hope."

My cheeks were burning as I ran to the foreman. No, I couldn't remember a single thing I'd done wrong recently—not like the time I'd dropped a big slab of slate when I was a new apprentice and it had cracked in two. That had cost me a day's wages. I'd followed all the safety procedures when we'd been blasting, unlike Dai Evans, who had left his hammer at the face and was lucky he didn't get it through his head.

"Over here, young fellow-me-lad." The foreman was looking quite jolly. "Got a job for you. You're the one who's batty about art, aren't you? Always drawing in your spare time, they tell me. Well, we've got a little project you can help on."

When I heard that the pictures from the National Gallery were coming, I couldn't believe my luck. This was it, my lucky break, the thing I'd been dreaming of. I imagined they'd let me help look after the pictures. I'd be able to help hang them and then dust them every day, which would give me a chance to study them close up. And who knows, maybe I'd meet someone from the National Gallery and he'd be impressed with my paintings and offer me a job after the war—providing there was an after the war, of course.

Just shows you what daft dreams you have when you're young, doesn't it?

And to prove how naive I was, I thought they were going to hang the pictures all over the walls of the slate caverns—a giant art gallery in total darkness. But then I found they'd put me on the team to build huts. It seemed the pictures were going to be stored in there—just like army huts, with central heating in them too, keeping the pictures at just the right temperature. And they were equipped with an alarm system. They were taking no chances, even deep inside a mountain with only one way out.

*When the pictures arrived, I had my next disappoint-
ment. They were already in crates. I helped carry them
into the huts and stack them under the watchful eye of
National Gallery men. It was torture knowing that I might
be carrying a Rembrandt or da Vinci and not even be
able to peek at it.*

*That's really been the story of my life—being so close
to something I really wanted and never being able to
make it mine.*

"Is that him?" Sergeant Watkins stared down at the body.
He had come with the ambulance team, in response to
Evan's emergency call from the mine office at the front
entrance. Reluctantly Evan had had to lead the way back
down to the body and now stood beside the sergeant, feeling the weight and horror of the mine pressing on him
again.

Evan couldn't see the face, but the dark curls, the black
leather jacket, and tight black jeans on long limbs were
easy enough to identify. Lying sprawled out like that, he
looked like a giant spider. He shuddered. "Yes, I'm pretty
sure it's him."

"Stupid bugger," Watkins said, still staring down in fas-
cination. "He must have blundered down here and not
realized the passage went to the left and stepped straight
into the bloody water."

"I wonder why he didn't manage to get out again?"
Evan asked. "It should have been easy enough to haul
himself out."

"He might have tripped and hit his head on a rock and
fallen in unconscious. Or maybe he couldn't swim," Watkins said. "Either way, we'll know as soon as we get a
postmortem. If he hit his head first, he probably won't
have water in his lungs."

"And we'll see the wound," Evan added.

Watkins turned to the ambulance men, who were standing uneasily in the shadows. "Okay, boys. You can bring him out."

The youngest member of the crew leaned over the side in an attempt to grab the body.

"Watch it, boyo," the older man warned, "or we'll be pulling you out, too. These bloody pools are deeper than they look."

He took a pole and stuck it down into the water. It reached nowhere close to the bottom. "I reckon it's twelve feet down at least. You'd better get your wetsuit on, lad."

The younger man began putting on a wetsuit. Watkins moved closer to Evan. "So how did you find him down here?"

"Process of elimination and some luck," Evan said. "The odd thing is that he had an appointment with Mr. Prys that morning. Why not wait and have a proper tour?"

"Bloody stupid, if you ask me," Watkins said. "How did he get this far, that's what I want to know? If he came in the back way, like you said he did, there'd have been no light at all, would there? And I don't see his torch anywhere."

"We checked out the area pretty thoroughly," Evan said. "We didn't find anything."

"It could be under him," the older ambulance man suggested. "We'll know in a minute when young Rob gets all suited up."

"I might need you to help me, Mr. Howells," Rob said as he prepared to lower himself into the water. "I don't know if I can bring him up alone."

"You get him moving and I'll use the hook when he comes within reach." Mr. Howells took off his jacket and started rolling up his sleeves. "I'm not getting in that cold water unless I really have to. Besides, if he's been there a while, he'll come floating to the surface easy enough. I'm rather surprised he hasn't already."

Rob put on goggles and lowered himself into the water. Then he took a deep breath and plunged downwards. The eerie light of the torch made his descent throw distorted shadows across the cave roof. He reached the body, tugged at it, then came back to the surface, gasping for breath. "Bloody hell, Mr. Howells, he's heavy. I can't move him."

"Have another try, lad. You've got the only good wet-suit. Just grab his arm and swim up with him."

Rob went down again. He grabbed the corpse's arm and kicked for the surface with all his might. The corpse hung beneath him like a rag doll. Mr. Howells reached in with the grappling pole and snagged the jacket.

"Bloody 'ell. He is heavy."

Evan took off his own jacket and reached in to help as the body came closer to the surface. He started as his hand closed around the wet tendrils of hair. At last, gasping with effort, the three of them managed to drag the body to the side of the pool, then lift it onto dry land. As they moved it, something fell from the jacket and tumbled to the bottom of the pool.

"No wonder he was so heavy," Rob commented. "That was a piece of slate. Look, he's got another bloody great piece inside his jacket, and more in his pockets."

Watkins looked at Evan. "Someone wanted to make sure he stayed down."

Evan stared down at Grantley's lifeless face, with its wide-open eyes staring up as if in surprise. "In which case his death wasn't an accident at all. Someone followed him down here and killed him."

Watkins nodded. "Not a bad place to hide a body. If that torch hadn't been waterproof, you'd never have seen him. He could have lain there for years." He turned to the ambulance men, who were now pulling off Rob's wetsuit. "Good work, lads. Now let's get him to the morgue and see what the postmortem shows."

As the men lifted him onto a stretcher, Grantley's head fell back. Evan nudged Watkins. "Look at his throat, Sarge."

Watkins looked where Evan was pointing at the areas of discoloration. "Badly bruised. Could mean he was strangled. I should call the D.I." He got out his mobile phone, then laughed. "Of course. It's not likely to work down here, is it?"

The somber procession set off back to the surface. Evan was surprised to find it was still daylight, a dusky pink twilight in which the smoke from fires hung in the still air. It felt as if he had been down there for days, weeks, years. He stood breathing in the crisp winter air.

Watkins tapped his arm. "You all right? You look like you could do with a drink."

"I'm fine now," Evan said.

"It must have been rough for you down there," Watkins muttered. "I remember how claustrophobic you were when we went through the Chunnel to France that time. It doesn't normally affect me, but I have to say that place gave me the willies. It must be something to do with knowing there are millions of tons of rock over your head."

Evan managed a smile.

Watkins snapped open his phone. "Right. I should call the D.I. and see what he wants me to do. Then I think I'll come with you and break the news to his mates. This is going to be rather a blow to them, isn't it?"

They hardly spoke as they drove the fifteen miles back to Llanfair. Evan, still recovering from being in the mine, was glad that he had to concentrate on driving the winding road.

"So, what do you think?" Sergeant Watkins asked as they walked across the Everest Inn car park together. "You're the one who's good at solving murders. What sort of bloke was Grantley Smith? Were you around him enough to get an impression of him?"

Evan nodded. "He was the sort who liked to push people's buttons. I think he got his kicks from antagonizing other people. He certainly got my hackles up and I hardly knew him."

"Ah, so you might turn up on the suspect list, might

you? You were the one who knew where to look for him, that's always suspicious."

Evan chuckled. "Unfortunately, I've got a perfect alibi," he said. "At the time he must have been killed, I was up at the lake with the film crew, waiting for someone to turn up so that they could start work."

"Someone to turn up—what do you mean?"

"I mean that nobody from the Everest Inn showed up that morning. Howard Bauer wasn't feeling well and decided to stay in his room. Edward Ferrers arrived around midday, having left Grantley Smith in Blenau, and Sandie, the assistant, had walked out in a huff a few days before but suddenly turned up again."

Watkins's eyes lit up. "So they all had time to nip up to that mine, strangle Grantley Smith, and dump him in the water. The question is—would any of them have wanted to?"

"All of them, possibly," Evan said. "There was no love lost between Grantley and Howard, or between Grantley and Edward. And Sandie was last seen stomping out and saying that she hated him."

"Interesting." Watkins nodded. "So I think this visit might be a little more than expressing my condolences. I might just ask a few subtle questions as well, while they're off guard, and before they've had a chance to think up alibis."

Evan grabbed the sergeant's arm and held him back as he went to walk into the Inn. "Look, there are a couple of things you ought to know before you meet them. Grantley Smith had a near-fatal accident a few days ago. He fell out of a train."

"He did what?" Watkins gave him a startled look.

"The Blenau Ffestiniog line. He was leaning out to shoot a film and the door came open."

"Bloody 'ell," Watkins muttered. "And he was all right afterward?"

"A few bruises and cuts. But he was very lucky. He landed on bracken and rolled into an oak tree. A few inches in the wrong direction and he'd have gone right to the bottom of the ravine."

"So you're thinking that it might not have been an accident, after all?"

"It did cross my mind," Evan agreed. "And there's one more thing. When I was asking questions up in Blenau, several people reported that they'd seen Grantley having a heated argument around nine in the morning. They gave me a description of the person Grantley was fighting with. It sounded an awful lot like Edward Ferrers."

Watkins nodded. "Right. Okay, let's go and see how they take the news of his death, shall we?"

He pushed the revolving glass door into the foyer of the hotel. Evan followed. The group was sitting by the fire in the bar again, as if they had never left. Howard was nursing a whisky and soda, Edward had an almost full beer glass in front of him, and Sandie was sipping a white wine. They sat like statues, not talking, lost in their own thoughts, and didn't even notice the approaching policemen until Evan spoke to them.

"Mr. Ferrers? I'm afraid we've got bad news for you."

Edward jumped to his feet. "You've found him? Something's happened to him? Is he hurt?"

Sandie let out a wail. "Oh my God. He's dead, isn't he?"

"Dead?" Edward looked bewildered. "Grantley is dead?"

Evan nodded. "I'm afraid so."

Edward sank to his chair again. "I knew. I knew it."

Watkins pulled up a chair beside Edward. "Excuse me, sir. Detective Sergeant Watkins. If you don't mind my asking a few questions."

Edward focused on him as if he hadn't noticed him until now. "What? Oh no. No, of course not."

"How did you know, sir?"

"What?" Edward frowned. "How did I know what?"

"That he was dead. You just said you knew it?"

"I meant that he would have called us, wouldn't he?

He wouldn't have let us sit here, worrying about him. Even Grantley wouldn't have done that. So I knew something terrible must have happened to him."

Howard Bauer cleared his throat. "How did he die, Sergeant? Not something like an overdose, was it?"

Watkins looked up at him. "He was found in a pool of water in a slate mine."

Sandie sobbed. "Oh, how terrible. Poor Grantley. He hated cold water. I am so sorry. I just wish I could have told him how sorry . . . but now I never can." Edward put an awkward arm around her shoulders and she continued to sob noisily.

Watkins got out his pad. "If I could just get some details from each of you. I know you must be upset but—"

"Of course," Edward said.

"Let's start with your names."

"I'm Edward Ferrers. This is Howard Bauer. Sandie Johnson."

"Thank you, sir. And you were all part of the same film crew, is that correct? Constable Evans says you're shooting a film about a World War Two plane in a lake."

"That's correct," Edward said. "I'm actually not part of the film crew. I'm the expedition leader, so to speak. I'm the expert on World War Two planes. I was given a grant and permission from the Ministry of Defense to raise this plane and display it in a new air museum. Then I persuaded my friend Grantley Smith that it might make a good documentary. He's been looking for a way to break into filming. He was lucky enough to get Howard, who is an Oscar-winning director, to join us and lend us credibility."

"I see." Watkins turned to Sandie. "And you, Miss?"

"I'm just the production assistant," she said, blushing.

"Would you happen to know the names of his next of kin? We'll need to contact them."

Edward looked down at his coffee cup. "His parents live in London," he said. He produced a small diary from his inside pocket. "Thirty-two Brunner Road, Waltham-stow."

Evan suspected from Edward's expression that the address wasn't in one of the better parts of the city.

"No other next of kin that you know of. No wife?"

"No," Edward and Sandie said at the same moment. They shot each other a quick glance.

"And I understand that you were the last person to have contact with him, Mr. Ferrers," Sergeant Watkins went on. "Could you tell me where and when you last saw Mr. Smith?"

"I already told all this to the constable," Edward said. "I left him around nine o'clock in the morning up in that place I can't pronounce."

"Blenau Ffestiniog, sir," Evan said.

"What were you doing up there?"

"A new idea of Grantley's. He wanted to feature the slate mine in his story."

"So you went up to Blenau Ffestiniog to look at a slate mine?" Watkins looked at Evan for help. "I may be dense, but what does a slate mine have to do with a plane in a lake?"

"The film's going to be called *Wales at War*," Evan explained. "I told Mr. Smith about the National Gallery pictures being stored in a slate mine during the war."

"Were they? I didn't know that." Sergeant Watkins nodded appreciatively. "It just shows, you learn something every day. So Mr. Smith wanted to see the slate mine for himself?" He directed the question at Edward.

"That's right."

"And did he?" Watkins was still looking directly at him.

"Did he what?" Edward shifted uneasily on his seat.

"Did he go and see the slate mine for himself?"

"I couldn't tell you that. I know he had an appointment with the man who had the keys to take a look later that morning."

"And you left him around nine o'clock, you said?"
Watkins asked.

"That's right."

"You didn't want to stay and see the slate mine?"

"I had more important things to do, Officer. Someone
had to supervise the work on the plane—the work we are
supposed to be doing up here."

"So you came back alone?"

"That's right."

Watkins leaned his elbows on the table. "If you don't
mind my asking, sir. Was Mr. Smith not able to drive
himself for any reason?"

"No. Why do you ask that?"

"Only that it seems a bloody long way to drive with
Mr. Smith and come straight back again on your own,
before you'd seen anything."

Edward's fair skin flushed pink. "If you must know, we
had a bit of a tiff. I thought he was wasting our time and
money on something irrelevant and I told him so. Grantley had a minor tantrum. He always liked to get his own
way. I didn't want to be around him when he was in that
kind of mood, so I came back."

"I see, sir." Watkins looked around the table. "And you
others, Mr. Bauer and Miss—uh—Johnson. You weren't
involved in this jaunt to the slate mine?"

"I was ill that morning," Howard said. "I had some kind
of twenty-four-hour bug, so I stayed close to my bath-
room. I still feel pretty rotten, come to think of it."

"And I wasn't here," Sandie said. "I was down in Bangor. I just got back yesterday afternoon." She gulped another sob. "So I never saw him to say good-bye."

Watkins closed his notebook. "Well, that seems to be
that. Thank you for all the helpful information. I must ask
you not to go anywhere for the present—just in case we
need to ask you any more questions."

"We'll be here, Sergeant. We still have work to do,"
Edward said. "There is a plane in that lake waiting to be

raised. It will help take our minds off . . ." Edward's voice cracked and he swallowed back emotion.

Watkins got to his feet and looked at Evan, who had been standing quietly in the shadows by the fire. "Oh, one more thing I wanted to ask you. About that accident the other day—Constable Evans tells me that Mr. Smith had a brush with death only a few days ago. He fell out of a train, is that right?"

Three bewildered faces looked up at him.

"Yes, but that was an accident," Edward said. "I know. I was in the carriage with him. I saw him fall out. Nobody was anywhere near him. It was his own stupid fault. He was leaning out of the open window, which is specifically forbidden. The door came flying open."

"So you were in the carriage with him, sir?" Watkins turned his attention to the others. "And you two?"

"I was in the next compartment," Howard said. "I saw him lean out and fall. He must have triggered the door handle somehow."

"And you, Miss?"

Sandie's blue eyes looked enormous in her white, tear-stained face. "I'd already gone. I didn't even take the train ride with them. And anyway, are you suggesting that someone tried to kill Grantley? Why would anyone want to do that?"

"That's what we're going to find out, Miss." Watkins got to his feet. "Ready, Constable Evans?" he asked.

"I tell you one thing," he muttered as they came out of the bar. "They were all bloody jittery, weren't they?"

Evan looked back at the figures silhouetted against the firelight. He tried to picture any of them creeping up behind Grantley, strangling him, and then weighting his body with rocks before throwing it into a pool.

FOURTEEN

THE SIGN OF the Red Dragon looming out of the evening mist was particularly welcome to Evan. It had been a long, tough day. His legs felt as if he'd gone up and down Snowdon a few times, and the horror of being in the depths of that mine still lingered.

He tried to push open the pub door and was surprised to find it locked. He stared at it, confused for a moment. After the strange events of the day, it wasn't hard to believe that he had slipped into a twilight zone. Then he heard Evans-the-Meat's loud laugh coming clearly from inside the pub. He rattled the door, but it wouldn't move. Then it dawned on him—it was Sunday, of course! Even though pubs throughout Wales were now officially allowed to open on Sundays, Llanfair was one of the communities that still observed the Sabbath and kept the pub shut—at least shut to outsiders. The locals had always taken the back path from the chapel to the back door of the pub and had clearly done so tonight.

Evan went around to the back door and let himself in. The lounge was deserted tonight. Ladies were not supposed to drink on Sundays. But the main bar was as full as usual. Evan stood taking in the comforting, familiar sights and sounds—the big fire flickering in the fireplace, the oak-paneled walls, the low hum of conversation, and the pleasant hiss of Betsy filling a pint glass. This was how the world should be. Every time he felt frustrated about not getting that promotion, he should remind himself that a promotion would mean moving away from this, working in the towns.

As he edged through the crowd toward the bar, he anticipated Betsy's usual excited yell. Instead, he reached the long oak bar without making any impression at all—almost as if he'd become invisible—adding to the sense of unreality he was already feeling.

He leaned on the bar. "*Noswaith dda,* Betsy *fach.* How about a pint of Guinness for your favorite policeman then?"

Betsy's wide blue eyes looked up at him coldly. "I don't happen to see my favorite policeman at the moment. That would be Constable Dawson from Caernarfon, wouldn't it? I think he's ever so handsome, and friendly too." She went back to the pint she was pouring. "There you are, Mr. Roberts. Get that down you and you won't feel the cold."

"Betsy," Evan said. "Have I done something to upset you?"

"You know very well what you've done." Her gaze was still icy.

"I'm sorry, but I don't. I've been so busy the past few days. . . ."

"You stopped me from breaking into show biz, that's what. If it hadn't been for you, I might have been discovered by now."

"I told you, they're not Hollywood producers. It's a documentary about a plane."

"The older one is." Betsy pouted. "He won an Oscar, they said."

"Yes, for a documentary about civil war in Africa. Do you see yourself running around in his next film wearing a loincloth and waving a spear then?"

Evan was only conscious that the other men had been listening in to this conversation when there was general laughter behind him.

"I wouldn't mind seeing that," Barry-the-Bucket chuckled. "You know what women wear on their tops in Africa, don't you?"

"Yes, and men have to kill a lion single-handed before they can be men!" Betsy retorted. "Which means you'd stay a boy all your life, Barry-the-Bucket."

"Anyway, they don't hire actors for those kind of films," Mr. Parry Davies, the minister, explained, leaning out from his chair in the corner. Although he condemned the demon alcohol from his pulpit as heartily as his rival at the other chapel, he wasn't averse to following his flock down the back path to perdition after evening service. "Documentaries are shot from real life. No actors."

"Oh, I see." Betsy was quiet for a moment, then her face lit up again. "But he'd know real directors, wouldn't he? If he's won an Oscar and all that. I saw him walking down the street yesterday. He's got a real American accent and everything, hasn't he? Next time I'm going to speak to him."

"Yesterday?" Evan asked.

Betsy nodded. "I would have run out and spoken to him then, but Harry had me cleaning the windows and the American looked like he was in a hurry."

Interesting, Evan thought to himself, as he took the pint of Guinness Betsy put in front of him. Hadn't Howard claimed he was too sick to leave his room?

"Didn't I hear one of those film people was missing?" Evans-the-Milk asked.

Evan nodded, surprised that he was ahead of them with the news for once. "He's been found—dead, I'm afraid. His body was found in a slate mine."

"Ooh, how terrible," Betsy said. "It wasn't the lovely dark one, was it? I thought he was ever so sexy."

"That's right. Mr. Grantley Smith."

"Was that his name?" Betsy looked up with interest. "We had someone in here the other day asking about him, didn't we, Harry?"

Harry-the-Pub looked up from the glasses he was wiping. "Grantley something? Yes, that was the name. We sent him up to the Inn."

"Who was asking about him—was it an Englishman?"

Betsy looked at Harry for inspiration. "No, he spoke Welsh, didn't he?"

"He did." Harry frowned in concentration.

"Did he say why he wanted Grantley Smith?" Evan asked.

Harry shook his head. "I've no idea. We're not the bloody police force, you know. We don't interrogate them." He grinned at Evan. "And we'd never heard of this Grantley Smith bloke."

"So he had an accident down a slate mine, did he?" Evans-the-Milk asked. "Dangerous places, those old mines."

"What was he doing down there?" Evans-the-Meat asked. "I thought they were here to get a World War Two plane. Not too many planes crashed into slate mines, did they?"

The other occupants chuckled, but Evan stood staring at his Guinness. What was Grantley Smith doing in a mine? he wondered. What could have been so important to him that he'd risked going down there on his own, half an hour before he was scheduled to go on a full conducted tour?

As these thoughts passed through his mind, Evan was back down there, ducking through those low passages, feeling the darkness pressing down on him, hearing the faint dripping of water, knowing there were three hundred steps between him and the outside world. He felt beads of sweat forming on his forehead again and his heart started to race. It was no good. He needed to be out in the fresh air. He drained his glass and put a couple of pound coins on the counter.

"Thanks, Betsy love, but I've got to go."

"They're surely not making you work at this time of night?" Harry-the-Pub demanded. "They don't pay you overtime, do they?"

Betsy was gazing at him with concern. "Are you all right, Evan? You've gone awfully white. Harry's right. They've been working you too hard. Why don't you sit down for a moment. Harry will bring you a brandy, won't you, Harry?"

"Always giving away my liquor, she is," Harry commented good-naturedly. "She's too generous by half when it's someone else's money."

"Thanks, but I think I'll just go home," Evan said. "The fresh air will do me good."

He pushed his way out of the room and came out into the cold night air. The mist had thickened and the cottages along the village street loomed as unidentifiable shapes. Evan didn't feel like being indoors. He turned up the street and began to walk fast. Cold strands of mist blew past him. He passed the rows of cottages and the shops. Then he came to the school playground. The schoolhouse was invisible in the fog, but Evan could see the glow of light from Bronwen's window.

A whole weekend had gone by without his seeing her. He had stayed away because he hadn't wanted to know the truth about her dinner date with Edward and Grantley. But now he needed to see her. He had to talk to someone about what he had been through today and Bronwen was the only person he could talk to. And he wanted her comforting arms around him.

The playground gate squeaked as he pushed it open. His footsteps echoed as he crossed the playground to Bronwen's living quarters at one end of the school building. He was about to knock on her front door when it swung open. Evan shook his head, smiling, as he went in.

"Hey, Bron, did you know you hadn't shut your door properly? And you're the one who's always complaining how hard it is to heat . . ." He broke off in midsentence. Bronwen was standing on the far side of the room, at her bedroom door. Her back was to him and her arms were wrapped around Edward Ferrers. As Evan watched in horror, she raised her face to be kissed.

FIFTEEN

CLASSICAL MUSIC WAS playing on the radio. She hadn't heard him come in. Evan began to back away. All he wanted to do now was to get out without being seen. But a gust of wind swirled in from the open door, sending the candle flames flickering.

Bronwen spun around and Edward looked up at the same time. For a second her eyes met Evan's. He turned away and hurried out into the night.

"Evan!" She shouted his name as he strode across the playground. "Evan, wait, don't go, please!"

He reached the gate and pushed it open. He heard the sound of her light footsteps echoing over the concrete behind him. "Evan, please, wait!" she shouted again.

He slipped through the gate and out into the street as she caught up with him, breathing hard from her sprint. "Don't go, please." She grabbed at his sleeve.

"You want me to stay and watch?" he demanded, finding it hard to get the words out.

"It wasn't the way it looked," she said. "I was just comforting him."

"Oh yes? Is that what it was?"

"You don't understand." Her eyes were pleading.

"No, no, I don't understand."

"Please come back inside and I'll explain. Edward came to me because he was desperate and he had nowhere else to turn."

Her breath came out as puffs of smoke, like a dragon's, and hung in the cold night air. Mist swirled around them. Evan shivered. Bronwen was hugging her arms around herself now.

"Evan, Edward is terrified they'll think he killed Grantley. It looks really bad for him. Please come back and say you'll help him."

"You want me to help Edward Ferrers?"

"At least listen to his side. I know it sounds bad, but let him explain."

"You mean because he and Grantley had an argument in public before he disappeared? Lots of people get into disagreements. That doesn't mean they end up killing each other."

"It's worse than that." Bronwen was still hugging her arms to herself, rocking in the cold. Evan wanted to comfort her and put his arms around her, but he couldn't make the move. She looked up at him with big, hopeless eyes. "You know I told you that Edward left me for someone else?" She was chewing on her lip, like a little child. "He left me for Grantley."

He hadn't been expecting this. It had never crossed his mind and it hit him like an unforeseen left hook. "Grantley? You're saying he and Edward? And yet you married him?"

Bronwen shrugged. "I was terribly naive, I suppose. We both were. I don't think Edward even realized he was gay until Grantley—I knew that our marriage was never great, but I thought that had to be something to do with me. That I wasn't sexy enough maybe."

"Oh, I don't think I'd say that," Evan said before he remembered, and Bronwen managed a weak smile.

"But I thought that Grantley and Sandie . . ."

"She probably thought so too," Bronwen answered. "Grantley was good at giving someone just enough encouragement to get what he wanted. He wouldn't have minded flirting with Sandie to make sure he got a willing slave. He did that with me for long enough."

Evan began to feel that he had stepped into an empty lift shaft and was just gathering speed. "You're telling me that you and Grantley?"

"I was madly in love with him all through Uni. I used to do his washing, mend his socks, help him with his papers. He used me. I saw that later."

"And you never caught on that he was gay either?"

"I know I sound completely stupid, but in Grantley's case I think he's a genuine AC/DC. I don't think he actually finds women unattractive. Found." She corrected herself. "I mean, found. I can't believe he's dead. I'd no idea it would affect me like this, after all this time. . . ."

Her voice wavered and she hugged herself more tightly. "I suppose that makes me a suspect too, doesn't it? I have no alibi for yesterday morning. I was out and about shopping in Bangor."

"I don't think you'd be my primary suspect at the moment," Evan said, trying to mask the tenderness he felt. "It would have had to be someone pretty strong to strangle a man and then throw his body into that pool. You'd have needed a strong accomplice." He forced himself to stop thinking what came into his mind: Edward was big and strong enough. Bronwen and Edward, teaming up to get rid of Grantley? Absurd. Bronwen would never harm anyone. She looked so frail, so vulnerable, standing there in her light sweater, with the mist swirling about her, hugging her arms to herself.

"You'd better get back inside," he said. "You'll catch cold out here."

She nodded. "Won't you come back inside with me and talk to Edward? Please?"

He had to force his mouth to form the words. "All right," he said.

She spun and hurried ahead of him to the open front door. Evan followed, still feeling that he hadn't yet reached the bottom of that lift shaft. This was Bronwen, Bronwen that he had thought he knew and loved, and yet she had been in love with Edward Ferrers and with Grantley Smith. Had she and Grantley been lovers, too? He couldn't bear to think about it.

Edward was sitting by the fire in Bronwen's armchair, staring into the flames. He got to his feet as Evan came in.

"It's very good of you," he muttered. "You see, I know they're going to come back and ask me more questions and I really don't have an alibi and it will look as though—" He ran his hands through his thick wiry hair. "Oh my God. They're going to think that I did it. I know they are."

"Why are you so sure of that?" Evan asked.

"Because we had a horrible, flaming row in public. People will have overheard what we said."

"And what did you say?"

"Among other things I think I told him that he'd better stay away from me or I'd break his bloody neck."

Evan pulled over one of Bronwen's kitchen stools and perched on it. Without being asked, Bronwen poured a glass of red wine and handed it to him. "Here, drink that."

"Thanks." He took a sip. "Okay, Edward, so you had an argument in the street and you exchanged some heated words. Were you really fighting about the film?"

"To begin with, yes. I thought all of this business of the mine was a silly waste of time. First the train, then the mine. Grantley had the attention span of a small child. He was always being distracted and dropping one toy for a bigger and better one. He was all excited about this mine business. I reminded him that he wouldn't have a job at all if it hadn't been for my involvement and my money. That's when he got very upset." He looked across at Bronwen. "Bronwen told you about us, did she? We fought a lot over money. He was unemployed; I had a good job, you see. Grantley hated being dependent, but at the same time he wasn't above spending my salary without telling me. It was one of the reasons we split up."

"When was this?"

"Right before we came here. We had just broken up. Grantley moved his stuff out of my place the night before we left on this little jaunt. That's why it's going to look so bad for me."

"I see." Evan took another sip of wine. "So go on about the fight."

"Grantley got upset when I mentioned that it was my money that was funding it. He told me what I could do with my bloody plane. He'd make his own movie. He didn't need me anymore. He'd got something much better."

"Which was what? The pictures in the slate mine story?"

Edward shrugged. "I presumed that was it. But it could be something quite different again. I know he made a lot of phone calls the day before. Maybe he'd come up with a new story entirely. That would have been like him."

"Edward." Evan paused. "Have you any idea what would have made Grantley go down that mine on his own—to find a back door and break in, when he was about to go down with the caretaker later that morning?"

"I have no idea at all. He didn't mention wanting to go down alone. All he told me was that he was meeting this chap who was going to give him a tour. Mind you, we hadn't exactly been in a very sharing mood. We hardly said a word to each other unless we had to."

"So why didn't he just drive up alone? Why bring you along?"

"That was me, I'm afraid, being petty. He asked to borrow the Land Rover. I told him it was mine—lent to me specifically. I was afraid he'd take it for the whole day if I let it out of my sight and I didn't want that to happen. So I said I'd drive him."

"So you fought and then what happened? You drove back alone?"

Edward studied his hands again. "No. I took a taxi. He kept the vehicle."

"Why didn't you drive back in the Land Rover?"

"I wasn't quick enough." Edward blushed. "We parted company with a few last hurled insults. I told him to go to hell. He wished me the same. Then he ran to my Land Rover, jumped in, and drove off before I could stop him. I had to get a taxi home." He looked up at Evan. "It doesn't look good for me, does it? People will have heard what I said. And the police will find out about us, and that we just broke up."

"No," Evan said. "It doesn't look good. But if you really didn't kill Grantley, then you don't have to worry. We'll find the person who did."

"But they're always picking on the wrong person." Edward sounded close to panic. "You read about it all the time in the papers—how some poor sod spends years in jail for a crime he didn't commit."

Bronwen put her hand on his shoulder. "But you've got Evan on your side," she said. "He's the best. If anyone can find out who really did it, he can."

"But he's only a P.C.," Edward said, glancing at Evan. "No offense, but I don't think you'll have too much say in a murder investigation, will you?"

This was his way out, Evan thought. He could say, "You're right. I'd be no help at all in a murder investigation. I'm just a village constable, nothing more."

But Bronwen reached out at that moment and laid her hand on his. "Evan will get to the truth for you—won't you, Evan?"

And he heard himself mutter, "I'll do what I can."

SIXTEEN

Ginger had never taken much interest in my work before, apart from telling me that I tasted of slate and needed a bath. "I don't know why you put up with it, Tref, I really don't," she used to tell me. "I wouldn't do anything I didn't like."

"What else could I do?" I asked her.

She laughed. "There's a war on. There's labor shortages all over. A girl I work with at the convalescent home, her boyfriend got a job driving lorries down to London. Sometimes it's sheep and sometimes it's butter or produce. Either way, they don't count too exactly and nobody notices if a pound or so of butter goes missing."

"I don't know how to drive, do I?" I said. "And no chance to learn either. Who do I know with a car?"

She grabbed my shoulders and shook me. "You're a defeatist, Trefor Thomas. When I want to do something, I find a way to do it. Like dancing lessons—there's this bloke at the convalescent home who used to be a ballroom dancing instructor before the war. He's been teaching me to tango. Lovely, it is."

I shook her hands from my shoulders. "I told you, I

don't want you mixing with those servicemen, and I certainly don't want you dancing with one of them."

She looked at my angry face and started laughing. "If you could only see us, Tref. He's in a wheelchair, you dope. Had his legs shot off, didn't he? He tells me the steps and I dance with his wheelchair. It's a riot. We have good laughs." She moved closer to me. "And I'm doing it for us, aren't I? For our future. How am I going to get a job in films if I can't do all the latest dance steps?"

"Well, I don't want you dancing with any man with legs," I said.

For some reason she thought this was awfully funny. "I could dance with you," she said, moving very close to me. "You've got legs, and everything else that matters, too. I could teach you the tango. It's ever so romantic. You press your body against mine, like this, and our lips are only this far apart, and then we start to sway, like this. . . ."

She was driving me insane. I could feel the points of her nipples digging into my chest and she was thrusting her leg between mine as we moved. I tried to kiss her but she broke away, laughing. "It's a dance, Tref. Don't get carried away."

"Come on, Ginger, stop teasing. Do you know I've been alone all week down that blasted mine, thinking about you?"

"Oh poor sweetie-pie, honey lamb." She turned her face up and kissed me. "You know, Tref, I've been thinking about those paintings."

"My paintings, you mean? I haven't had time recently. . . ."

"Not yours, you dope. The famous paintings down your mine. It was Pamela's boyfriend got me thinking—the way he said he could nick a pound or so of butter and they never noticed. If you could slip out with one of those famous paintings under your shirt, we'd be made for life."

I laughed. "Oh yes. No problem about that. Only alarms on all the sheds and a guard at the door, too."

"Pity it's not me down there. I always find a way to get what I want. You would too if you wanted it bad enough."

In his dream he was drowning in deep, cold water. He could feel it pressing down on him, meters of water over his head. He fought his way to the surface, but as he came up, he saw that someone else was above him, kicking and thrashing and preventing his escape. Through the water he could see Bronwen standing on the shore. He tried to shout her name but no sound would come out. He tried reaching out his hand to her. Help me, Bron, I'm under here. But when she reached out her hand, it was to the thrashing man above him, not to Evan at all.

"Up early and off to work again, is it, Mr. Evans?" Mrs. Williams greeted him as he came into the kitchen on Monday morning. "And they had you on duty all weekend, didn't they? No wonder they're finding it hard to get good men to join the police. I'd like to give them a piece of my mind. Working you to the bone like this." She poured boiling water into the teapot, then placed a red knitted tea cozy over it. "You're looking peaky, too."

"I didn't sleep well last night."

"I'm not surprised, all the things you go through." She leaned closer to Evan. "It's true what they're saying then, is it? That they found that poor man drowned down a mine in Blenau? I heard about it last night and I've been feeling so guilty."

"Why would you feel guilty, Mrs. Williams?"

"Well, it was me told him about it, wasn't it—that day you brought him to see me? If he hadn't talked to me, he'd never have known about the mines and he'd never have gone there and got himself drowned." She took out a handkerchief and held it up to her eyes. "I'll never forgive myself."

Evan patted her shoulder. "It wasn't your fault in any way. You wouldn't feel guilty if you'd told someone the way to Beddgelert and then he got himself in a traffic accident, would you?"

She managed a watery smile. "No, I suppose I wouldn't. But what a week of tragedies this has turned out to be. First poor old Mr. James dying, and then the young man."

"Mr. James-Fron-Heulog? He died, did he?"

Mrs. Williams nodded. "Oh yes. He didn't last the night after his heart attack. Such a terrible shame. A nice God-fearing chapel man if ever there was one. You shouldn't speak ill of the dead, I know, but that young man ought never to have stirred up the past—bringing that woman there. Like I said, no good ever comes of it. Look where he is now. Look where both of them are now, God rest their poor souls."

Evan was staring thoughtfully at the mist swirling past the window. So Mr. James had died. His son had been pretty upset before—had the news of his father's death been enough to make him go after Grantley? Evan remembered Betsy saying that a man had come into the pub asking for Grantley Smith. A farmer, Harry-the-Pub thought, from Dolwyddelan?

Evan turned back to Mrs. Williams. "Does the Jameses' son live at Fron Heulog with them?"

"Oh no, he has his own property. He used to come over and help his folks out when they needed it, with the lambing and shearing, you know, but he didn't live with them. He married a girl from over Dolwyddelan way and they inherited the place from her father."

"Dolwyddelan? Do you know the name of it?"

"I can't say that I do. But you can't miss it. If you're on the road between Dolwyddelan and Blenau, you'll see fields of sheep on the right, where the railway goes through. And a pretty white farmhouse not too far from the train lines. Right after the road dips down from Blenau. That's them."

"Thank you, Mrs. Williams. Most helpful." Evan got up.

"You're not going out before your breakfast?" she asked. "I was going to do kippers for you this morning."

"I don't think I've got time for kippers," Evan said. "I will have a cup of tea, though, and maybe some toast with your homemade marmalade."

"Just as you like, Mr. Evans. Coming right up then." She poured him a cup of tea. Evan sipped at it, putting his thoughts in order. He remembered that Robert James had put his hands around Grantley's throat and had to be dragged away. A man for whom violence came naturally. And then he had called in obvious distress when his father was admitted to the hospital. And he lived only a stone's throw from Blenau. He might easily have spotted Grantley Smith there and followed him to the mine.

This was a definite lead that he and Watkins should look into when they started the investigation today.

He gulped down a slice of toast, then hurried up the hill to the Everest Inn. He had been all business when he left the house, but as he drew level with the school, a bleak depression swept over him again. He had promised Bron that he'd help Edward Ferrers. Given his word. He had never wanted to do anything less in his life. For one thing, he wasn't at all sure that Edward Ferrers was innocent. He had the classic two "m's"—means and motive. What better way of claiming innocence than playing on the sympathy of someone as sensitive as Bronwen, and through her, getting the local copper onto his side.

Evan paused and stared across the empty schoolyard, his mind still racing. If he actually managed to prove that Edward didn't kill Grantley, what then? Might Edward want to come back into Bronwen's life?

"Blast and damn the lot of them," he muttered. Now it looked as if he was going to be part of another murder investigation. He had half expected Sergeant Watkins to call him at home with the latest news, telling him where to meet, but Watkins would definitely show up at the Inn sometime during the morning, probably with the results of the postmortem. Evan expected that Detective Inspector

Hughes would be with him. He wasn't looking forward
to that encounter and he doubted that D.I. Hughes would
be too thrilled to see him either. He suspected that the
D.I. saw him as something of a smart alec who always
seemed to be poking his nose into murder cases.

Evan smiled to himself as he reached the gateway to
the Inn. Lucky that he had been assigned to assist the
filmmakers by his own chief inspector. So this time he
had a legitimate reason for being on the spot. D.I. Hughes
might even welcome his help. After all, he was the only
policeman who had been on the spot from the beginning
and who knew all the details.

Evan reached the Inn and went inside. No sign of a
police car in the parking lot. Also no sign of any of the
film people in the dining room. He didn't blame them. He
would be dreading today if he were in their shoes. It
crossed his mind to call Edward Ferrers's room and find
out if he came home last night. Then he decided he'd
rather not know.

It wasn't until about ten o'clock that Sergeant Watkins
showed up at the Inn. By that time, Edward, Howard, and
Sandie had surfaced and were now sitting drinking coffee,
discussing what they should do next. Edward was the only
one who felt that they should go on with their work immediately. "I'll have to let the salvage crew go in a couple
of days. We'll have run out of money, and you won't get
paid, Howard, if we don't have a product to sell."

Howard reached forward for his coffee cup and drained
the dregs. "To tell you the truth, Ed, I'd just as soon be
on a plane back to California at this moment. The sooner
the better for me. I was only doing this as a favor to young
Grantley and now he's gone. . . ." He let the rest of the
sentence hang in the air.

Evan, sitting alone behind the morning paper, glanced
at Howard. So Howard was anxious to leave as soon as
possible, was he? Anxious to get out of the country and
far away from the scene of the crime, maybe? Evan re-

membered Howard's reaction the day before. What had made him think that Grantley's death might be due to an overdose? Did he know something that Evan didn't, or was that deliberately planted to disconnect himself from any suspicion?

"Well, I think we should finish the picture in his memory," Sandie said. "It's what he would have wanted. And it's not as if Howard couldn't do it without him, is it, Howard?"

"Honey, I've directed a cast of thousands, as they say," Howard said. "That's not the point. The point is, will the movie be worth finishing? So far we've got a couple of interviews and a sunken plane. Not the stuff that epics are made of."

"It will be exciting when it comes to the surface, Howard. You'll see. Especially if those German flyers are still in their seats, as the cameras have indicated."

Evan looked up again. The old German—they had all forgotten about him. He'd been very angry that day. In fact, he'd told Grantley that he'd stop him at any cost. And he looked very fit and agile for an elderly man. Could he have been staying nearby, possibly spotted Grantley going down the mine, and seized his chance? Another suspect to discuss with Watkins when he got here.

Just as his gaze went to the door, it opened and Sergeant Watkins came in. It must have started raining because his collar was turned up and his head and shoulders were wet. "Ah, there you all are." Watkins nodded and headed toward the group at the table. "The inspector is just finishing up his notes in the car. He'll be right in to talk to you."

Evan put down his paper and went over to Watkins. " 'Morning, Sarge. I was waiting for you to call. Did you get the results of the PM?"

Watkins nodded. "Yeah. Clear case of strangling. The hyoid bone was broken and there was quite a bit of internal bleeding of the neck muscles. Must have been a strong bloke. Did it with his bare hands." For some reason, Watkins was uneasy. He was shifting from foot to foot and kept glancing back at the door.

"So the D.I. is taking over the case himself?" Evan asked.

Watkins nodded. "For the moment. We've just been down that bloody slate mine and shown him where the body was found. He's got the crime scene boys there, going over the place, although what he expects to find in a slate mine, I'm not sure. Now he wants to talk to this lot."

"So what's the plan then, Sarge? Do we have to wait for him to finish up here?" Evan asked. "I've got a couple of leads we should . . ."

He broke off. The D.I. was coming through the revolving door with someone else following him. Watkins shuffled his feet uneasily again. "Look, Evan, I meant to tell you before this, but I've been assigned a partner for this case, so I'm afraid . . ."

"Ah, there you are." D.I. Hughes's crisp, high voice echoed through the foyer. He paused to brush raindrops from the shoulders of his well-tailored trench coat and ran a hand over his graying hair, although every strand was already in place. Then he came to join Watkins and Evan. "Everyone assembled? Good man, Evans. I don't know if you've met our latest addition, have you? This is Detective Constable Davies. I've assigned her to Watkins for this case."

Glynis Davies was crossing the foyer, looking stunning as ever in tailored navy pants and a dark blue raincoat that accentuated her sleek copper hair. She smiled at Evan. "Hello again. I gather you're the one who found the body for us. Brilliant." She went and stood beside Sergeant Watkins. "My first murder case," she said, beaming at everyone. "I'm so excited."

"Right, let's not waste any time then." D.I. Hughes clapped his hands together. "I'm going to have a little chat with these good people and I'd like Watkins to take a look at the victim's room. Make an inventory of anything that might be important, Watkins—correspondence, addresses, notes, bills."

"Right you are, sir." Watkins started for the reception desk.

"Should I go with him, sir?" Glynis had already produced a notebook from her bag.

The D.I. turned to her with his most charming smile. "I think you should stay and observe when I interview the victim's associates. A good interviewing technique is something that takes time and practice to acquire. It is that fine line of getting the information we need without putting the suspect on his guard, or making him feel he is being interrogated."

"He or she," Glynis corrected.

"Quite." D.I. Hughes nodded tersely.

Evan glanced at Watkins, but the latter was already getting the key from the girl at reception.

"So let's get started, shall we? I take it that the people at the table are Mr. Smith's associates, Evans?"

"Yes, sir," Evan said.

"Splendid." He smiled benignly at Evan. "Well, we won't detain you any longer, Constable. I expect you have work to do."

"I was assigned to assist these people with their project, sir."

"Well, I don't foresee them being free to get back to work before this afternoon, so I'll let them know that they can get in touch with you at the police station when they need you. Come along, my dear." He put a hand on Glynis's back and shepherded her over to the waiting filmmakers.

SEVENTEEN

EVAN CAME OUT of the Inn into the fine morning rain. He had been dismissed; not wanted. Not needed. Watkins had a new partner. Now Glynis would be doing all the things he had expected to do. She'd probably solve the case single-handed in a couple of hours and be promoted to sergeant by the end of the day, he thought angrily, then grinned at his own childishness.

As he drew level with the two chapels, he heard his name called and Mrs. Powell-Jones came running down her driveway, apron flapping and hairpins flying. "Ah, there you are, Constable Evans. I wondered if you'd gone on holiday or something."

"No such luck, I'm afraid, Mrs. Powell-Jones." He stood with resignation, waiting for her to reach him. "Why did you think I'd gone on holiday?"

"Because you are never at the police station when I phone and you haven't answered any of the important messages I've left in the past few days."

"I'm sorry. I've been assigned elsewhere."

"I know. To that very rude young man who never turned up for tea when he was invited. Well, you can tell him from me that he's lost his chance to find out the true details of Llanfair in the war now. Invitations to tea at my home with homemade scones do not come lightly."

"So was there a problem, Mrs. Powell-Jones?" Evan asked, anxious to get to the station and shut the door behind him.

"More than one. Several problems, in fact. Major problems. It's all thoughtlessness, of course, and a very warped view of Christianity."

"What is?"

She pointed dramatically at the other chapel. "That star. I'm lodging an official complaint."

"Star?" As so often when talking to Mrs. Powell-Jones, Evan found himself floundering.

"On the roof, man. They've had the gall to put up an electric star on their roof. To announce Christmas to the world, so Mrs. Parry Jones says. It's not that at all. It is purely an act of jealousy." She leaned closer to Evan as she glanced across at the other minister's house. "She has always been very put out that I do such a wonderful Christmas pageant. So obviously she has come up with this ridiculous flashing star in an attempt to draw attention to herself."

"But surely a star is a nice Christmas symbol for the whole village to enjoy, isn't it?" Evan suggested.

"A Papist symbol, Constable Evans. Not the sort of thing you'd expect to find on a good Nonconformist chapel, and a traffic hazard to boot."

"A traffic hazard?" Evan glanced up at the star on the chapel roof. It didn't look as if it might fall off at any moment.

"I understand that the lights are going to flash on and off. Approaching motorists will be distracted. They might think it is some kind of traffic signal, slow down, and run into each other. It can't be allowed, Constable Evans. It has to go. If it doesn't, I will personally com-

plain to the Public Safety commissioner—an old
friend, I might add."

"I'll register your complaint and pass it on to my
superior," Evan said. "Now if you'll excuse me, I have
work to do."

"And ask her about the holly," Mrs. Powell-Jones
called after him. "I had some particularly fine holly
berries in my back garden. Now they have all mysteriously disappeared and that Parry Jones woman has a
holly wreath on her front door. Very strange, since she
has no garden of her own to speak of and certainly no
holly bushes. Ask her about it, Constable Evans. Get
her to confess."

Evan sighed as he continued down the street. Was
this why he had become a policeman, to mediate dis-
putes between feuding ministers' wives?

So what are you going to do about it, boyo? he asked
himself as he shut the station door behind him and put
on the kettle for a cup of tea. Are you going to sit there
and let them all walk over you? Or are you going to
show them that you're as good as any of them? The
problem was he had no idea how he was going to show
them anything at all . . . unless he used his initiative
and started doing a little snooping on his own. Anyway,
he wasn't going to sit there all day, waiting to be summoned to play nursemaid. He unplugged the kettle
again and strode out to his car. It wouldn't do any harm
if he had a talk with Mr. Robert James, and maybe
asked if an old German had turned up in Blenau Ffestiniog recently.

Robert Jameses' farm looked prosperous, with lush
green water meadows beside a rushing stream and a
large two-story farmhouse set among larch trees.
Smoke was curling up from the chimney and a big
bonfire of leaves added a delicious smell as Evan drove
between dry stone walls to the house. A pretty woman
came to the door, slim and fine boned, with blond hair

and blue eyes. Although she wore jeans and an old sweatshirt, she managed to look elegant, and much younger than she really was, Evan suspected. A toddler emerged from behind her legs and was promptly grabbed before it could escape.

"Sorry about that," she said, smiling at Evan. "My daughter's off helping my husband with the funeral arrangements and I'm stuck here with the grandkids."

"I'm Constable Evans, Mrs. James. I'm sorry to trouble you at this difficult time, but . . ."

A flash of fear crossed her face. "Nothing's wrong, is it?"

"No, I just came to see your husband, actually. My condolences about his father. I didn't know him personally but he was obviously well respected."

"He was indeed—a lovely man. Robert says he used to be quite stern when they were kids, but turned into a big old softie. You should have seen him with the grandchildren, giving them rides on his back." She paused, fished for a tissue, and wiped her eyes. "Robert's really taking it hard. His father was doing so well after the heart surgery, look you." She smoothed down her apron. "But I mustn't keep you here, chattering on. I don't think Robert will be back for a while. There's so much paperwork to be done and his mother's not really up to it—well, she wouldn't be, would she?"

Evan wondered when she might stop for breath. When the grandchild tugged at her skirt and said, "Nain, I'm hungry," she looked up at Evan and smiled apologetically.

"I'd better go and feed the multitudes. Always hungry at this age, aren't they? So what was it you wanted to ask Robert? Maybe I can help you?"

"It's about a man called Grantley Smith."

"Grantley Smith—don't mention that name around here," she snapped. "Robert told me all about that Englishman and what he did. He blames him for his father's death. Well, he would, wouldn't he? And I have

to agree with him—bringing that terrible woman to
visit him. I mean, you don't shock somebody who's
had heart surgery, do you?"

"Would you happen to know if Robert went to see
Grantley Smith after his father died?"

"He talked about it," she said. "But he always talks
big, does Robert, when he gets riled. He was going to
give that Grantley Smith the whipping of his life.
Teach him to come interfering where he wasn't wanted.
That kind of thing, you know. But it's all talk, isn't
it?"

Evan thought it prudent not to tell her that Robert's
hands had been around Grantley Smith's throat at least
once.

"On Saturday morning, did either of you go out?"

"On Saturday? Why yes. I always do my week's
shopping on Saturdays. I dropped Robert off in Blenau
and I went on down to Porthmadog."

"What was your husband doing in Blenau?"

"He usually pops down on a Saturday morning and
ends up at the Wynnes Arms, of course with all his
cronies." She paused and then asked cautiously,
"What's this about then? Nothing's happened to Robert, has it?"

"Just routine inquiries," Evan said. "I wondered if
your husband might have bumped into Grantley Smith
on Saturday morning, that's all."

"He didn't say anything about it," Mrs. James said,
sweeping the toddler up into her arms, "and I'm sure
he would have, knowing how he feels."

Evan gave her a friendly smile. "Well, I won't keep
you any longer then."

He'd have to report this to D.I. Hughes and his
merry men, Evan decided as he drove away from the
Jameses' farm. He didn't want to, but he didn't have
much choice. The fact that Robert James was in Blenau
when Grantley Smith met his death was something they
couldn't overlook—although Evan couldn't really pic-

ture Robert James as Grantley's killer. Robert reminded him of Evans-the-Meat, all bluff and bluster, but he cooled down just as quickly as he heated up. He could imagine Robert strangling Grantley in the heat of the moment, but sneaking down a mine after him, strangling him in a dark passage, and then weighting down his body before dumping it in a pool of water—that took a different kind of temperament. It was an opportunistic, clever sort of murder.

But he would have to pass on the facts to the D.I. And he'd have to tell them about the old German as well. Not that he thought the German was a likely suspect. He had been angry enough. He had vowed to stop Grantley at any cost, but stopping someone at any cost didn't usually mean killing them. Evan couldn't picture that old man following Grantley down a mine and sneaking up behind him. Besides, the project to raise the plane would go on without Grantley. No—Evan suspected that the answer lay closer to home, among Grantley's colleagues. He had felt the undercurrent of tension when he first met them. So many little remarks he didn't understand. So many sneaked glances. The best thing he could do right now was to stay at his assigned post and observe.

That afternoon he was summoned up to the lake, where work on raising the plane was going to resume. The D.I. had apparently finished interviewing all of the filmmakers without leaping to conclusions and arresting anyone—which was a distinct improvement on his usual modus operandi, Evan decided. When he arrived at the lake site, the generators were humming, the winch was turning, and so were the film cameras. It was as if Grantley Smith had never existed.

Evan sat on a rock and watched them. Sergeant Watkins had been right—they were all jittery. Howard kept glancing up at him as he scribbled furiously on his yellow pad, then leaped to peek into the camera. Sandie must have dropped her pen at least ten times, each time looking across at Evan. And Edward was a bundle of nerves, pacing up and down, bringing out his handkerchief to mop his forehead, snapping at the crew when they didn't follow instructions immediately. Evan supposed it was understandable that they would all be on edge. After all, they had just lost someone who had been close to them. But was their behavior showing their guilt, or was it possible that they suspected each other? Evan watched even more closely. Sandie was doing a lot of glancing at Edward, but then Edward was glancing at Howard, and Howard was taking care to avoid eye contact with either of them. Interesting.

Evan waited until Sandie sat down to write up some notes. He went over and sat beside her. She started nervously as he perched on the rock. "So you had to face D.I. Hughes grilling you this morning, did you?" he asked, giving her a friendly smile.

She nodded.

"I can't imagine that was too pleasant. Our D.I. isn't known for his subtlety or tact."

Sandie shuddered. "It was the way he looked at me with those piercing blue eyes. And once he leaned across to that woman detective and muttered something and she looked directly at me. But when it came to my turn, he didn't really ask me anything at all." She picked at the hem of her sweater, twisting it into a knot. "Maybe they know more than they're letting on."

"About what?"

"About who killed Grantley, of course."

"Do you have any ideas yourself?"

She jumped again. "Me? No, why should I?"

"You've been working very closely with these people. When I first met them, I sensed things going on that I didn't understand. An awful lot of tension, wasn't there?"

"I suppose so. Grantley was the sort of person who

thrived on tension. He wasn't always easy to get on with."

"Had you been with him for long—as his production assistant, I mean?" Evan asked tactfully.

"As his production assistant? This is the first thing he ever produced." She glanced at him shyly. "I'd known Grantley for about a year. We were taking classes at the film institute together. When he told me about this, I jumped at the chance to be part of it—even if it meant being his maid of all work. Grantley had hardly paid me any attention before, but when I said my family came from North Wales, he was suddenly very attentive and asked me to join his team.

"I was flattered, I suppose. It's not easy to break into films these days—too many qualified people, and I didn't have a degree in media or anything. And when he said Howard Bauer was going to be directing, well, that clinched it. I'd have scrubbed floors or served tea to work with Howard."

"And has he turned out to be as good as you thought he was?"

She stared at Howard with a puzzled frown. "That's the weird thing. He hasn't really done anything much. He's been content to leave all the decisions to Grantley when I'm sure he knows much better. Maybe he was just being nice and letting Grantley run the show here."

"What made him decide to join this venture?" Evan asked. "It can't have been the money."

"Hell, no. None of us has been paid yet. We were doing it for Grantley, and Grantley, I suspect, was doing it for Edward." She made a face.

"So what made you walk out?" Evan asked her suddenly. "You said it was a personal matter."

"It was." She got to her feet again.

"You were in love with Grantley, weren't you?"

"That's none of your business."

"It's all going to come out in the investigation, you know. They're looking for someone with a motive, and a jilted lover who storms out yelling, 'I hate you,' is going to be something that interests the D.I. It gives you a pretty strong motive, doesn't it?"

"That's what I'm afraid of," Sandie said. She pushed her blond hair back from her face and suddenly looked very young and vulnerable. "I knew they'd suspect me. And when they find out I was there . . ." She looked up at him appealingly. "You seem like a nice sort of bloke. You look as if you'd understand."

Evan nodded. "Where were you, Sandie?"

"Up in that bloody place I can't pronounce. Blenny something. I was so angry and upset when I stormed out. Then I thought that maybe I got it wrong. Maybe it was just Grantley being Grantley."

"What was?"

"I found a photo of him and Edward. They were— you know—it was disgusting. I couldn't believe it. I confronted Edward and he said it was true. He said he and Grantley had been living together—you know, like a couple. I couldn't believe it. I mean I thought that Grantley—that he fancied me. He certainly acted that way when we were alone."

"So you left?"

"Yeah. But I couldn't make myself go away. I kept thinking they'd taken that photo for a joke, or that maybe Edward was that way but Grantley was just playing him along. So I decided I'd make Grantley tell me the truth. If I heard from his own lips that he was gay and he wasn't interested in me, then I'd leave.

"I rented a car and came back here, looking for him. Howard told me that they'd gone up to the Blenny place. So I drove up there. I saw the Land Rover parked at one end of the High Street. I looked everywhere but I couldn't find Grantley. So I came back again." She looked up at him hopelessly. "But they'll find out I was up there. I asked people if they'd seen him. They'll remember me. And they'll think I did it." She shook her head, squeezing her eyes shut to stop the tears from escaping. "Not that I care anymore what happens to me. Now that he's gone. Nothing matters anymore. I just pray they catch the bastard that did it."

Howard called her and she hurried over to him. Evan watched her go. Someone with a motive and means, he thought. She had been betrayed and humiliated. She might have seen Grantley. He might even have invited her down the mine with him. But after that . . . Evan studied her slender frame. The wind was blowing her fine blond hair out behind her and flapping her jeans around her spindly legs. If she had wanted to kill Grantley, she'd have hit him over the head with a rock, not grabbed him around the throat and strangled him. And she certainly wouldn't have had the strength to drag his body and drop it into the water.

"I'd never met Grantley until recently." Howard lowered himself to a rock and stretched out his legs, today clad in black cords. There was a hitch with the underwater cable and they were taking a break. The sun had broken through the clouds and was pleasantly warm when the wind dropped. Howard took out a hip flask, took a swig, and then offered it to Evan.

"Not when I'm on duty, thanks," Evan replied tactfully.

"My only vice these days." Howard gave a sad little smile. "I've given up on cigarettes and women. I've had three wives. Now I stay well away. Too expensive." He grinned at Evan. "Are you married?"

"Not yet."

"Keep it that way. Less complicated."

Evan laughed. "I'm curious," he asked. "What made you sign on for a project like this? I mean, I'd imagine a bloke with your reputation would be pretty much in demand. And this can't be too exciting after the kind of high excitement things you've done. So were you doing a favor to a personal friend?"

Howard grimaced. "As I told you, I only met him

earlier this year. I was teaching a course at the film institute in London and he was in my class. He was really interested, really keen to get on, you know. He even volunteered to be my intern, which really meant my gopher. He helped me out with my filing and editing for a while. So, when he called me about this project, he said it would only take a couple of weeks, and I thought, Hell, why not? Give the young guy a break. I wasn't keen to fly back to California in a hurry. Wife number three has an alimony suit going. She can't live on what I pay her, apparently. The poodles all need shampooing twice a month."

"So you agreed to do this just to help Grantley get launched in his own career?"

Howard nodded. "He thought my name would lend the project credibility and get us backing. And I'm always happy to pass on what I've learned to the next generation."

"That's very nice of you," Evan said.

Howard got to his feet. "Oh well. I suppose we should get back to work while the sun's out. It makes it seem kinda pretty up here."

Evan got to his own feet and strolled down to the edge of the lake, where the two divers were still struggling to attach a cable. No motive there, apparently. Howard Bauer wasn't even closely connected with Grantley Smith. He had the means all right. He had been seen walking through Llanfair when he claimed to be struck down with a virus and in bed all day. He could easily have taken a bus or taxi to follow Grantley to Blenau Ffestiniog. But what for?

All the same, something didn't make sense. Howard had said that he agreed to help out with the project as a mentor figure. He hinted that Grantley idolized him— had even helped with his office filing. And yet the exchanges Evan had witnessed were not those of master and pupil. It always seemed that Grantley was the one in charge and that Grantley took perverse pleasure in needling Howard—almost talking down to him on occasion. Howard clearly hadn't enjoyed those exchanges, which made one wonder why he put up with Grantley.

And then there was Edward Ferrers. Evan looked back at the young man as he shouted and gesticulated. Edward was showing definite signs of stress. Obviously, the death of a close friend might have made him act that way, but Evan remembered the day Grantley went missing. He remembered Edward arriving at the lake in a very agitated state. Was it just because they had fought and then Grantley had driven off in Edward's car? Or had Edward followed Grantley, found him down the mine, and done what he had threatened to do? Of all of them, Edward had the strength and a compelling motive. The collapse of a relationship, Grantley's constant humiliation and teasing. Yes, Evan could well understand if Edward had finally snapped. Of course, proving it would be another matter, and he had promised Bronwen that he'd prove Edward's innocence. What if all facts pointed to his guilt instead?

EIGHTEEN

After that, she kept harping on those blasted pictures.

"You helped build those sheds, didn't you?" she asked me out of the blue one day, a week or so later. I'd met her down in Llandudno and we went to the pictures. Joan Fontaine in Suspicion *was playing, and Joan Fontaine was one of her favorites, right up there with Ginger and Betty and Carole Lombard. But the B movie was really bad. A stupid cops and robbers.*

"What sheds?" I whispered back.

She dug me in the side. "You know, the ones for the pictures."

"You know I did. I told you."

Someone behind leaned forward and made shushing noises. Ginger grinned at me. She leaned against me, nestling her lips against my cheek, as if to give me a kiss.

"You know what I was thinking," she whispered. "I was thinking that someone who put them together would know how to take them apart again."

"It was a good picture, wasn't it?" I said as I walked her back to the hostel where she was living.

"I suppose so. I was thinking of other good pictures. Pictures that are lying there down a mine."

"Would you shut up about them," I snapped. "I've told you the sheds have alarms on them and there's a guard. So I couldn't get at them, even if I wanted to—which I'm not at all sure that I do."

"Not even for me?" She moved closer to me, rubbing her hip and thigh against mine. "I thought you said you'd do anything for me once. And this isn't for me. It's for us. It's our ticket out of here, Tref. You and me. Our ticket to Hollywood."

"You're crazy. You're always dreaming about impossible things."

We were walking along the promenade. In peacetime that promenade used to be very glamorous—all the posh hotels and strings of fairy lights and bands playing. Now, of course, it was all dark. We carried a little torch with us, just to find our way, but it had to have a paper shield over it and it was the only light for miles around. To our left we could hear the crash and hiss of the waves, breaking on the sandy beach. You could taste the salt in the air.

Ginger paused and leaned on the railings, looking out over the sea. "I don't see why it's so impossible," she said. "There are ways around everything, if you look for them. Like I said in the cinema, you put the sheds together. You must know how they come apart again. You could take off a back panel and get in that way, and the alarm would never go off, right?"

"And the guard? You don't think he'd notice me with a bloody great crowbar?"

"What happens at night? Is there a guard then?"

"No. They lock up the place at night. There's a night-watchman on duty for the whole mine."

"There you are then. Simple as pie." She snuggled against me, rubbing her face against my collar like a cat. "You just stay down there one night. You hide out and don't come up with the rest of the quarrymen."

"Stay down there alone all night?" I could feel my heart starting to race at the thought of it—alone, in all that blackness, all those hours. "I don't know if I could do that." Then I remembered and let out a sigh of relief. "And anyway, I have to sign out. They'd know I was missing."

"You couldn't get one of your mates to sign for you?"

"I haven't got any mates now. It's just old blokes and me down there. All the young ones have been called up. I couldn't ask any of them. They're all my father's friends. They'd tell him."

"Yeah. I suppose you're right. Too bad. That would have been so easy. All right. Let's think again. Just one guard, is it?"

"One at a time."

"Then he must need to pee occasionally. Or he could be a few minutes late on duty one morning, if he got delayed. I mean, if someone delayed him . . ."

"How?"

"If a really gorgeous girl stopped him and asked him for help." She grabbed my arm. " 'Mister, I'm in terrible trouble. The heel just came off my shoe and now I've dropped my purse and all my money's spilled out and my mum's going to kill me for being late. Please . . .' You don't think he'd stop and help me?"

She was very convincing. I knew then that she'd be a great movie star if she ever got there.

"See?" She laughed, breaking the spell. "Then you just pop in and get one of the back panels loose. After that, you can take your time. Watch him. See when he's paying attention and when he's not. It's my betting that it's bloody boring down there. He might even doze off. Then you can just slip in, pinch a painting, and hide it until we're ready. There are plenty of places to hide something down a mine, aren't there?"

"No problem about that. Little caves, and piles of slate cuttings all over the place."

"There you are then. Piece of cake. No one will ever know."

"When they come to take the paintings back to London, they will. They'll notice one is missing, won't they?"

"We'll be long gone to Hollywood by then. I'll probably be a famous movie star."

"Doesn't matter. They'd still get us. We'd still go to jail."

She laughed. "I don't think so. I'll be rich and famous. We'll just pay them off. You can bribe people really easily in America, you know."

I laughed nervously. "This is stupid. It's bloody daft."

"Don't swear. It's not nice." She slapped my arm.

"It's playing with fire. We're just asking to get burned."

"I like fire." She looked up at me. I could see her eyes sparkling in the moonlight. "And I like getting burned."

The village was already nestling in its smoky haze as Evan came from the Everest Inn. There had been no sign of a police presence when he dropped off Howard, Edward, and Sandie. He wondered how their investigation was going, whether the crime scene boys had turned up any clues in the slate mine. It was so frustrating not to know what was going on. The village street was deserted, even though it wasn't much past five o'clock. The temperature was dipping rapidly and his footsteps clattered on the frosty pavement.

He hurried past the chapels, before he could be assaulted again by Mrs. Powell-Jones, and kept up his quick pace as he passed the school. He was almost past when he heard his name called. Bronwen must have been watching for him from her kitchen window. She came running across the schoolyard, a red wool shawl wrapped around her and her braid over one shoulder, looking like a heroine from a fairy tale.

He waited, patiently, not knowing how to react to her. Maybe last night had been a bad dream. Maybe he had overreacted at finding her ex-husband in her home—in her arms, he reminded himself.

"Any news?" she called as soon as she was within hailing range. "Have they found out who might have killed Grantley?"

"I wouldn't know. I'm not on the case, am I?"

She looked confused at his bluntness. "I know you're never officially on any case, but Sergeant Watkins relies on you; even that pompous little inspector . . ."

"Not this time," he said. "Sergeant Watkins has been assigned his own detective constable. The D.I. told me to go home and be a good boy."

"Oh Evan, that's so stupid." There was sympathy in her face, or so he thought. But then she went on, "Poor Edward—he has to be the most obvious suspect. I don't know what it will do to him if they put him in jail."

"The British police don't make a habit of throwing the wrong man into prison," Evan said stiffly.

She came closer and touched his sleeve. "But you could still do something unofficially, couldn't you? Remember that time when those climbers fell to their deaths. You were sure it wasn't an accident, even though everyone else wanted to call it one. You stuck your neck out, did your own investigating, and found the killer."

"Yes, and it nearly cost me my job."

"But it didn't. You're still here. And you know that they were impressed, even though they wouldn't admit it."

"That doesn't mean I can keep on poking my nose in where it's not wanted. I'm sure Sergeant Watkins and his new D.C. will do a good job."

"They won't get at the truth, I know it." She was gripping his arm now. "Please help, Evan. I can't let him down." She let go and turned away, as if aware that she might have gone too far. "Of course I realize you can't go bursting into the crime lab or anything like that, but you're the one with the instincts. You're fantastic at making connections other people can't see. You're a better detective than any of them, and you know it."

He had to smile. "Flattery will get you nowhere."

"It's the truth. Look, I know Edward is a bit of a pompous prig, but he's very vulnerable underneath."

"And what if he did it, Bron?" Evan asked. "Have you thought of that?"

She shook her head. "I just can't picture Edward killing anyone. He's the sort who faints at the sight of blood." Then she pulled the shawl around her more tightly and took a deep breath. "But either way, I'd rather know the truth."

"All right," he said. "I'm not sure if there's anything I can do, but I'll do what I can."

"Thank you."

As he went on his way down through the village, Evan had the horrible feeling that he had already lost her.

There were no messages on the answering machine at his police station. He locked the door and went home.

As he came in the door, he met Mrs. Williams adjusting her hat in front of the hall mirror.

"Oh there you are, Mr. Evans. Sorry to be dashing out, but I've got a meeting at chapel for the Christmas bazaar. There's a shepherd's pie in the oven and some mashed turnip to go with it. I've no doubt you can fend for yourself this once, is it?"

"Don't worry about me, Mrs. Williams," he said. "I'll be just fine."

"Oh, that's good." She gave him a relieved smile. "I'll be going then. Mrs. Powell-Jones doesn't like us to be late."

The door slammed and he was alone in the house, conscious of the silence. He went through to the kitchen and took the shepherd's pie from the oven, looked at it, and put it back. He had no appetite tonight. He didn't even feel like going to the Dragon for a pint. He poured a cup of tea from the pot Mrs. Williams always kept going under a cozy and sat at the kitchen table. It's not the end of the world, he told himself. But it felt like it.

He was just telling himself not to be so bloody stupid and to get on with his dinner when there was a knock at the front door.

"I'm not disturbing some culinary masterpiece, am I?" Sergeant Watkins was standing there, his coat collar turned up against the cold.

"I was about to eat some shepherd's pie and turnip. Not my favorite."

Watkins indicated with his head. "Come on, get your coat. I'll buy you a drink."

"Is Glynis with you?"

"Last seen being shepherded out by the D.I. to 'a little place he knows where they can produce quite a decent Chardonnay,'" he imitated the inspector's Anglicized tones. "He's going to catch it when Mrs. Hughes finds out." Watkins gave him a knowing grin.

"Look, sorry about today," he said to Evan as they walked together to the Red Dragon. "It was sprung on me, too. D.I. just shows up with her and says, 'Watkins, meet your new partner.' She's a nice enough girl, but . . .'"

"I expect she'll make a brilliant detective," Evan said. "Go right to the top. She's got the brains."

"And the legs. And the connections, too."

They exchanged a grin.

"She's already driving me barmy, she's so dead keen," Watkins said. "She's told me about ten times how excited she is to be on her first murder case. Lucky the D.I. is so keen on giving her his Hercule Poirot imitation that he's kept her with him for most of the day."

They pushed open the pub door and were met with a blast of warmth, smoke, and Frank Sinatra on the jukebox.

Betsy's eyes lit up when she saw Evan come in—something that had been lacking in his last couple of appearances.

"Here he is himself then," she said loudly. "You can tell us all about it."

"About what?"

"Why, the murder, of course. It was murder, wasn't it?

That's what we heard, anyway. That poor man found down in the slate mine. No wonder you looked so terrible last night. I thought you were going to pass out on us. All right now, are you?"

Evan was conscious of Sergeant Watkins's amused gaze. "I'm fine thanks, Betsy. Now if we could just have . . ."

"So you've got yourself another murder to solve, is it?" She was leaning over the counter, smiling at him. "You'll like that, won't you? Liven things up a bit."

"Betsy, I'm not solving any . . ."

"Pity it had to be the handsome one, though. I thought he was ever so good-looking. All dark and brooding, like. Of course, I never got the chance to really meet him, because someone spoiled it for me every time. . . ."

"Betsy, I've got things to discuss with Sergeant Watkins, so if we could just have a couple of pints?"

Betsy's smile faded. "Oh well, if you're too busy. Still, I suppose you're not meant to be chatting when you're on duty. What will it be, then?"

Watkins stepped forward. "I'm buying. Guinness, is it? Let's go through into the lounge. We can't hear ourselves speak in here."

They seated themselves at a table against the far wall. The lounge was deserted except for a couple of older women, who looked up and nodded at Evan.

"So how's it going so far?" Evan asked. "Any promising leads?"

"Nothing really," Watkins said. "The D.I.'s been in touch with the Met and we've notified the next of kin. A Mr. and Mrs. Arthur Smith, of very 'umble origins, I might add. It seems our boy was christened plain old Arthur Smith after his dad, who works on the railways. The Grantley bit appeared when he got a scholarship to Cambridge. Started signing his name A. Grantley-Smith, hyphenated. That was also when he stopped visiting the old folks, or even admitting to their existence."

"Interesting," Evan said. "So are they going to be looking into his background further?"

"What, and see if anyone might have had a big enough grudge to come up here and bump him off?"

Evan smiled. "It does sound rather stupid when you put it like that."

"Who knows? I gather he's being thoroughly checked out, but I tend to agree with the D.I. for once. It had to be someone up here who did it. Someone close to him."

"One of his colleagues, you mean. The D.I. was about to work on them when I left," Evan said.

Watkins grinned. "That's right. But apparently he didn't manage to make any of them break down weeping and confess. Must be losing his touch." He took a long drink of his bitter, then put his glass down again. "So, tell me—what do you think? You've been working with them. You must have ideas."

"I'd say that any one of them could have done it," Evan said. "Edward Ferrers had a violent row with him and they parted hurling insults, but he swears he took a taxi back and didn't kill Grantley."

Watkins made a note. "Should be easy enough to find the taxi and get the exact time. We've got a time for their very public fight, so we can easily see if he had long enough to strangle someone and drop the body into the water. So what about Howard the Yank?"

"He's a strange one," Evan said. "I haven't quite made him out. He's a famous director, he claims Grantley offered to act as his unpaid intern and he was only directing this as a favor to his pupil, but—"

"But what?"

"But to hear them talking, you never got the impression that Howard was the mentor and Grantley his adoring pupil. It was definitely Grantley who called the shots."

"Maybe the power was going to his head."

"Then why did Howard stay? He didn't have to. He hadn't even been paid."

"Did they like each other?"

"I can't say I ever got that impression," Evan said. "In fact, I'd say that Howard definitely disliked Grantley. Grantley enjoyed needling Howard, but then he enjoyed needling everyone. That's probably what got him killed. He pushed one person too far. That person overreacted and lost his temper. They happened to be down a mine with nobody else around."

"That would point to Edward Ferrers," Watkins said. "Who else would he take down a mine with him since we know it wasn't Howard?"

"It might have been Howard claimed he didn't feel well and stayed in his room all day. But Betsy at the bar saw him hurrying down the village street. So he was out and about that day. It wouldn't have been hard to get a taxi up to Blenau Ffestiniog. Maybe he showed up saying he'd changed his mind and wanted to see the mine after all."

"But that would be premeditated murder. That's a different kettle of fish altogether, isn't it?"

Evan shrugged. "I'm only giving you possibilities."

"And what about the girl?"

"Sandie? She'd make a good suspect—unrequited love, had a big shock."

"*Fatal Attraction* all over again, you mean?"

"But I don't think she'd have had the strength. She's so thin and frail, she looks like the wind would blow her away. It's not easy to strangle someone."

"Had some experience, have you?" Watkins chuckled.

"No, but I can think of a few people I'd like to try it on."

Watkins drained his glass and leaned toward Evan. "So you think it has to be one of them, do you?"

"Not necessarily," Evan said, and told Watkins about Robert James.

"And you say he always goes to Blenau Ffestiniog on Saturday mornings?" Watkins scribbled notes. "Now that's very interesting. And you actually caught him a few days earlier with his hands around Grantley's throat?"

"Yes, but . . ." Evan began. "I think he's one of those

people who is all bluster when he's het up and then quickly calms down again."

"Like your friend the butcher in there." Watkins indicated Evans-the-Meat's broad back. "Come on, drink up. How about another?"

"Let me get them this time." '

"Nonsense. You've already earned it, giving me that information on Robert James. I like to be one up on the D.I. when I come in to work in the morning. And now I've got young D.C. Davies to impress too, haven't I?"

He went into the main bar and returned with two new pints.

"*Iechyd da,* boyo. One of the few bits of Welsh I can say really well."

"So, did anything turn up today during the search?" Evan asked.

"Only one thing of interest. A bloody great footprint, halfway down the path to the mine. It's pretty recent and that path's not used anymore. It's not the caretaker's. It's not Grantley Smith's, either. He was wearing fancy Italian shoes, size nines. This is a boot—a big boot."

"Not that it means anything much," Evan said. "Anyone could have been walking a dog, or gone courting along a disused path."

"Except this path only leads to the mine and there is a big sign posted saying, 'Keep Out, Trespassers will be . . .' and all that stuff."

"So you're going to try and get a match?"

"First thing tomorrow."

"And nothing turned up in his room?"

"Nothing I could see. It was such a bloody mess in there. He liked to live in a pigsty, didn't he? I asked the maid if it might have been ransacked, but she said it had been like that since he moved in." Watkins took a big gulp of beer. "It was hard to know where to start. Clothes all over the floor. Photos and papers all over the bed . . ."

Evan paused in mid-swig. "Here, hang on, Sarge. Photos and papers all over the bed, you say?"

"And the floor, some of them."

"Then someone *had* been in there. When Grantley was first missing, I went in that room with Edward Ferrers. The place was a pigsty all right, but the photos were in a folder, in his briefcase."

"Now that is interesting. I can get the boys to go over the room for prints, but . . ."

"But his colleagues have probably all been in there at one time or another."

"Oh really?" Watkins's smile hinted at funny business. "All of them?"

"I didn't mean it like that. When you're away at a hotel, you pop into each other's rooms for a chat from time to time, don't you? Grantley could have called them all in for a meeting."

"But there was some funny business too, I get the feeling."

"Grantley and Edward had been partners. Just broken up. Sandie was madly in love with Grantley—devastated to find out about Edward."

"And Howard? It's getting to be like a soap, isn't it? It will take over in the ratings from *Pobl y Cwm.*"

"I don't think Howard was involved . . . but on the other hand, he could have been."

"A bit on the poncy side, isn't he? Silk shirts and all that?"

Evan grinned. "The D.I. wears silk shirts. Howard talks about ex-wives, but then Edward had an ex-wife, too."

"Told you about her, did he?"

Evan had only just realized that Watkins didn't know. He wanted to keep it that way, if at all possible. The last thing he wanted was Watkins's sympathy.

"Yes, he mentioned it."

"So we could have been dealing with a very knotty love-knot. Knotty and naughty!"

He glanced at Evan, expecting a smile. "What?"

"I was just wondering what someone might have been looking for in Grantley's room."

"Something incriminating? Drugs?"

"Why take out the photos? Maybe there was a particular photo that was incriminating to somebody." He looked up. "Did you just leave them where they were?"

Watkins nodded. "I thought we might want the lab boys to go over the room, so I gave orders for it not to be touched."

Evan drained his glass. "Could I take a look, do you think? I saw those photos when we were looking for a picture of Grantley to show around. I can't say I remember them all, but maybe I took in enough to know if one of them is missing."

As he was speaking, he remembered something that hadn't seemed too important at the time—he had suspected Edward Ferrers of taking a photograph the last time they were in Grantley's room. It might have been purely a matter of embarrassment or vanity. He wouldn't mention it at the moment, but it could well turn out to be one more nail on Edward's coffin.

Watkins drained his own glass and got up. "It's a long shot, but worth trying. Come on, then."

"Going so soon?" Betsy called as they passed the big oak bar.

"We might be back," Evan said. "We've got a piece of evidence we have to check on."

"How exciting." Betsy's eyes lit up. "I bet it's great when you're on a case like this. Not as exciting as being in a movie, of course." So she hadn't completely forgiven him.

They drove up to the Inn in Watkins's police car and got the key to Grantley Smith's room. It looked as if a tornado had recently been through it. The briefcase was open on the bed; the file was lying empty and its contents were scattered. Evan took out a handkerchief and lifted the photos, one at a time. It wasn't as easy as he had thought to remember what had been there before—a lot of head shots of Grantley in various poses, of course, and various press photos, World War II shots of the plane. He shrugged. "I don't think I'm quite in Sherlock Holmes's league yet. Nothing struck me before as odd, and nothing does now. Sorry to have wasted your time. Let's go and have another round—this one on me."

"I should be getting home," Watkins said. "I get it from the wife if she has to wait dinner for me. And our Tiffany will be starving after football practice. Did I tell you she got two goals on Saturday? Too bad she's not a boy— she'd have Manchester United hammering on our door by now."

They closed the door and started down the stairs. Various animal heads lined the stairway, looking down at them in a supercilious sort of way. An attempt to attract the huntin', shootin', and fishin' crowd, no doubt, Evan thought. Then he stopped dead. "I know one photo that was missing, Sarge. There was a picture of Howard Bauer, surrounded by African tribesmen."

Watkins laughed. "Who on earth would want that? You're not trying to tell me that I'm to be on the lookout for Africans who came over to kill Grantley for stealing their sacred idol, are you?"

Evan laughed. "It's probably nothing at all. The picture might have fluttered under a piece of furniture when they were all tipped out."

Watkins headed to his car. "If you remember any other missing pictures—shots of scuba divers with dolphins, men scaling the Pyramids, Miss World beauty contests— don't disturb my sleep with them, will you?" He waved and got into his car. Evan walked back down the hill.

NINETEEN

I couldn't stop thinking about what Ginger had said. I took a look at those sheds. They weren't too solidly built. Some of the blokes who helped build them were less skilled with the hammer than I was. There were a lot of crooked nails. It wouldn't be impossible to ease off a board or two and get inside.

I started spying on the guards, too. There were two of them. They did an early shift and a late shift. When the mine was shut for the night, there was no guard at all. But they really didn't pay too much attention when they were on duty. They seemed to enjoy a chat when miners on their break stopped to talk. One of them was very keen on comics. He was always sitting under a lamp, reading. I suppose he thought it was quite safe because anyone would have had to walk past him to get into the cavern.

That was true enough. He sat between the cavern and the staircase to the surface. The area where we were still working was down another level of steps. Nobody would have any reason to cross the cavern with the sheds in it and if anyone came up the staircase, he'd see them.

Which got me thinking—if someone could hide out in

the old workings beyond the cavern before the guard came on duty, then that someone could get at the back of the nearest shed quite easily, as long as he was quiet about it. Of course, if that someone was me, I'd be missed at my job. There were few enough miners on duty now that someone would notice I wasn't there.

And anyway, it all came back to the same thing—the painting would be missed. And I—the only one there with any interest in art—I'd be the most likely suspect. I wasn't going to jail, not even for Ginger.

During the night a front came in from the ocean, bringing freezing rain that peppered Evan's window with such violence that he woke. He lay there, listening to the moaning of the wind in the chimney, and the rain hammering on the roof. Unable to sleep, he let his thoughts drift to the murder of Grantley Smith.

What were the facts, he asked himself. Undisputed facts were that Grantley and Edward drove together to Blenau Ffestiniog, where they quarreled in public. Grantley went down a mine and was killed. The more he thought about it, the more everything pointed to Edward—the strongest motive, the opportunity, his subsequent nervousness. Evan wondered how Bronwen would take it if Edward were found to be guilty. Grantley's death had obviously upset her. Evan didn't want to be the one who caused her more grief.

You know what you've got to do, don't you, boyo, he said to himself. You have to get to the truth as soon as possible.

He stared at the pattern of bare branches dancing wildly in the streetlight and tried to put his thoughts in order. There had to be a pattern somewhere. Either it was a simple crime of passion, or it wasn't. Either Grantley was killed because someone lost control—either Edward or Robert James—or this was a carefully planned attempt to lure Grantley down a mine alone and then get rid of him.

Another fact that should be considered: Grantley fell

out of a train two days before he died. People didn't fall out of trains every day, did they? It would be an amazing coincidence if a near-fatal accident and Grantley's death two days later were in no way connected, and Evan didn't believe in coincidences. And the train was going to Blenau Ffestiniog again. And Edward Ferrers was in the same compartment.

Wait a minute, he said, shaking his head as he took this thought further. If Edward had pushed Grantley out of the train, why wouldn't Grantley have made a fuss about it, confronted him with it? And would Grantley have been so relaxed about riding in a vehicle with him again?

Evan supposed it might be possible that Edward could have reached across and opened the train door while Grantley was leaning out filming, but wouldn't Grantley at least have suspected? There was obviously not going to be any filming going on as long as this weather lasted. It might be worth going down to Porthmadog and having a closer look at the train in which they traveled. It might also be worth taking a look at the spot where Grantley fell from the train.

The next time I saw her, it was just before Christmas 1940. After a long period of waiting, the war had started in earnest, although not much had changed in Wales. We heard that London had been bombed. We had celebrated the Battle of Britain and cried over Dunkirk. But it all seemed very far away, apart from the empty seats in chapel where my friends would have been sitting.

Everyone at home was excited because some of the boys in uniform would be home on leave. My mum was trying to make Christmas puddings without half the ingredients and getting in such a tizzy about it.

"How do they expect me to do anything with no butter and no eggs?" she demanded. "It won't taste of anything."

"Put in a good drop of rum and nobody will care," my father muttered, looking up from his evening paper.

"And where are you going to find me a good drop of rum, that's what I'd like to know? You're always complaining there's a shortage of beer. And I hear the navy has all the rum."

That got me thinking about Ginger's friend who drove the lorries. If only I could drive a lorry right now, maybe I'd have been able to come home with butter and rum in my pocket and be the family hero. But I was still too young to get a driver's license, even if I knew anyone with a car who could teach me. I still had a year to go before I would be called up. Maybe there was something else I could do that wasn't tapping away at bloody slate all day. Ginger was the one with the ideas. I'd have to ask her.

I didn't see much of her these days, and I was looking forward to her having a whole week at home for Christmas.

The Sunday before Christmas there she was, standing on my doorstep, looking like a peacock in the middle of a henhouse. She was wearing a bright blue coat and a red knitted beret and gloves, and the way she stood there, against the backdrop of the gray cottages and gray slate, she was like the one splash of brightness in a gray world. When she came rushing into the room and threw her arms around my neck, all sensible thoughts went out of my head. All I could think was how lovely she was, and how proud I felt that she was kissing me.

"I've had the most wonderful idea and I've been dying to tell you about it," she whispered, her arms still wrapped around my neck. She paused and looked at me, her eyes sparkling. "Tref. I want you to paint me a picture."

I was flattered. She'd never shown that much interest in my art before.

"You do? You want me to paint you one for Christmas, is it?"

She laughed again. "No, silly. A lot more than Christmas."

"What are you talking about?"

She glanced around, to see if any of my family was in hearing range. My mother was singing hymns to herself in the kitchen while she cleaned the brussels sprouts. My dad was outside with the hens he had started keeping for eggs. So far, it hadn't been a huge success. We had had a total of three eggs between them. My dad reckoned the rats got the rest. My mum reckoned the hens were just plain useless and they cost a fortune in feed.

"The painting we're going to take," she whispered. "You were so worried about getting caught. I've found the perfect answer. Listen—how does this sound? You sneak it out of the hut. Then you take it out of its frame and hide it under your shirt. Then you bring it home and make a copy. Then we put the copy back in the frame, the picture back in the shed, and no one will know we've got the genuine one."

I started to laugh.

"What? What's so funny about that?"

"You are. Do you think the experts couldn't tell the difference between one of my paintings and an old master?"

"You're good, Tref. I've watched you. You can copy anything. I bet you could do it."

"Some of the modern painters, maybe. But not the old masters."

"You never know what you can do until you try. And this is the perfect time to put our plan into action. I'm home for a week. Everyone will be feeling festive. They'll be drinking more than usual." She sat down on the sofa and patted a place beside her for me to sit. "Tell you what. I'll be waiting for you at the mine tomorrow. Show me the guard, so I'll recognize him when I see him again. Then next morning you get to work very early and I'll delay him, so that you have time to get the back of the shed opened up. If you still have time, sneak a painting out and hide it."

I was trembling all over. My mother had stopped singing hymns. It seemed to me as if the whole world must have overheard what we were planning. I glanced at the door. "I can't, Ginger. I can't go through with it. Just think of the trouble if I'm caught. It will be all right for you. They won't catch you. But I'd go to prison. Think of my family—I can't do that to them."

She tossed her head so that her blond curls danced. "Only stupid people get caught." She grabbed my arm and squeezed it until it hurt. "You've got to learn to think on your feet, Trefor Thomas. If you're caught, tell them that you're looking for the cufflink you must have lost when you were building the sheds."

"And what if they find me with the picture in my hands? How will I explain that then?"

She laughed again. "Easy. Say that you did it for a dare—to prove how easy it would be to pinch one. You were going to turn it in to the mine manager."

"You think of everything, don't you?"

"I told you. I'm willing to do what it takes. You just have to be willing to do anything for me, like you promised."

The amazing thing was how easy it was! On Christmas Eve, I left the house while the rest of the family were still finishing breakfast.

"What's your hurry, Trefor bach? Hold on, I've still got a slice of toast to go," my father called as he saw me putting on my cap and scarf.

"I just want to get there early today," I said.

"Nice to see you keen as mustard for once," my mother commented.

"Won't do you any good," my father said. "They won't let you out of there any earlier this evening. It won't make Christmas come any quicker, you know." He laughed as if he'd made a joke.

"I just feel like walking on my own this morning, Tad," I said. I could feel my face glowing with embarrassment.

"He wants to meet that no-good girl, that's what he wants to do." My mother smoothed down her apron, which was her way of showing disapproval. Everyone in Blenau knew of Ginger's reputation for being too free and easy with her affections.

"Let the boy have a bit of fun," my father said. "He'll be seventeen soon enough. Lord knows how long he's got."

They exchanged a glance. I took my cue and ran out.

I was standing outside the mine when the whistle went off and they opened the grille for us to sign in. I had passed Ginger by the gate. She was wearing a short pleated skirt that kept blowing up in the wind, causing even the oldest miners to stop and gape at her. I reckoned she'd do her part pretty darned well.

I signed in and went down all those steps lickety-split. Some of the miners waited to take the lift down, so I found myself running down the steps alone. When I got to the big cavern level, I glanced around, then sprinted across to the nearest shed. After that it was easy to make my way to the very back shed. I took the chisel out from under my shirt, stuck it between the wood planks, and prised. It didn't take much strength before the board popped open. I wrenched it free and stepped inside.

It smelled different inside the shed. I suppose it was because the sheds were kept warm, but the paintings somehow made it smell old and musty in there—almost as if someone had lived in there for a long while. My heart was hammering so violently that I found it hard to breathe. All around me there were stacks of packages. Some of them were really huge. It didn't make sense to take anything but the smallest painting. For one thing, it would take too long to copy. For another, I'd never be able to hide it under my shirt without being noticed. I knew I only had a few more precious minutes. I grabbed the smallest package from the pile in the corner and ran out. Then I pushed the panel gently back into place. It wasn't on very securely, but you'd never notice unless you shone a torch at it. It was pretty dark back there at the far side of the cavern.

No sense in trying to do too much and getting caught. I took the package with the painting in it and stood it behind a pile of slate in the first tunnel. Now I could come and pick it up when a good moment arose.

It seemed as if it was destined to be my lucky day. That afternoon the mine manager, Mr. Arthur Jenkins, sent down a message to say we were all invited up for sherry and mince pies in the office. Just as I got up to the guard's chair, one of the blokes clapped him on the back. "Come on up with us, Alun. You're invited to the celebration too, you know."

"Oh, I better not, thanks all the same," the guard muttered.

"It's Christmas, man. You've got to enjoy yourself. Come on—the office is right there at the entrance, isn't it? Who's going to walk out with a bloody great painting right past us, eh?"

The guard laughed and started up the staircase with him. I took my chance. I dodged into the darkness and waited. When they'd all gone, I crept over to the painting and unwrapped it. It was really well wrapped up, let me tell you. In a wooden case and all wrapped in soft cloth inside, too. The gold frame glinted in the dim light. I took out my torch and shone it on the painting. "Bloody hell," I muttered. I'd picked a Rembrandt!

I might not have been an expert, but let me tell you, he certainly knew his stuff, that old Rembrandt. I had given myself an impossible task. There was no way I could ever copy that painting. Still, it came out of the frame without too much effort and I rolled it up in soft cloth and carried it home under my shirt without anyone even giving me a second look.

That night, when Ginger and I went for a walk, I showed it to her by the light of a street lamp.

"It's a bit dark and gloomy, isn't it?" she said. "Couldn't you have found something more cheerful, like?"

"Ginger! This is a painting by one of the best painters ever. Mr. Hughes said that Rembrandt was the master. He lent me a book once with all his paintings in it. He said if I could ever learn to paint like that, I'd do just fine."

"So I suppose it's worth a lot?" she asked dubiously.

"A lot? Thousands and thousands."

"So we're rich?"

"First I have to copy it, then the war has to end, and then we have to sell it. Apart from those small details, we're rich."

She laughed and flung her arms around my neck. "My clever Trefor," she said. "I'm very proud of you. How soon do you think you'll get it copied?"

"I don't know if I can," I said. "I'm not good enough."

"Give it a try. You can copy anything you set your mind to," she said, giving me a gentle peck on the cheek. Then she pressed herself closer against me. "Pity it's too cold up on the moors right now, isn't it? It's been a long time, hasn't it, Tref? I bet you've been missing it as much as I have."

If she knew how much I'd been missing it! I tried to think of a place we could go, but everywhere was bustling with people doing their last-minute shopping before the shops closed.

"There's always the chapel," she whispered and laughed at her own wickedness.

"You're a wicked woman, you know that?" I nuzzled against her cheek.

"Then it will just have to be up at the mine," she said. "It's not too windy below the cliff, among those rocks, and you've got a nice big jacket we can lie on."

So we went up to the mine and she was right. We didn't notice the cold at all.

TWENTY

IT WASN'T THE sort of weather to go mucking about with trains on Tuesday morning, but Evan knew he might not get another chance. Eventually, even Watkins and Hughes would put two and two together and start wondering if an accident two days before Grantley Smith died might be more than coincidence. Especially if they wanted to find yet more reasons to book Edward Ferrers.

The driving rain took his breath away as Evan crossed the parking lot to the deserted Porthmadog station. One good thing about today, the railway personnel wouldn't be too busy to talk to him. He found the elderly engine driver sitting with the rest of the employees in the cafeteria having a cup of tea.

"Yes, I can show you which carriage it was, if you like," he said.

"You can just point it out to me," Evan said. "No sense in two of us getting wet."

"Oh, I'm used to it, boy." The old man grinned. "I've had my head rained on for seventy years until it's washed away all my hair." He rubbed a bald pate and cackled with laughter. "Besides, rain's good for the complexion, so they say. I might want to impress the ladies."

He put on his cap and cape and went out with Evan into the storm. "This is a good 'un, isn't it?" he shouted over the wind. "A few weeks ago, the farmers were bleating about a drought. I knew they'd be eatin' their words soon enough."

They walked to the end of the platform and then down onto the narrow-gauge tracks where several carriages waited. "If I remember correctly, it was this lot here," the driver said, pointing at some brown and cream rolling stock. "And the gentleman fell out of the second from the end." He looked up hopefully at Evan. "I remember you—you came here asking about him the other day. Nothing's wrong, is it? I mean, it was just an accident?"

"Just a routine check," Evan said.

He walked along the track to the compartment, closely followed by the old man. He jiggled the latch and then pressed it open. It was the type of old-fashioned latch that had to be drawn back sideways. It did indeed seem loose. He opened it a few times and slammed it shut. On the last occasion, it didn't snap shut properly.

"You see," the old man said. "Nothing to do with foul play. These carriages are older than me, and that's saying something. I'm just surprised an accident like this hasn't happened before now. You should see what the young hooligans get up to. Anyone would think this was a train going to a football match, the way they bash everything about."

"But this wasn't a lager lout, this was a respectable man," Evan said.

"But he was leanin' out, isn't it? These are old doors. Not meant to be leant out of. See what the notice says? It says, 'Keep your head inside the car.' He could read well enough, couldn't he?"

"He was leaning out to take pictures," Evan said.

"Leanin' bloody far out. I saw him, right before he fell," the old man said. "I think he got what was comin' to him."

Evan climbed into the tiny compartment. It was built like a real train, but to a smaller scale, so that he had to duck his head. He searched the compartment but found nothing. He didn't actually know what he might be looking for and he was sure that the floor would have been swept by now anyway, but at least he felt that he was doing something. He lowered the sash and leaned out, as Grantley would have done. His large frame filled the window. It would have been very difficult for Edward to have pressed open the catch with Grantley's body in the way. And surely Grantley would have felt Edward doing it.

So this was one line of inquiry that looked as if it was coming to nothing.

"Nothing in here." He jumped down beside the old man.

"What did you expect to find? A few terrorists under the seats?" the old man cackled again. "Tell you what. If you're so keen on your investigation, you can ride up with me in half an hour. I'm going to take a train up, whether there's any passengers or not. That old engine gets restless, cooped up in a shed, and there might be someone along the way waiting for us—though I doubt it. Everyone has cars these days, isn't it?"

Evan smiled. "*Or gore*. All right, I'll ride with you, and you can show me exactly where he fell."

"I will indeed," the old man said. Clearly, this was spicing up an otherwise dismal day. He'd be able to brag in his local pub about helping the police for weeks to come.

They went back into the cafeteria for another cup of tea, then the old man fired up a diminutive steam locomotive, shunted it to pick up the carriages, and invited Evan to hop up beside him. Evan had never been one of those small boys who dream about trains, but he had to admit it was an experience standing behind the old engine driver, watching him coax life into a piece of metal until it became a living, fire-breathing monster.

"Some of the other chaps, they wouldn't show up on a day like this," he said. "But I'm here all the time. Rain or shine. You can't keep me away. These engines are my life, see." He turned knobs and a satisfying hiss of steam escaped.

"The others don't show up if it's raining?"

"Don't have to, do they? We're all volunteers."

"I didn't know that."

"Oh yes. All volunteers—put in our time to keep this old equipment running. Labor of love, I suppose you could say."

Evan looked at him, impressed. It must be wonderful to have a passion that drove you still when you were over seventy. They pulled out of the station and started on the narrow bar across the estuary. Wind was whipping up waves on the normally placid stretch of water and the spray came into the engine cab. On the other side, they plunged into gloomy oak woods. Then they started to climb. The old man coaxed the engine as the gradient became steeper. Soon they were hugging the edge of the mountain while the land to their right fell away steeply. Through tunnels, over bridges, across level crossings where the driver let Evan sound the warning whistle. They passed through several tiny stations without seeing a soul. Now they were really high. Cloud swirled around them, parting from time to time to reveal the gray waters of the estuary and miniature cottages, far below.

Then the train began to slow. "We're coming to the place now," the old man shouted. "I'll slow and maybe you can jump down. I don't want to stop completely unless I have to. It's not the best place to get going again."

Evan nodded and moved to the steps of the cab.

"You want me to pick you up on the way down?" the driver asked.

"Yes, please."

"About an hour, I'll be. I'll toot so you know I'm coming."

The train slowed with much hissing and grinding of brakes. Evan stood on the lowest step.

"Right here, it was," the old man called. "That tree stopped his fall."

The train was barely moving. Evan stepped down and heard the engine give a series of puffs before it picked up speed again and disappeared into a tunnel. Evan stood alone on the windswept hillside, wondering what on earth he was doing there. Just what did he expect to see? He looked around him. One thing struck him right away: If you were going to push somebody from a train, this was the spot to do it. The drop-off was the steepest so far—a long, steep slope all the way down to an angry torrent leaping over rocks at the bottom. And the track was at the very edge of the slope, so there was no possibility of someone falling out and lying beside the rails. Whoever fell would roll and keep on rolling, if there hadn't been one sturdy oak tree to prevent it.

Say it was done deliberately, Evan thought. How could you ever prove it? You couldn't attach string to the latch to control it remotely. That meant Edward would have had to reach past Grantley's body and somehow grab the latch. Almost impossible.

Moving carefully over the rain-slicked grass, Evan slithered down the slope to the big oak tree, looked around, then climbed back up again. "You've done it this time, boyo," he said aloud. "Of all the daft things. Now you've got to sit and wait an hour before he comes back. You'll get soaked through and probably catch a cold into the bargain."

He reached out his hands to steady himself as he climbed back onto the track and noticed a spot of yellow between the clinkers. A little late for a flower this time of year. He moved the clinkers apart and picked up a scrap of paper. It was folded into a neat square, about an inch across. It was completely sodden, of course. He opened it carefully, wondering if anything might have been written on it. Nothing was. It was an ordinary scrap of lined yellow paper. Evan held it in his hand, staring at it. If it had just been tossed from a window, why fold it so very exactly?

Then a clear picture came into his head—Howard Bauer standing at the film site, scribbling notes to himself on his yellow pad. That yellow pad went everywhere with him. Probably just coincidental that it fell here. Howard couldn't have had anything to do with Grantley's fall. He hadn't been in the same compartment. He'd been next door—too far to reach across and grab Grantley's door handle. So there was probably a very mundane reason for the yellow paper lying folded up by the track. Most likely Howard had been sitting with his yellow pad on his knee. Maybe he'd torn out a sheet, started to write, changed his mind, and folded up the sheet to put it in the rubbish container. It was the kind of thing a neat sort of person would do. Was Howard meticulously neat? Evan couldn't say. He also couldn't think why Howard would want to push Grantley Smith out of a train.

The wind started blowing with renewed force, driving Evan away from the edge. He went to sit under a rocky overhang, wrapped his raincoat around his knees, and thought. And during the long hour it took the train to come down again, he had a very good idea just what that yellow paper had been used for.

On Christmas morning, I woke to find a stocking beside my bed. It had a new pair of gloves in it and an orange and a sugar mouse. I had bought my mum Lilies-of-the-Valley scent in Woolworths and my dad a diary for 1941. He liked to record what he did every day, even though every day of his long life had been the same.

We had mince pies for breakfast, then we went to chapel. As I sat there on the hard cold pew, I felt as if the eyes of God were boring right into my soul. I was certainly destined for hell now. I'd broken two rather major commandments on the day before Christmas—although I hadn't exactly committed adultery. I was so overcome with guilt that I couldn't even join in "Hark, the Herald Angels Sing."

As we walked home, it started to snow, which made it feel nice and Christmassy. I left my parents and ran over to Ginger's house with my present for her. I'd spent too much money on a scarf. She smiled and said she liked it, but then she said she'd been hoping for a ring—still, next year, maybe?

I don't know how much she thought I earned in the mine. Not enough for the sort of ring she'd want. She gave me the Picture Post Annual, *with lots of pictures of Hollywood stars in it. On one page there was a picture of Fred and Ginger, and she'd crossed out the word "Fred" and substituted "Tref." I thought I was a lot better-looking than him, and I had more hair too!*

We had a chicken for dinner—the one Dad suspected of laying the least. Turkeys had disappeared from the face of the earth. And Mum's plum pudding wasn't half-bad. She confided she'd used the last of the medicinal brandy in it.

We sat around the fire and listened to the king's message on the wireless. He didn't have any good news, just a lot of rubbish about everyone pulling together through these dark days. The sort of stuff they're always telling you, as if we didn't know that the days were dark and we'd all got to pull together!

After Christmas dinner, my mum and dad both fell asleep in their chairs by the fire. I sneaked upstairs and

*got out my paints. No sense in waiting. I had to get to
work on that picture right away. Every time I looked at
it, I knew it was a hopeless task, but I'd promised Ginger
that I'd try.*

*But I'd hardly done more than put on an undercoat
when my mother came charging up the stairs. "Are you
using those smelly paints in the house, Trefor Thomas?"
she demanded. "What did I tell you? Paints belong outside."*

*"But, Mam, it's freezing out there and there's some-
thing I really want to paint today—it's a sort of Christmas
present for Ginger."*

*"If you want to give her a present, go to Mr. Jones-
the-Cloth and get a yard or two of his best flannel, so
that she can make her skirts a decent length," she said.
There was nothing for it. I had to stop painting.*

*The next few weeks I was a bag of nerves. Every day at
the mine, I expected to hear that there had been a break-
in. Every night I expected to hear hammering on the front
door as the police came to take me away. But as the weeks
passed, and nothing happened, I began to relax. Now that
I was aware of it, the security was really not too hot. I
could have taken a whole lot more paintings if I'd put my
mind to it.*

*I might tell you I was very tempted to sneak back into
the shed and take another painting instead of the one I'd
got. I must have picked the bloody hardest painting in the
whole National Gallery to copy. As Ginger had said, it
was dark and gloomy, but the gloom had such shape and
texture to it that the figures became part of the darkness.
I just didn't have paints in my palette to even attempt
those shades of darkness. I suppose they must have all
been in Rembrandt's head.*

*But I kept working at it, every time I had a spare mo-
ment. When my parents were out at one of their many
chapel meetings, I even painted in my room. I kept the
window open and smoked cigarettes all the time to hide*

the smell. Bit by bit, a fairish copy came into being—nothing like the quality of the original, mind you, but you could tell what painting it was meant to be.

Finally, by March, it was finished. I took it outside and looked at it in the bright light. It was a passable imitation at best. But Ginger was very impressed.

"It's just like the real thing, Tref. It's lovely, just. I'm very proud of you. One day when we're in Hollywood, I'll let you paint the walls in my mansion and everyone will want one of your paintings. You'll probably be more famous as a painter than I will as a film star."

I laughed. "Get away with you. Such big ideas."

She started dancing around. "But we have our ticket out of here now. Don't you see? All we have to do is wait for this stupid war to end and then we're away from this place for good."

But the stupid war didn't look as if it was going to end soon. The news on the radio was never good. More cities bombed, the London docks set on fire, our troops battling Rommel in the African desert. More telegrams bearing bad news to cottages in Blenau. My own time was getting closer. I tried not to think about it. I tried not to think about the painting and the row there would be when they discovered my copy. I tried not to think about Ginger with all those servicemen all day. The trouble was that I was working alone down a dark mine most of my life and all you do down there is think.

TWENTY-ONE

THE RAIN HAD eased slightly by the time the train returned, its piercing whistle echoing from cloud-draped crags and invisible valleys. Evan stood impatiently behind the engine driver all the way down to Porthmadog, listening to the old man sounding off about hooligans and day trippers who ripped his seats to pieces and even tried to scratch their initials on the polished flanks of his beloved engines.

When the train finally stopped, the old man shook his hand. "Nice to have a bit of company for a change, I must say," he said. "Sorry if it was a wasted ride for you, but I enjoyed it. Like I said—your man was leaning too far out as we went around a bend. Lucky to be alive, if you ask me. We've had cameras and handbags and kiddies' dolls fall out before now and they usually end up a thousand feet below."

Evan decided not to tell him that Grantley hadn't been so lucky the second time around. He waited until the old man had gone back into the cafeteria before he tested his theory on the railway carriage. It worked exactly as he had thought.

His mind was racing as he made his way across the car park to his car. If Howard Bauer really had engineered Grantley's death—why did he do it? Grantley and Howard had supposedly hardly known each other. Grantley had been Howard's intern in the hopes of learning more about the business. Howard had agreed to direct this movie to do Grantley a favor. There was something wrong with the story, but Evan wasn't sure how he was going to find out what it was. Were Howard and Grantley connected in another way altogether? Was this another gay relationship gone sour? And yet Howard had mentioned multiple wives and alimony complaints. Gay men married, but did they marry several times? So could it be something to do with drugs? Howard had asked if Grantley's death was an overdose. Had he suspected that Grantley abused some kind of substance? Was he somehow linked in a chain of supplier, pusher, user?

Evan shook his head. There was no way he could pursue a broader inquiry like this without getting into serious trouble. He'd have to hand over the piece of folded paper to Sergeant Watkins and let him follow up on it while Evan went back to the village and Mrs. Powell-Jones.

Damn. He slammed the car door behind him, none too gently.

"You are feeling sorry for yourself, aren't you, boyo?" he said out loud. "Must be the weather. And the important thing is that the killer is found. It doesn't matter one bloody bit who finds him." Having given himself this pep talk, he drove out of the car park and through the center of Porthmadog. The High Street was lacking its normal bustle, due to the rain. Women with head scarves, plastic macs, and shopping bags darted across the street and into the shelter of another shop, sometimes dragging reluctant toddlers behind them. Suddenly, another figure came out of the post office, stopped to turn up his collar and jam his beret more

firmly onto his head before he walked out into the
storm.

Without a second's hesitation, Evan pulled over to
the curb and wound down a window. "Hello, Howard.
Going somewhere? Like a lift?"

Howard Bauer's face lit up in recognition. "Are you
driving back to the village? Boy, what a stroke of luck.
I thought I'd have to wait for a bus."

He opened the passenger door and climbed in.
"Filthy weather. Is it often like this?"

"Most of the time," Evan said. He grinned as he put
the car into gear. "So what were you doing in Porthmadog?"

"I got a little stir-crazy up there," Howard said. "I
mean, it's a nice place, that Everest Inn, but dead—
like a morgue. So when the bellhop said he was driving
down to Porthmadog, I asked if I could ride along. Not
that there's anything down here, is there?"

"What were you hoping for?" Evan asked.

"I don't know. Movie theater? Internet café?"

"There are movie theaters in Bangor and Colwyn
Bay, but I don't think there's an Internet café anywhere
in North Wales yet."

"Too bad. My damn roving feature won't work for
some reason. I've been without e-mail since I got here.
It's driving me mad, not being connected to the outside
world." He looked at Evan. "How can you stand it,
cooped up in a dump like this?"

"Most of the time I stand it pretty well," Evan said.
"I don't feel cooped up. Just sometimes."

Howard shook his head. "I'm an L.A. kind of guy.
I'm lost without my car and my freedom. How much
longer do you think we'll have to stick around here?
I'd just as soon scrap the whole damn project and go
home. It was Grantley's thing after all, not mine."

"Until you're ruled out as a suspect, I should think,"
Evan said, trying to sense some reaction from the man
beside him. Be sensible, he told himself. If you are

sitting beside a man who has killed, you're at a distinct disadvantage. You have two hands on the wheel and a winding road to contend with. And if he really did kill Grantley, then he has to be damned strong.

Evan glanced at Howard's hands. They were artistic, with long, white fingers. There was a signet ring on his little finger. His nails were immaculate. Were those the hands of a strangler? He forced himself to take long, deep breaths. Play it easy. Don't jeopardize the investigation by shooting your mouth off, boyo. But he was bursting with curiosity. Howard Bauer just didn't add up. Were those the hands of a man who enjoyed roughing it in the African bush? Who was famed for his tough documentaries of tribal warfare?

The road had passed through the last of the coastal settlements and was entering the narrow pass where the river Glaslyn flowed between tall cliffs. It was usually a somber place. Today, with the rain dripping from oak trees and running down the walls of rock, it felt overwhelmingly melancholy.

"So what were you doing down here today?" Howard asked pleasantly. "Getting some shopping done on your day off?"

"No, I went for a train ride," Evan said. "You know, the little train up the mountain. The driver is an old friend of mine. I like keeping him company from time to time, especially on days like this when he has no passengers. He was glad of company today, I can tell you. Showed me exactly where that accident happened—you know, when Grantley fell out of the train. Lucky, wasn't he? A few more inches to the right, and he'd have been a goner."

He turned to look at Howard. The latter's face was ashen. "Yeah. Damned lucky," he said.

"My friend the engine driver reckoned there was something fishy about the whole thing. He says he's never known a door to come flying open like that before. But I think I have to disagree with him. Some of those catches don't really lock properly unless you slam them really hard—and if something was wedged into the lock—something as simple as a piece of paper . . ." He glanced at Howard again. "I notice you're not carrying your pad with you today, Howard. Don't you need to make any more notes, or is it all used up?"

A big shuddering sigh went through Howard Bauer. "Oh my God. You know, don't you?"

"Know what?"

"About Grantley falling out of that train. I never really thought—I mean, it was just a crazy idea. I don't know what made me do it. I never thought it would really work and then it did. He came flying out, like a rag doll. Oh my God!"

They emerged from the gloom of the pass. The village of Beddgelert was ahead of them. Evan began to breathe more easily. Here was potential help if needed.

"Why did you do it, Howard?" he asked.

Howard Bauer had buried his face in his hands. "It seemed like too good a chance to be missed," he said. "I don't know. I must have been crazy. I've never hurt anybody in my life. I just saw a chance to get him off my back and I took it. I've been sick with worry ever since, reliving it over and over again until I thought I'd go mad."

"Why did you need to get Grantley off your back?" Evan asked quietly. They were in the center of the village now, driving between solid gray houses, over a sturdy stone bridge. "Was it something to do with drugs? Was he supplying you . . . ?"

Howard laughed. "Drugs? No, nothing like that. Scotch is good enough for me. He was just an annoying little bastard. You saw him. If you must know, he was bugging the shit out of me. I have no idea why I ever said I'd do his stupid little movie. The moment I got here, I knew it was a mistake. So when I saw that that door didn't shut properly, the idea came into my mind. I thought, If he falls out of the damned train, he'll hurt

himself and we can stop shooting and I can go home.
They were all busy taking pictures of the locomotive.
I folded up a piece of paper and jammed it into the
lock to make sure it didn't shut all the way. Then I got
in the next compartment. I seriously never thought it
would work. I don't know what had gotten into me."

"But it did work," Evan said. "He almost died. Were
you disappointed, Howard, that you hadn't finished
him off? Did you follow him up to the mine to complete the job?"

Howard shot him a look of horror. "Me? You think
that was me? Jesus, there's no way I could ever strangle anybody. I hate violence. I abhor it."

"And yet you shot a famous movie about violence."

"Oh yes. That. I wanted to show the evil of violence.
The terrible destruction to lives."

They had left the village and the road had begun to
climb again, this time up the Nant Gwynant Pass to the
junction at the crest.

"What I don't get," Evan said, "is why you didn't
just walk out if he was bugging you. You weren't under
any kind of contract, were you? You said you were just
doing him a favor. Why were you doing him a favor
in the first place if you found him so annoying? And
why didn't you just walk away if he got too much for
you?"

"It's a long story," Howard said. "Let's say it was
part of the complicated relationship I had with Grantley—and nothing whatever to do with his death, okay?
Can we leave it at that?"

"For the time being," Evan said. So it looked as if
Howard and Grantley were in some kind of relationship
that had nothing to do with mentor and pupil after all.
Was there anyone in this case who had not been ro-
mantically involved with Grantley Smith?

*Now I'd finished the copy, a couple of small problems
remained. I had to get the copy into the frame and back*

into the shed, and I had to decide where to hide the real painting so that it was safe. I thought about hiding it among the slate pilings in the mine, but I was scared there would be a flash flood, like there was sometimes, and it would be damaged. I wasn't too keen about hiding it at home. My mother liked a good snoop. She'd even found the pin-up magazine I hid under my mattress once.

Ginger, as usual, was full of bright ideas. "Why don't you hang it on your wall? You've got enough pictures there, so nobody would suspect anything. Might as well enjoy it while we've got it."

It sounded all right in theory. So I went out and bought a cheap frame in Woolworths and I hung the Rembrandt between a Turner I'd torn from a magazine and a Frans Hals I'd picked up at a jumble sale for two and sixpence.

But once it was up there, it haunted me. I was overwhelmed by the enormity of what I had done. Then I reassured myself that I could put it back anytime I wanted to. In fact, I could even put it back and keep the copy if my conscience got too much for me. Ginger couldn't tell the difference. Don't get me wrong. I wanted to get out of Blenau and go to Hollywood just as much as she did. Above all, I wanted to be with her, basking in her glory when she became a big star. I tried to picture myself in Hollywood, lounging by one of those fancy swimming pools. I could picture her there, all right. But never me. It just seemed too impossible, even to dream about.

You've heard that saying about the best-laid plans of mice and men, I suppose. There was I, thinking that the security was lax, and waiting to pick the ideal day and good weather to get the copy back into the shed. But before I could put the copy back, the mine manager called us all together into his office. "I've got bad news, I'm afraid, boys," he said. "The mine is closing."

There was a collective gasp, then silence. Not one of those men dared to ask why. The manager looked at us with sympathy. "I got the directive from the owners this morning. It's government orders, see. Slate's not a high priority in a war, is it? Not much new building going on. Just a lot of destroying. So the government is sending you where you are needed for the war effort—they're short of miners down in the Rhondda."

"Coal?" I heard a man behind me exclaim. "You want us to mine that filthy, dirty stuff? Gets in your lungs, coal does."

"And dangerous, too," another man muttered. "Always having cave-ins down there in the bloody coal mines, aren't they?"

"And they're all South Walesians, too," a third man protested. "Can't speak a word of Welsh down there, so I hear. And they don't wash."

The manager lifted his hands. "Boys. Boys. It's no good complaining. My hands are tied. I've been given my orders to close this mine, and you've been directed to report for work in the Rhondda. There's nothing else I can say. We all have to do our part to win the war, don't we?"

"I bet he's not headed down some bloody coal mine," I heard someone mutter behind me.

"So go and get any tools you've left down at the work face and then we're shutting down," the manager said. "Good luck, boys. Do your best for North Wales, won't you?"

The other men filed out, muttering and grumbling. I wasn't even thinking about being sent down a coal mine. I was in a panic because I hadn't managed to return the copy to the shed. Now I'd never get a chance. When the National Gallery came to get their pictures, they'd find one missing.

I wished Ginger was at home, but she hadn't had a weekend off for weeks. She said they were short-staffed and she had to work two people's jobs and they gave the women with families the weekends off. At the time I believed her.

I didn't know what to do. We got our tools, the big iron

grille was closed, and the mine was shut down. My father was philosophical about the whole thing.

"Had to happen sometime, I suppose."

"But, Tad—you don't want to work down a coal mine, away from home, do you?" I asked.

He grinned. "Won't affect me, boy. I've got a lung condition, see."

He'd never mentioned it before. He saw my horrified face and grinned. "Comes from breathing slate dust all those years. They'd never send me down a coal mine with my dicky lung."

"So what will you do?"

"Don't worry about me, boy. I'll find myself something to do. I wouldn't even mind working at the docks, or one of the RAF stations." He patted my shoulder. "It's you I worry about, down a coal mine. Still, it's not long until you turn seventeen. I reckon you can stick it out until then."

Later that week, my father had a chapel meeting at our house. He was becoming a deacon, so I gathered. The other men in our front room were all miners, apart from the minister, of course. And the talk moved, as one would expect, away from chapel to the closing of the mine. Most of those men were being sent south, with me, and they weren't very happy about it.

"I never thought I'd hear myself say this," Howie Jenkins said, "but I'm going to miss the old place. We've had some memorable times, haven't we?"

"Remember when Lloyd George came?" another man said. "Before your time, was it? My, but that was a splendid occasion. The town band played. I was playing the cornet, like I usually do."

"And no doubt off key, like you usually do," came the comment. Loud laughter followed.

"Was that right before the fire in 1922?"

"That's right, it was. We all joked that now the Prime Minister had been, we could burn the bloody place down—there was nothing more to live for!"

"A fire down the mine, was there?" one of the younger men asked. "Bad, was it?"

"Oh yes," my father said. "It was dreadful, just. It was the machinery in the lift that caught on fire, so there were flames and smoke all the way up the main staircase. If we hadn't managed to make it to the back exit, I reckon we'd have all been goners."

"We would indeed." Old Howie Jenkins nodded.

I had been sitting in the kitchen, half listening to what they were saying. Now I came hurrying into the front parlor.

"I just heard what you said about a fire in the mine," I said, as the men looked up at my entrance. "I never knew there was a back way out."

"Never needed it, did you?" my father said. "In fact, I don't think it's ever been used since. But I imagine it's still there."

"Has to be by law, I think," someone said. "You always need an escape route from a mine. Remember that, Trefor bach, when you're down in the Rhondda. First thing you do is find out how you get out of the bloody place."

"So this back exit is still there, at our mine?" I asked, trying not to sound too interested. "Where is it, then?"

They gave me a pretty good description of how to find it. First thing next morning, I was up at the mine. It was strange to see it silent and shut. There was a watchman on duty outside, but he was sitting in his hut, not paying attention to anything other than his morning paper. I found the path they had told me about and the passageway into the mountain. There was a door across it, but I pushed it open without too much effort. They obviously hadn't got around to locking it with the rest of the mine yet. I shone my torch on a narrow, dark staircase. Even a couple of years of working in the mine hadn't prepared me for this. I had never been alone into total blackness. The steps were damp and uneven. I went down carefully, step by step. If I took a tumble now, they'd probably not find me for months. My, but it was spooky down there.

No sound except the echo of my feet and the occasional drip of water into an unseen pool. My heart was racing a mile a minute. I was used to going up and down hundreds of steps every day of my life, but my legs felt as if they were made of jelly and I had to hang onto the wall for support.

At last I came out into a cavern. My small torch only lit a few feet in front of me, but I could feel the empty space. I really hadn't thought what it might be like down here with no light except mine. How was I ever going to find my way to the big cavern with the sheds in it? And find my way out again?

I crossed the cavern and found the opening to a passage on the other side. It looked broad enough to lead somewhere important. I picked up a piece of slate and scratched a line on the wall. I kept scratching until I came out into another chamber, then another. At last there was an eerie glow ahead and I came out into the big cavern. A couple of lamps were alight on the main staircase—so that someone could come down and check the paintings, no doubt. There was a faint humming sound that made my skin crawl until I realized that they'd kept the heating system running in the sheds. Well, they'd have to, wouldn't they? It gets awful damp and cold down there.

I held my breath and looked around, half expecting to see a guard slumped in his chair as before. But there was no one. I found the frame where I had hidden it, put the picture in it, then rewrapped it in its packing. Not as well as it had been done originally, but well enough. They were going to know it was a fake as soon as they opened the package anyway. There was nothing I could do about that except pray that I was far, far away. Then I hammered the back panel of the shed properly into place and made my way to the surface again. I had done it. For the first time I felt rather pleased with myself.

TWENTY-TWO

THE SKY WAS clearing as Evan drove away from the Everest Inn, where he had deposited Howard Bauer. There was no sign of the other members of his team. Evan couldn't blame them. At a time like this, facing more grilling by D.I. Hughes, he might also have chosen to stay in the comparative safety of his own room. He paused and toyed with the words that had just passed through his mind. Comparative safety? Had any of them a cause to feel unsafe? Did any of them know more than they were letting on? Did they, in fact, have their suspicions about who the killer might be? Another, more disturbing thought passed through his mind—had the killing of Grantley been somehow a joint effort, with Grantley lured to Wales to get rid of him?

"Ridiculous," Evan said out loud, and smiled at the sound of his own voice. The trouble with being shut out from the main investigation was that it meant he tended to grasp at straws.

The cloud was definitely breaking. Tantalizing glimpses of blue sky appeared and then were swal-

lowed up again. Going to be fine again tomorrow, he
thought. That meant back to work at the lake. Tomorrow might well be the day that the plane finally floated
to the surface, his last day to observe them interacting.

As he drove slowly down the hill, he noticed a figure
on top of Capel Bethel. It was old Charlie Hopkins,
and he was adjusting the star—no, he was replacing it
with a bigger one. That meant phone messages from
Mrs. Powell-Jones would already be waiting at the police station. Just past the chapels he braked as a
crossing guard stepped out, waving a stop sign. Several
small children sprinted across the road. The school day
must just have finished. He tried to make himself drive
on without looking for Bronwen, but he had already
spotted her, standing by the gate, talking to parents. He
was about to lift his hand in a sort of casual greeting
when Bronwen saw him and came flying out of the
gate.

"Evan, wait!" she shouted.

He waited and wound down the window.

"Where were you? I tried phoning but you weren't
at the station, and when I called your headquarters, a
rather snooty woman said you weren't on the case."

"She's right. I'm not."

"So you haven't heard, then?"

He looked up inquiringly.

"They've arrested Edward. They gave him one
phone call and he called me. I don't know what to do,
Evan. What should I do?"

"Get him a good solicitor, I suppose," he said, and
then was ashamed at his callousness. He opened his car
door. "Come on, hop in. We'll go down to the station.
This needs thinking about."

She looked back at the school playground. It was
almost empty now. Just a few older boys kicking
around a soccer ball. "I've left the building open. I
should go and lock up. You go on and I'll be down in
a few minutes."

"I'll put a kettle on," he said and was rewarded with a smile.

As soon as he had filled the kettle and turned up the heat, he dialed Sergeant Watkins's mobile.

"You arrested Edward Ferrers?" Evan demanded. "On what evidence?"

"What are you, his bloody solicitor? And it wasn't me who arrested him—it was the D.I., based on the fact that we identified the footprint outside the mine entrance. It came from Ferrers's boot. And when questioned, he went to pieces. Sobbed that it was all his fault and he felt terrible about it. That was enough to make the D.I. bring him in for further questioning."

"So has he confessed?"

"We're waiting for his lawyer."

"And do you think he did it?"

"Me? I'm just the sergeant, boyo. What I think doesn't matter. But I'll tell you one thing—he's not protesting his innocence loudly. And he lied to us about not knowing that Grantley went to the mine. He obviously followed him that far, which might lead us to think that he followed him the rest of the way." He lowered his voice. "Look, I've got to go. The D.I. has just come in, with Glynis in tow. I'll let you know if anything happens."

There was a click. The line went dead. Evan was just replacing the phone when Bronwen came in. She was wearing her Red Riding Hood cape and her cheeks were pink from the cold wind, but her eyes looked huge and hollow.

"Any news?" she asked.

Evan relayed his conversation with Watkins.

"They've arrested him just because a footprint matched?" she demanded. "Have they checked how many other people wear identical boots?"

"Apparently he said it was all his fault and he felt terrible about it," Evan said. "He's not saying any more until a solicitor arrives."

"Am I supposed to be finding this solicitor, do you think? He was quite distraught when he called me. He never did handle stress very well."

"I can call and find out, if you like," Evan said. "You'd think he had a family solicitor, bloke like that from a posh background. Or was he another pretender like Grantley?"

"Oh no. His family has money all right. Yorkshire wool industry from way back. But Edward and his father don't exactly see eye to eye. His father always thought he was too soft. Edward certainly didn't tell his father he'd gone to live with Grantley. He wanted me to lie if his family called. I couldn't do that. His father absolutely exploded, as one would have expected. So, no, I don't think the family lawyer would be available."

"They speak very highly of Lloyd-Jones in Bangor," Evan said. "You could call him in for now and then see if Edward wants to get someone else. He may have someone in London."

"I don't think Edward was the kind of man who retained a lawyer," Brownen said. "He was very naive in many ways. He told me he'd made a big mistake by getting joint credit cards with his and Grantley's names on them. Grantley was charging left, right, and center and Edward was afraid . . ." She paused in midsentence. "This all sounds very bad for him, doesn't it?"

"It doesn't sound too good." Evan poured the tea and handed her a cup. "I know you don't normally have sugar but you need it for shock."

"Thanks." She managed a smile. "He has a strong motive and he had the perfect opportunity. And he'll make a terrible witness. He'll stammer and say all the wrong things. I don't see any hope for him, unless you can find out who really killed Grantley."

"Why are you so very sure he didn't do it?" Evan asked.

She looked down at her steaming cup. "We had a

mouse once, caught in a trap. It wasn't quite dead and I asked Edward to finish it off, poor little thing. It took him ages to do it, and then he threw up. Then he insisted on burying it in the back garden. I'm not saying I can't imagine Edward killing somebody, but not physically, like that. And if he did, he wouldn't have the composure to weight the body with rocks and hide it in a pool. He'd be overcome with remorse and turn himself in instantly."

"So why did he follow Grantley to the mine, and deny having done so?"

She sighed. "I don't know. We'll have to wait until we have a chance to ask him." She managed a sip of tea. "All I know is that he needs my help and I have to do everything I can."

"Even after he walked out on you, you still love him?"

"I suppose I must do."

Evan took a deep breath. "All right," he said gruffly. "I'll do what I can. I'm not sure it will be any use, though. I know nothing of Grantley Smith's life and background. For all we know, someone could have followed him to Wales and decided the mine was a convenient place to finish him off."

"You make him sound like a high-powered criminal!" She gave a nervous laugh. "Grantley liked to project a grandiose image, but he was really only a small fry—a fairly ordinary person. He got bit parts as an actor. He wrote a couple of screenplays that he couldn't sell. Then he decided he'd try his hand at directing and he took a course at the film institute, which was where he met Howard, so I understand."

"And a relationship developed there, do you think?"

"That kind of relationship, you mean?" She looked astonished. "Surely Edward would have told me."

"Unless he was jealous. Unless Grantley was leaving him for someone else and he brought up the money problems to hide his pride at being jilted."

"Oh dear." She toyed with her teaspoon. "Jealousy. That's always a strong motive, isn't it? But maybe Howard was the one who was jealous. Has anyone looked into him?"

"I gave him a lift in my car just now. He swears he didn't kill Grantley and I think I believe him. Throttling is such a violent way to kill. If you were down a mine, you could creep up behind someone and hit them with a lump of rock. Much easier. Or you could creep down the stairs behind your victim and give him a good push. I could imagine Howard doing either of those, but look at him. He'd be no stronger than Grantley, would he, if it came to a wrestling match."

"And Edward would, of course." She toyed with the spoon again. "Oh dear, you've got me doubting now. I'd better get onto that solicitor right away. And I should call Edward's parents, even if they don't want to hear. I should be going . . . thanks for the tea. Sorry I didn't feel like finishing it." She got up, pulled her cloak around her, and headed for the door.

Evan felt he had just entertained a stranger.

Next day I was off down to South Wales and the coal mines. It was as bad as the men had said. Worse, in fact. We were used to working in large open caverns, but down the coal mine we were crouching like rabbits in dark, narrow tunnels. And hot? The sweat mixed with the coal dust to make us look like a lot of darkies. You never got the coal dust out of your nostrils or lungs, either. When you blew your nose, the snot was black. I'd thought that the slate mine was hell, but this really was.

They boarded me with a local family whose own son was off fighting in Africa. I can't say that they made me welcome. In fact, they seemed to blame me that I was there while their boy was far away and in danger. I gave them my ration book, but I don't know what they did with my rations. We hardly ever saw a piece of meat, or an egg, for that matter. It was a lot of stodge puddings, with scraps of streaky bacon in them, maybe, and toad in the hole, and cod, boiled until it was hard and gray.

I tried to picture Ginger as I worked down the mine. I'd see her laughing and dancing, like that time on the moors, and I felt as if my heart would break if I didn't touch her soon. But it wasn't until Christmas that I got a chance to go home. When I walked into our house, I got one hell of a shock—there, over the mantelpiece, was the Rembrandt I had stolen. I nearly passed out.

"What's that doing there?" I managed to stammer. "That's my picture."

"I noticed it when I was dusting your room," my mother said, "so I thought we might as well use it in here. A bit on the dark side, but a nice frame, isn't it? Looks quite posh, I think. I'd really like flowers, but this is better than nothing, isn't it? Where did you get it—one of those jumble sales?"

I didn't know whether to laugh or cry. My mother had one of the world's most valuable paintings on her wall and she liked the frame, which came from Woolworths. I couldn't think of a good reason to demand it back, so I left it there. At least it was safe and being dusted every day. When I told Ginger, she thought it was very funny. She only had the two days at home and no chance at all for us to be alone together, but it was better than not seeing her at all. I thought she looked even more beautiful than I had remembered.

It was a bleaker Christmas than the one before—that Christmas of 1941. Terrible bombing raids on lots of cities. Bath and Bristol had caught it, so had Cardiff docks. The war was getting closer all the time.

There weren't even any chickens this year, but Mum had managed to wangle a piece of boiled bacon from a farmer who kept pigs, so we had that instead, and Christmas cake made with dried eggs. The only good news was that the Americans had got their share, too—whole navy caught by surprise at Pearl Harbor and bombed to pieces, so we heard. I don't mean that getting bombed was a good thing. The good part was that it made the Americans come into the war. Everyone was saying that now the tide would turn. Soon we'd have bloody great American planes bombing the you-know-what out of Hitler.

Hardly any of our boys in uniform made it home for Christmas that year. Most of them were already fighting abroad, Egypt or in the Far East where there was no good news either. So I enjoyed being top dog at the few gatherings we had. I'd grown again, and you should have seen my muscles, working with that pickax all day. The girls clustered around me, but then Ginger came in and slipped her arm through mine. "It's stuffy in here, Tref," she said, glaring at the other girls. "What about you and me going for a walk?"

Since I knew where and how our walks usually ended up, I didn't need much persuading. There was snow on the ground, but we found a place among the rocks and it was as good as ever.

I didn't see her again until Easter. Then they gave us an extra day off again and I took the train up north straight to Llandudno. She'd already told me she couldn't get the weekend off—spiteful old cows, the sisters in charge at the home, making sure the young never had a chance to have fun.

I felt fully alive again for the first time in months as I strode down the promenade with the salty tang of the sea full in my face and the seagulls crying and the sun sparkling on blue water. It was like waking from a bad dream. Then I saw her—she was in one of the shelters on the front, with a tall, skinny bloke with a funny haircut. They were smoking cigarettes and laughing. I didn't know what to do. Part of me wanted to slink away and catch the next train home, the other part wanted to run right in there and punch the daylights out of him. I could have, you know. But before I could decide what to do, it was as if our minds connected. She looked up and saw me. For a second she blinked as if she was seeing a ghost, then a *big smile spread across her face. "Tref! It is you. Oh, my goodness. It is you!" Then she ran out of the shelter and threw her arms around my neck.*

"How long have you got?" she asked me.

"I have to go back tomorrow. I came all this way, just to see you, but I notice you're busy."

I looked back at the bloke, who was still sitting smoking and staring at me.

Ginger smiled. "Don't be silly. Hold on a minute." She ran into the shelter, said something to the man in uniform, and came out again. "It's okay. I told him about you. Come on, it's a lovely day. Let's go for a walk."

"Who is he?" I turned back to the shelter where the bloke was still staring at me.

"One of my patients, silly. He's American. His name is Johnny Gabbiano. He's been badly wounded."

"He doesn't look as if he's too crippled," I said suspiciously. "In fact, he looks pretty bloody healthy to me."

She laughed and rubbed against me. "You don't have to be jealous, you silly ha'pth. I try to be friendly to all the poor blokes. They're a long way from home and they're lonely. They like talking to a pretty girl. Johnny was shot down over the Channel, you know. He lost the sight in one eye and got badly burned, too."

When I didn't say anything, she stopped and gazed up at me. "He doesn't mean anything to me, you know. I'm only being friendly because I feel sorry for them. And you never know when one of them might end up being helpful. We have to find out how to sell that painting, don't we?"

Apparently it was true about her not getting time off that weekend. I had to be content with a quick kiss and cuddle in one of those shelters before she was back on duty again and I was catching the train to South Wales. But this time I didn't mind too much. The end was in sight. This coming summer I turned seventeen and I'd get my call-up papers.

TWENTY-THREE

EVAN SAT AT his desk, scribbling on a notepad, making bold black doodles around names and getting nowhere. Why shouldn't he believe that Edward Ferrers had killed Grantley? And why not Howard Bauer, who had admitted engineering his fall from a train, not to mention a relationship gone sour? Then there was Robert James, whose hands had been around Grantley's throat once before. Maybe the police investigation should be focusing more on him. And that old German had threatened to stop the raising of the plane, one way or the other; another name he should give to Watkins. Apart from that, there wasn't much that Evan could do except wait for Edward Ferrers to break down and confess— or not as the case may be.

He got up and decided to walk his usual afternoon beat around the village a little early. There was no point in just sitting in his office, becoming more and more frustrated, and he really didn't want to be in when Mrs. Powell-Jones rang—as she most certainly would. He put on his jacket and hat and went out. The clouds had now broken into wild gray threads through which the sun painted moving stripes of light on the mountains. He noticed that the hillsides above Llanfair were now white with new snow and wondered if snow had covered the site beside the lake. If there was too much snow on the pass, then they wouldn't be able to finish raising the plane this year.

Evans-the-Post was heading toward the post office, lost in concentration as he read a letter. He jumped guiltily when he saw Evan come out of the police station.

"It had the wrong address on it," he said defensively. "I was taking a look to see who it should have gone to. It's from someone's Auntie Gwen in Australia. Do you know anyone in Llanfair with an Auntie Gwen?"

"You're not supposed to open them, you know." Evan tried not to smile. "You're supposed to return them to sender."

"Wouldn't be no use in that, would there?" Evans-the-Post demanded. "Then the letter would be back where it came from. It's my job to see it gets delivered. But we don't have no Mrs. A. Jones at Number Twenty-nine and the lady at Number Twenty-nine don't have no Auntie Gwen in Australia." Then his large, lugubrious face lit up. "I know," he said. "They must mean old Mrs. Jones. Remember her? She moved to live with her daughter a few years ago." He glanced at the envelope. "Look, this was posted five years ago. I wonder where it's been all this time? Funny how it's caught up with her at last, isn't it? I'll just forward it to her daughter then."

He loped across the street with his strange jerky run, his postal bag bouncing at his side. Evan smiled and walked on. There was no reasoning with Evans-the-Post. He definitely marched to a different drummer.

Harry-the-Pub came out of the Dragon and tipped a bucket of dirty water into the drain. "Haven't seen you in a while, Mr. Evans," he called. "Busy hobnobbing with those film stars, is it?"

"Nothing like that. Just busy with my job," Evan called back.

"You'll never hear the last of it if you don't get our Betsy a part in that film," Harry said. "On about it, night and day, she is. Set her heart on it."

"Harry, I've tried to explain to her that it's not that sort of film," Evan said. "And anyway, it doesn't look as if it will be finished now. We've had a spot of bother."

"I heard. That good-looking bloke killed, wasn't it? And they say the other one did it. They lead wild lives, these movie types. I told Betsy, 'You're better off out of it, my girl. Stay behind the bar where you're safe and sound.' "

Evan walked on. Such a small place, Llanfair—so naive, so untouched by the world, so simple to understand. He was approaching the school. A light was already on in Bronwen's window. He wanted to find out if she'd managed to find Edward a solicitor, but he hesitated. It wasn't exactly easy to see Bronwen and know that she was pining after someone else.

He quickened his step and went to walk on. Then the door opened and Bronwen came out. "Evan!" she called. "Any news yet?" She ran across the playground, wearing only her indoor clothes and fluffy blue slippers on her feet. He came through the gate to meet her. "From the police, I mean. They haven't called about Edward, have they?"

"I haven't heard anything," Evan said. "Did you fix him up with a solicitor?"

"Yes, that Mr. Lloyd-Jones you recommended was going straight over to the police station. It's a pity I can't be there. He gets so flustered, you know. I could tell them what he really meant to say, not what was coming out of his mouth."

"I think that's called coaching a witness," Evan said.

Bronwen looked up at him and smiled. Their eyes met.

"Look, sorry I rushed off earlier. I've been so worried, I don't really know what to do. It's like a nightmare, isn't it—someone you care about arrested and you can't do anything to help them." She shivered and looked down at her slippered feet in surprise. "Gosh, it's cold out here, isn't it? Why don't you come in. I'll make you a cup of tea."

There were a thousand things he could have said. I'm afraid I'm on duty. I'm too busy. But he heard himself say, "All right. Thanks," and followed her across the schoolyard, watching those ridiculous fuzzy slippers flap on the concrete. Her kitchen was warm and smelled of baking bread.

She turned and smiled at him. "Madame Yvette's recipe for French bread. I'm trying it again. Somehow bread making is very therapeutic—all that kneading and punching."

She put a kettle on the stove and checked the oven. "Almost ready. You can be my guinea pig if you like."

"I suppose your guinea pig is better than nothing."

She came around the table to him and put her hands on his shoulders. "What did you say? Evan, Edward has been arrested for murder. You wouldn't sit by and let a friend flounder, would you?"

"No, but . . . I get the impression that he's still more than a friend to you."

"Of course he is. I was married to him once. You can't ever undo that, however badly it ended. I once loved him enough to marry him."

Evan turned away and looked into the fire.

"I'm sorry if I don't have time for us, but at the moment I can't think of anything else except getting Edward out of prison."

"And if we do get him freed, what then?"

"What do you mean? He'll go back to where he came from and get on with his life, I suppose—as well as he can without Grantley."

Evan found this mildly reassuring but decided not to

press it. Maybe she didn't really know in her own mind what she wanted to do next.

"I've been thinking." She went over to the stove and lifted the kettle. "Maybe we're looking at this the wrong way around."

"Meaning what?"

She looked up. "I can't help feeling that Grantley's death might have had something to do with the mine."

"An accident, you mean? He had bloody great marks around his throat and someone weighted his pockets with slabs of slate."

"No, I didn't mean that. I'm not really sure what I mean. It's just a feeling that maybe Grantley's death had nothing to do with him or the people who knew him. Maybe he was just in the wrong place at the wrong time."

"And found something he shouldn't?" Evan shook his head. "I was down there. There was nothing but a lot of slate piles and pools of water."

"But those old mines are huge," Bronwen said. "An awful lot of space to hide anything, or to have an assignation. Maybe Grantley stumbled into something going on down there."

Evan smiled. "A Satanist cult meeting? There are more accessible places, I should think. And if you wanted to meet someone in private, you could do it on a desolate mountain road—much easier than all those steps."

Bronwen shrugged. "Maybe I'm clutching at straws because I don't want it to be Edward. Tell me something, Evan. What do you think makes someone kill?"

"In my experience, people kill only if there's no other way out. I'm not talking about drug dealers or organized crime bosses who'd gun you down without a second thought. I'm talking about ordinary people, like Edward. If someone has embarrassed you, blackened the family name, stolen your money or your girl, you might want to kill, but you won't. Because we've all been brought up with a set of manners and they kick in before we do anything too daft. Ordinary people only kill because they have no choice."

Relief flooded across Bronwen's face. "If you put it that way, then Edward had plenty of choice, didn't he? He could have broken all ties with Grantley and lived happily ever after. So it doesn't look as if it was him, after all."

Evan's pager beeped for him. "Can I use your phone?" he asked. "It might be important."

"Of course."

He dialed the number and Watkins answered.

"Hello, Sarge. Any news yet?" Evan asked.

"Not really. He's got a solicitor in there with him and it looks like we're getting nowhere fast. It's Lloyd-Jones from Bangor. Know him, do you? Very slow and methodical. He's driving the D.I. up the wall, making him repeat every question three times and then not letting Edward answer it."

"So he hasn't done anything daft like confess?"

"Why, did you expect him to?"

"I understand he doesn't do well under pressure. Look, Sarge, I think you should maybe check into Howard Bauer a little more closely, and into Robert James, too. Find out if either of them were seen near the mine on Saturday morning."

"Now then, what are you getting at? What do you know that we don't?"

"Nothing, Sarge. But I don't feel too easy about Howard Bauer and I know that Robert James went for Grantley Smith once before. I don't think we should neglect other likely suspects, that's all."

"Why exactly are you so sure we've got the wrong man here?"

"Because someone who knows Edward Ferrers very well is sure he couldn't have done it." Evan's eyes met Bronwen's.

"He's the best suspect we have so far. Everyone

heard him threaten Grantley Smith only a short while before he was killed. His footprint was found just outside the mine when he had told us he caught a taxi straight home. It would have taken a pretty strong bloke to kill Grantley Smith and dump him single-handed. Again, Ferrers fits the bill. And he was very, very flustered, babbling on about how sorry he was."

Evan looked up to see if Bronwen could overhear.

"So, has he said anything about why his footprint was found outside the mine?"

"Oh yes. He admits now that he went there. He said he didn't want to leave Smith with such bad feelings between them, so he changed his mind and went looking for him. He found the Land Rover parked, but no keys in it. He looked around, even went to the mine to see if he was there, but couldn't find him. So he got angry again and went home in a taxi."

"Sounds plausible enough to me," Evan said.

"Forensics are working on the body," Watkins said. "It's just possible they might find something that would point to Ferrers. Of course, being underwater like that has spoiled things for us, but something might come up. If not, the evidence is all circumstantial and we'll have to let him go."

"Maybe you're looking in the wrong direction altogether," Evan said. "Have you thought that maybe someone came to the mine to meet him—someone we don't even know about yet?"

"The mysterious stranger theory? Or, how about the butler? That usually works well in old books." Watkins chuckled.

"I'm serious, Sarge. What about Smith's mobile? Did he make any calls the day before he died?"

"Plenty," Watkins said. "But no mysterious strangers, I'm afraid. A couple of calls to the consortium that owns the mine, asking for permission to have it opened up for him, so I gather. And several calls to the Na-

tional Gallery in London. A call to the *Daily Express*.
But no calls to individuals."

"Any possibility that I could have those numbers?"
Evan asked.

"I don't see why not. There's nothing private about
any of them. Here, hold on a second." Evan scribbled
as the sergeant dictated.

"Right. Thanks a lot, Sarge," Evan said. "So you
won't be releasing Ferrers before tomorrow morning,
will you? Which means work can't go on at the plane
and I'll have a little time to myself."

"Be careful, boyo," Watkins said.

"I'll be careful." Evan glanced at Bronwen, who was
eyeing him with interest.

"Anything good to report?" she asked as he hung up
the phone.

"Nothing bad either. Lloyd-Jones has arrived and is
driving the D.I. crazy with his slow, methodical ways."

"Is that good?"

"It means that they can't get Edward rushed and flustered, which is what you were worrying about."

She nodded. "You're right. So what are you going
to do now?"

"Check on the last phone calls he made from his
mobile. I think they were all pretty routine, but you
never know."

She went to the oven. "The bread's just about ready.
Would you pour the tea, please?"

Evan picked up the teapot, poured one cup, then put
it down again. "I think I should skip the tea, if you
don't mind. There are some phone calls I should make
right away." Then seeing her disappointment, he added,
"But you can save me a piece of bread for later,
please."

"All right." She managed a smile. "You're onto
something, aren't you? You've just found out something important."

"I'm not sure. It's just a hunch. I'll tell you later."

He went to kiss her, thought better of it, and waved
awkwardly as he headed for the door. His footsteps
echoed back from the steep valley sides as he strode
down the street. The National Gallery, he thought. It
had to have something to do with the National Gallery
and those pictures stored in the mine during the war.
Edward had said that Grantley Smith was excited about
something and wouldn't say what. He had wanted to
change the focus of the whole film because of something he'd just learned. What if he'd discovered that
pictures were stolen and never recovered all those years
ago? What if he had come up with a clue as to where
they were hidden?

He had almost broken into a run by the time he
reached the police station and fumbled with his key.
He glanced at his watch. Only just after four. That
meant that nobody would have gone home yet. He dialed the number Sergeant Watkins had given him.

"Archives." The woman's voice sounded young,
crisp, and efficient.

"Do I have the National Gallery?" Evan asked cautiously.

"Gallery Archives. What department did you want."

"This is North Wales Police here." He took a deep
breath. "A Mr. Grantley Smith made several calls to
this number a few days ago. Would you have been the
one who took the calls?"

"Grantley Smith? Was he the man who was making
the film about the war?"

"That's right." Evan felt his pulse quicken. "I wonder if you could tell me what he wanted to know and
what you told him."

"Oh, he was just asking general questions about how
we moved the collection, how well it survived. I don't
think we were able to help him much. We've got all
the documentation in the archives, of course, but
there's nobody still working here who was alive then."

"Did he ask whether any paintings were stolen?"

"Yes, he did. And they weren't."

"Nothing was stolen? You're sure?"

"Very sure. Security was very good, you know. I understand the whole operation went remarkably smoothly."

"Oh. Oh, I see. Well, thanks for your help."

He hung up, deflated. It had seemed like such a promising lead. He called the other numbers Watkins had given him. The mine company merely confirmed that Grantley Smith had been insistent about being allowed to film inside the mine. He had told them it was for a major BBC production, and sounded very important, so they had agreed. But he hadn't said anything about why he wanted to film there.

The other call was to the *Daily Express*. The recipient, a Mr. Dan Raleigh, just happened to be at his desk, writing up his day's stories. Yes, Grantley Smith was an old Cambridge pal. He had called to say he was going to let Dan have the scoop on a great story. He needed to check the facts for himself and he'd call back the next day. He never did.

"He couldn't," Evan said. "He was lying dead at the bottom of a mine."

"Killed? Do we know how and why?"

"We're still trying to find out. He didn't give you any sort of hint about what this scoop would be, did he?"

"Grantley loved drama. He was suitably mysterious. Actually, he didn't say much at all. I took it all with a pinch of salt. Grantley was a little prone to exaggeration, you know—and he liked to pose as the expert when he wasn't. Oh, I suppose I shouldn't speak ill of the dead. I liked the chap, actually. He was a lot of fun at Cambridge. It's just that that kind of thing doesn't always transfer well to real life, does it?"

Evan decided he had had enough for one day. He was going nowhere with his investigation. He might just as well go home. Soft pink wintry light was flooding the valley. If he hurried, he might have time for a short hike before it was completely dark. Walking in the hills often helped him to sort out his thoughts.

"Is that you, Mr. Evans?" Mrs. Williams called from the kitchen. "Home early, aren't you? And your dinner not even cooked yet."

A rich herby smell wafted along the passage, almost making him change his mind about the hike.

"No hurry, Mrs. Williams." Evan poked his head through the kitchen doorway. "I thought I'd just change and go out for a short walk while it's still light. It's lovely out there right now."

"It is indeed, lovely just." She nodded agreement. "And snow up on the peaks already. Just like a Christmas card, isn't it?" She stirred a large pot on the stove. "Well, you take your time, Mr. Evans, and I'll have the dumplings ready by the time you get back. I'm doing hotpot tonight."

Evan's mouth watered. Mrs. Williams was famous for her dumplings—light, fluffy, floating daintily on top of a rich, brown gravy.

"You need to get out and have some fresh air," Mrs. Williams said. "It's been a hard time for you, all those tragedies. That poor man dying down the mine and old Mr. James having the heart attack. My, but it's been a sad week, hasn't it? And I was talking to my sister today and she says that the man I told you about, old Trefor Thomas, he's just taken a turn for the worse. They're going to have to put him in a home right away."

"Oh no, I'm sorry to hear that. He seemed quite bright when we visited him."

Mrs. Williams shook her head. "It's very up and down at this stage, isn't it? They say he never fully recovered from the stroke. A shame really. Before that, he was as fit as a fiddle. Never had a day's illness in his life—after he recovered from the war, of course."

"He was wounded in the war?"

She lowered her voice. "Captured. By the Japs. He was all skin and bones when he came back. Lucky to have survived at all, if you ask me, and knowing what happened to so many of our poor boys. And he was never the same. Before the war, he used to be really fun-loving, the life and soul of the party, and a great one for the girls. But when he came home, he didn't go out, didn't mix at all. I'd imagine being in a prison camp does that to you." She sighed and wiped her hands on her apron. "My sister said his son has been wonderful to him. Showed up the moment he got out of hospital and has been taking care of him ever since. He'll likely be relieved when his father has full-time nursing in a home."

"What? Oh yes, I'm sure he will." Evan's brain had been wandering onto an unlikely path. Everything had happened after Grantley had gone to see Trefor Thomas. Trefor Thomas had also been an artist—albeit a very amateur one. And Trefor Thomas had helped move the pictures into the slate mine. Could there possibly be a connection?

TWENTY-FOUR

The next summer, the summer of '42, I turned seventeen. I waited anxiously for my call-up papers to arrive, half-excited, half-dreading the moment, but anything was better than that bloody mine, even a battlefront. At least I'd see some excitement. Finally, a few weeks after my birthday, the foreman called me aside and said I was to go home. I'd got a week's leave before I reported for duty with the Royal Welch Fusiliers.

I was excited and impatient all the way home, but as I lay in my own bed that first night, it really hit me. Now that I was about to go off to fight, everything seemed different.

If you want to know the truth, that picture was starting to play on my conscience. What if I died with a sin like that against me? My dad had dragged me to chapel enough to make me believe a little bit in hellfire. Thou shalt not steal. Thieves went straight to hell, no questions asked. I made up my mind that I'd put the picture back where it belonged. But it was only fair that I went and told Ginger what I was going to do. It wasn't right to have her counting on something that wasn't going to happen.

I was a bundle of nerves as I sat in the bus on the way to Llandudno. I could imagine how upset she was going to be and I really didn't want to let her down. But I didn't particularly want to go to hell, either.

I went into the convalescent home, found a girl washing the floor, and asked for Mwfanwy Davies. I imagined she'd have to use her proper name at work.

"Ginger, you mean? I think she's up in the linen room."

"Where's that?"

"Up the stairs and at the end of the hall on the right, but you can't go up there. No visitors allowed until two o'clock, and no gentleman callers."

"I'm not a gentleman caller. I'm family." A small lie. I hoped to be someday.

"Even so, you'd get her in terrible trouble with Matron if anyone saw you."

"I'm only staying a minute. Don't worry. I won't get anyone in trouble." I flashed her my biggest smile. It worked. She fluttered her eyelashes at me. "My name's Margaret. Do you have a girlfriend?"

"Yes, and I'm off to join up on Saturday."

I ran up the stairs and along the hall as she had directed. As I approached, I heard Ginger's rich sexy voice, talking to someone. "Don't worry about it, Peggy. I'm not. He's a nice bloke, honestly. He said he'll do the right thing and I know he will."

I wondered if she was talking about me. For a horrible moment, I thought she might have been telling someone about the painting. I pushed open the door. Ginger and another girl were standing there with armfuls of clean sheets. There was a look of total shock on both their faces.

"Tref—what are you doing here?" Ginger stammered. "You won't half get it if Matron sees you."

"I've only got a couple of days and then I'm off into

the army. I've got to talk to you, Ginger. It's very important. It's about you know what."

She looked around anxiously. "Not here and not now. I'm on duty until nine tonight." She must have seen my disappointed face. "Look, I'll trade shifts and I'll get the day off tomorrow and come home, okay?"

"All right. I'll be waiting."

Next morning, she showed up about eleven. It was a lovely warm, sunny day and we went for a walk, away from the town up onto the moor. Larks were singing and the heather was in bloom. It was just beautiful up there. Ginger looked beautiful, too, but different somehow. She was wearing different sort of clothes, for one thing. She used to go in for tight sweaters like the girls in the posters, but today she was wearing layers of clothes as if it was cold, which it wasn't. I studied her. Her face was different, too.

"You've put on weight," I said. "You won't get discovered in Hollywood if you're chubby."

"It's the damned stodge they feed us at the home," she said, making a face. "Every day it's nothing but stodge, stodge, stodge. And I have to eat it because I'm always so ruddy starving, the way they make us work. Don't worry. I'll go on a diet as soon as I can." She gave me a wonderful, warm smile. "So you're really going away, Tref. Into the army, is it?"

I nodded. "No sense in the navy or air force," I said. "If I'm going to be blown to pieces, I'd rather it happened with my two feet on the ground, not in some tin can of a ship or plane."

She shivered. "Don't talk like that. You'll be just fine. Remember what I said about telling them you're a good artist."

Which reminded me. "Ginger. We have to talk about the painting. I've decided. I can't go through with it."

"What do you mean?" Her voice was sharp, her eyes dark and dangerous.

"Like I said, I can't go away to fight with that on my conscience. If I die, I'll go to hell."

She actually laughed. "You don't still believe all that stuff, do you? Of course you won't go to hell. And you're not going to die." She grabbed my arm. "Come on, Tref. Think of the future. Think of us. How will we get out of here if you throw away our one ticket to happiness?"

"But it's wrong, Ginger. I've been doing a lot of thinking. Great art is a national treasure. It should belong to everyone."

Her eyes were still flashing dangerously. "Belong to the English, you mean. We don't exactly get much of a share in it, do we? The moment the war's over, it's off back to London. Not to Caernarfon, or even Cardiff, is it? No, the English make sure they keep all the good stuff for themselves—and grab poor sods like you to go and fight their wars for them. They owe it to you, Tref."

"Even so, I can't go off with that on my conscience. I've been thinking about my family. I don't want to get them in trouble. What if I'm killed and they find that painting in our house? They'd go to jail, wouldn't they? I'm going down the mine today to put the painting back."

She grabbed my shoulders then, her nails digging in so that they hurt. "Listen, you dope. You can't back out now, when everything is about to work for us. I was going to tell you some good news. Listen to this—I've found a way to sell the painting." Her face was alight and her eyes glowing. "Remember that Yank you saw me with when you came home last? I told you his name's Johnny Gabbiano. His dad's some kind of boss in the underworld over there. Johnny says he can sell that picture for us, no problem. And he's been invalided out. He was a bomber pilot and he got shrapnel in one eye, so now he can't fly anymore and they're shipping him home. He says he'll take the picture with him. They fly home on military aircraft and nobody really checks what's in their kit bags. He'll send us the money."

I laughed. "Oh yes, does he think we're stupid?"

"He's a nice bloke, Tref. He's all right. His old man might be crooked but Johnny's as straight as a die. He won't cheat us, I promise."

I stood there, wrestling with myself. I wanted to please her so much, but then ... "I can't," I said at last. "They're going to know when they find the copy. They're going to trace it back to me. I don't want to put my family through worry."

"So you care more about your family than you do about me—about us? Is that what you're trying to tell me?"

"No. Of course I care about us, but ..."

"You do want to come to Hollywood with me, don't you, Trefor? You want to be with me and not stuck here for ever and ever?"

"Of course I do. But it won't work. I know it won't. Even if you manage to sell the picture, the National Gallery will know they've got a fake and they'll come after us. I don't want to live worrying about that every day, and I don't want to die with it on my conscience either."

She turned away and started walking across the moor, her feet swishing through the heather. Then she turned around suddenly. "All right. I've got another idea. It's pretty wet down in that mine, isn't it? Often gets flooded when there's a storm?"

"Yes, it is." I couldn't see what she was getting at.

But she looked excited. "So, if a picture got damaged, damaged beyond repair, it would just be bad luck. The water could come in through a badly fitted back panel on the shed. Such a pity."

Now I saw what she was hinting.

"It might just work," I said.

"Of course it will work." She stood there, her eyes sparkling now, her loose jacket blowing around her. She looked so beautiful. I went up to her. "All right. I'll give it a try. And since there's nobody watching ..."

She pushed me away. "Not now, Tref. I have to get back."

And she was off, ahead of me, across the moor to town.

• • •

"I'll be back in a while, Mrs. Williams," Evan said. He started up the stairs, then glanced at his watch and changed his mind. He had to find out before they went home for the night.

"Archives," the efficient voice said again.

"It's the North Wales Police again. Look, sorry to disturb you, but I was just thinking. Is it possible that one of the paintings you stored down the mine could be a forgery?"

She laughed. She had a nice, musical laugh. "I really don't think so. They were all checked over by our experts for signs of damage before they were rehung. Unless it was an absolutely incredible forgery, it would have been noticed. It's the whole age thing, isn't it? Our experts can date a picture from looking at the age of a canvas."

"Oh, I see." He felt rather stupid again. "So the whole collection came through intact. No problems at all."

"I wouldn't exactly say that. Water got into one of the huts during a storm. It was rather unexpected as the huts were supposed to be waterproof. Three pictures were damaged, one beyond repair."

Evan hung up and stood staring at the phone. One picture was damaged beyond repair. Knowing what incredible restorations could be made these days, that was very badly damaged indeed. Maybe damaged too badly to know it was a forgery? He was annoyed that he had forgotten to ask the name of the damaged picture, but he didn't like to call back again.

All right, he said to himself. Obviously, Tref Thomas hadn't taken the picture—he wasn't exactly living in luxury and he'd gone back to work in the mine right after the war. Then he remembered the girlfriend Mrs. Williams had mentioned, the one who had run off with an American G.I. She could have taken it with her, or—what if she had switched the painting, damaged the copy so that it wouldn't be recognized, and then had to leave the original behind at the last minute? It was unlikely that she'd come

back to find it after all this time. After all, she'd be close
to eighty these days and hardly likely to be tramping
around in mines. But she could have told someone else
about it. She could have sent one of her relatives to find
it. Maybe she'd kept quiet all these years and then on her
deathbed she had told her son, or her nephew. An image
began to form in his mind. Someone who was about the
right age and who had come from California. The image
that formed in his mind was that of Howard Bauer.

He had never been able to find a satisfactory reason for
Howard Bauer's involvement in this film. Maybe he had
it planned all along and was just biding his time and
Grantley caught him at the wrong moment . . . maybe
Howard wasn't who he seemed to be.

Evan hurried back into the kitchen. A startled Mrs. Williams looked up from the stove. " 'Deed to goodness, Mr.
Evans. I thought you'd gone out on your walk!"

"Listen, Mrs. Williams. Remember when you first told
us about Trefor Thomas. You said his girlfriend had run
off to America and left him?"

"That's right. Oh, he was so cut up about it. Treadful,
it was. She left him a note to say she'd run away with a
Yankee airman. They were getting married and she was
going with him to America." Mrs. Williams shook her
head. "She got what she always wanted, I suppose. Always talking big about going to be a Hollywood star."

"And did she make it—in Hollywood, I mean?"

"Not that I ever heard, and I never saw her in a film,
but then nobody heard from her again. She sent her family
a note when she sent one to Trefor, then she never wrote
to them again. Of course, she and her mother had never
really seen eye to eye, but it fair broke her mother's
heart."

"What was her name again?" Evan asked.

"Mwfanwy Davies. But she used to insist on calling
herself Ginger, after Ginger Rogers. Always gave herself
airs, Mwfanwy did. A thoroughly bad lot, if you ask me."

"Is any of her family still around?"

Mrs. Williams sucked on her lip for moment. "Her parents are long gone, of course. And her brother was killed in the war, God rest his poor soul. But she has cousins. Her mother's family farmed down the valley in Dolwyddelan. It would be her cousin who's got the farm now. You know her. She's the one who married Robert James."

TWENTY-FIVE

SERGEANT WATKINS ANSWERED his mobile right away. "You again, Evans? What now?"

"Is it a bad time to talk, Sarge? You're not in with the D.I., are you?"

"It's a rotten time to talk, but only because I'm about to attack a plate of egg, beans, and chips. I haven't had time to eat all day. What are you onto?"

"It might be nothing, but I wondered if you'd found out anything about Howard Bauer or Robert James yet?"

"What do you think I am, bloody Superman?" Watkins demanded. "I've only just managed to get away for a minute and now my egg yolk's running into my chips while I'm talking to you. Look, we've got someone onto Bauer's background, just in case there's anything fishy. And you can go up to Blenau Ffestiniog tomorrow and ask about Robert James, if you've a mind to. He was involved in a little spat on your turf, wasn't he, so you won't be out of line."

"All right, I will."

"Look, boyo," Watkins said, more kindly now. "If

you were anyone else, I'd tell you to lay off the hunches and leave us to get on with our work. My only advice is to be careful. Don't stick your neck out, okay? If you find anything, call us. I don't want to fish you from the bottom of a pool with rocks in your pockets."

"Don't worry about me, Sarge. As I say, it might not be anything at all. I'll keep you posted."

"You do that." Watkins hung up.

Evan glanced at his watch. There was nothing more he could do that night. All government offices would be closed. But he made a list of places to call first thing in the morning. Then he set off for a brisk walk before dinner. The wind blew in his face as he strode up the side of the mountain. Sheep scattered as he passed them. He was onto something, he could feel it. But he had no idea what it was. It was like groping about in a dark room, knowing that something you want and need is lying somewhere and not being about to put your hand on it. But it was definitely somewhere in that room and by tomorrow he'd be able to grab it.

Light faded fast. He reached the snowline and paused to scoop up a handful of freshly fallen snow. Then he threw it at a stunted bush and ran down the hill again to supper.

In the morning, he was at his desk, ready to go with pen and paper at nine o'clock. The American Embassy was first on his list.

"North Wales Police here," he said. "I wanted to know if you had a list of war brides from World War Two. Presumably they were given some sort of visa before they could enter the United States?"

"Yes, we do have records," the clerk said. "A lot depended on whether they got married in the U.K. before they left for the States. If the young woman married a serviceman during the war, then she'd have come to the States on one of the special bride ships."

Evan must have made a surprised noise because she

went on, "That's right. They had whole shiploads of girls they transported to the U.S. But if she'd waited until the war was over and then gone under her own steam to marry, she'd have needed a visa and a British passport. You could check with the British Passport Office as well. What was the name you were looking for?"

"I'm checking on a Miss Mwfanwy Davies from North Wales," Evan said and spelled the name out slowly. "I understand that she married a U.S. airman, but we don't know his name or what part of America she went to."

"I'll see what we've got and get back to you," the clerk said.

"Could you check on the name Bauer?" Evan added. "She might have married an airman called Bauer."

"Okay. I'm not sure how long this will take. Is it very urgent?"

"It's part of a murder inquiry," Evan said. "If you find out anything, would you leave a message on my machine? I'll check in during the day."

"Sure. We'll get someone onto it right away."

Evan hung up. At last he might be getting somewhere. He was tempted to call Watkins and see if anything had turned up on Bauer, but he didn't like to keep annoying him. So the next thing to do was to follow up on Robert James. He drove to Blenau Ffestiniog. More snow had fallen here on the high exposed hillside, and the bleak gashes of slate quarries were blanketed with a soft white coating, making them rather pretty. Evan's first stop was the police station. It wasn't smart to tread on someone else's turf without his knowledge or permission.

Another constable was sitting at the desk. "Meirion's out, I'm afraid," he said. "In court in Colwyn Bay. I'm Bob Pugh. Can I help?"

Evan explained.

Constable Pugh grinned. "Robert James? What's he been up to now?"

"Know him then, do you?"

"Everyone does around here. I've had to step in and calm things down a few times at the Wynnes Arms."

"So he's a real hothead, is he?"

"You could say that. He gets riled up easily, when he's been drinking."

"I understand he comes into town every Saturday morning."

"Yes, and ends up at the pub to watch the football game. He's a big Liverpool supporter, which doesn't always go down well. Most of the lads are Manchester United fans around here."

"You didn't happen to see him last Saturday, did you?"

"Last Saturday? I don't think I did. I popped in to the Wynnes Arms myself, Saturday. There was a rugby match on—Wales against the All Blacks. Did you watch it? We got clobbered."

"No, I was working," Evan said. "Pity. I'm a rugby man myself."

"Me too. Anyway, I'm pretty sure Robert James wasn't in there."

"What time was that?"

"Oh, two? Two-thirty?"

"I'm more concerned with Saturday morning. His wife said he went into town to do some shopping. I just wondered if anyone had seen him earlier."

"Not me, but I was off duty. I had a bit of a lie-in and a big breakfast. Meirion was on. He'd know."

"I'll come back later then," Evan said. "But in the meantime you don't mind if I look into whether anyone saw Robert that morning, do you?"

"You're welcome," Constable Pugh said. "Why, what's Robert done now? Broken another nose? Or another window?"

"Probably he hasn't done anything," Evan said. "I'm

just trying to eliminate him from my list."

"Nothing to do with that body down the slate mine, was it?" Constable Pugh asked as Evan was about to leave. "Funny business that. Still, I hear they've got the bloke. The one he was fighting with, wasn't it? My, but they were going at it. You should have heard the language. I reckon our children learned ten new English words that morning—all words you wouldn't want them to know!" He chuckled.

Evan took the cue to leave without having to go into details. He realized that he had been looking for reasons to prove Robert James's innocence, but he had come away feeling disquieted. Anyone who had got into a fight because Manchester United beat Liverpool could easily have strangled someone, especially a man he blamed for his father's untimely death. And it could have been more complicated than that. If Robert had recently had cause to suspect that a famous painting was hidden down the mine, he would have been doubly enraged if Grantley Smith was the one to have found it.

He walked up the High Street, stopping to ask at all the shops. Several people had seen Robert on Saturday morning. He had ordered a ham from the butcher and several cases of booze from the off license for his father's funeral. He had seemed quieter than usual, upset about his father's death. The last place he had stopped was the garage, to ask about a part for his tractor. That was after eleven, when Grantley Smith must have already been dead. Would a man who had just killed, particularly a highly spirited man like Robert James, have been able to discuss tractor parts? Would he have stayed near the scene of the crime? If he had burst into the Wynnes Arms and demanded a large drink, Evan would have found it more plausible, but the barman at the pub thought that he hadn't even shown his face that morning. "I thought it was quiet like," he said. "Must have been because Robert didn't show up."

Nobody could place Robert nearer the mine than the garage. Close enough, but not the same as seeing him sneaking down the pathway itself. Evan stood looking at the path to the mine, not quite sure what to do next. Then he decided that he ought to pay another visit to the Thomases. Would it be too crass to try and find out the name of the American that his girlfriend had married?

Evan wasn't quite sure what he was going to say when Tudur Thomas opened the door. He had forgotten what a strapping chap Tudur Thomas was. And Mrs. Williams had said how well he looked after his father. Did old Trefor have a secret and was his son trying to protect him?

"Yes, what do you want?" Tudur was eyeing him uneasily.

"Just routine, Mr. Thomas," he said. "I wondered if I could have a word with your father—about the war. Oh, and I could take back the tape recorder, since it won't be needed now."

"Oh, right." He glanced into the house. "Look, now's not a good time to talk to the old man. I've just got him off to sleep. He's been very difficult lately, but the Social Services have managed to find a place for him in a home." He lowered his voice. "That's good news, isn't it? I'm driving him there on Friday. He doesn't know yet. He's not going to like it, but it's for the best. He's got beyond my care, I'm afraid."

Evan nodded. "It's very hard, I'm sure. But everyone says how wonderfully you've looked after him."

Tudur Thomas actually blushed. "Well, he's my father, isn't he? I'm all he's got in the world." He glanced around again, as if listening, but all was quiet in the house. "I'll go and get you that tape machine." He disappeared into the house, then reappeared a few minutes later holding the recorder. "Here it is, but I couldn't find the tape. I don't suppose it matters. He must have thrown it away or hidden it somewhere daft.

He's always doing things like that these days. I found
his shoes in the refrigerator." He handed Evan the tape
recorder. "So what exactly did you want to talk to him
about?"

"Oh, just routine stuff. Maybe you can answer some
questions for me. I'm checking on where everyone was
last Saturday. I think you said you were in Porthmadog?"

"That's right." Tudur Thomas's gaze was challenging. "We did what we always do Saturday mornings. I
drive the old man down to get his pension. He collects
it from the post office in Porthmadog. Always has.
Then we do our shopping at the big Tesco's. He likes
that. Makes a bit of a change. And he likes to stop for
a cup of tea and a bun in the cafeteria there."

"So you got home when?"

"Around lunchtime, as usual. I didn't look at the
clock."

"I see. Well, thanks a lot, Mr. Thomas. Good luck
with your father."

"Thanks." Tudur Thomas had visibly relaxed.

"So your dad didn't have anything more to say about
the old days then?" Evan said. "He didn't mention an
old girlfriend who ran off to America?"

"A girlfriend who ran off to America? No, I can't
say I ever heard that one." A smile twitched at his lips.
"You saw my dad, Constable. His mind has gone.
When he talks, it's just a lot of rambling. I can't make
head nor tail of it, but I tell you one thing—I don't
want you asking him any more questions and upsetting
him. He's a sick old man. There's nothing he can help
you with."

No, Evan thought as he walked back to his car.
Maybe not. But he was certainly going to double-check
Tudur's alibi. Although he couldn't see how either of
them could be involved with any painting heist. If old
Trefor had helped steal a painting, he wouldn't be liv-
ing in such sad poverty now. And he wouldn't have

kept working down the same mine for forty more years. And if his girlfriend had jilted him and run off with a painting, wouldn't he have blown the whistle on her?

This is stupid, he said to himself as he slammed the car door behind him. There was no painting heist. The National Gallery said so. I'm letting my imagination run away with me. More likely to be Robert James's hot temper. Even more likely to be Edward Ferrers. Evan sighed.

Right. No time to waste. On with the job. He'd drive down to Porthmadog and check out Tudur Thomas's alibi. At least that was something positive to do. He eased the car down the steep hill, out of the village. The sky was heavy and gray with the threat of more snow. It matched the desolation he felt.

The postal clerk in Porthmadog nodded brightly when Tudur Thomas's name was mentioned. "He was in here, like he always is, same time, regular as clockwork, to get the old man's pension for him."

"What time was that?"

"Oh, nine-thirty? Quarter to ten, maybe. We're awfully busy around that time."

"Thanks," Evan said. It was a half hour's drive between Porthmadog and Blenau Ffestiniog. So it looked as if the Thomases were safely out of the way as Grantley was entering the mine. And if they had been to the supermarket as they said, then they wouldn't have returned home until long after Grantley was dead.

Evan went to a pay phone and checked his messages. The American Embassy had come up with a Sandra Davies from Merthyr Tydfil. Also two U.S. airmen called Bauer who had married English girls, neither of whom were called Davies. None of these was promising. Even if Mwfanwy was using an alias, she'd never have claimed to come from South Wales. No North Walesian would.

There was the predicted message from Mrs. Powell-Jones, who had just noticed the bigger, better star on

the other chapel's roof. Then one from Mrs. Parry Davies, saying she had heard that the Powell-Jones
woman was planning to use live animals in her Christmas pageant and she suspected it was against health
regulations as well as very sacrilegious to bring animals into a chapel. Evan sighed. More trouble brewing.
Then Watkins's brusque voice. "Listen, boyo. Thought
you'd like to hear this. Several large sums were paid
from Howard Bauer's account to Grantley Smith. And
I mean large sums. Interesting, eh? I'm going to have
a little chat with him later today if I get the time. Don't
think of getting there first."

The messages clicked off. Large sums paid to Grantley Smith. Grantley had been Howard's intern, but in-
terns didn't get paid large sums. Which made it sound
like some kind of hush money. Had Howard Bauer told
Grantley what he planned to do and paid Grantley to
keep quiet, or had Grantley found out and demanded
hush money? Evan would have liked to question Howard Bauer right away, but Sergeant Watkins had made
it very clear that he was to keep away. He certainly
didn't want to upset his one ally in the plainclothes
division.

Just as he was returning to his car, he saw Constable
Roberts coming down the street. Evan eyed his car,
wondering if he could sprint to it undetected. He didn't
feel like an encounter with Roberts right now. But Roberts saw him.

"Hey, Evans," he called. "I was going to call you.
We came up with something." Evan waited patiently
for Roberts to catch up with him. "Not that it's likely
to be any use now. I heard they've got a man in custody
for the murder of your missing bloke. But I finally
came up with a woman who saw someone parking the
Land Rover."

"You did? Fantastic."

Roberts looked pleased with himself. "Yes, and it
wasn't Grantley Smith."

"Was it a big fair chap?"

Roberts shook his head. "The one who's in custody, you mean? No, it wasn't him. This woman says it was a local man, she's sure she's seen him around. Big chap, wearing a cap. Couldn't describe his face. Just ordinary, but local. That's how she put it. I don't know if that's of any help?"

"It might be. Thanks, mate. If you can give me her name and phone number, I'll pass it along."

"Not that they'll give us any credit if it does help," Roberts said as he wrote down the details on a sheet of notepad and handed them to Evan.

"Still, it's catching the perpetrator that counts, isn't it?" Evan said tactfully.

"What are you, the bloody police training manual?" Roberts grinned. "Good luck, anyway."

"That's what I need right now. Luck." Evan got back in the car. Big chap, wearing a cap. Robert James fitted that description pretty well. But why was he driving Grantley's Land Rover—unless he wanted it to be thought that Grantley had gone away from the area? Whoever drove the Land Rover down here did not expect the body to be found.

Evan drove to Tesco Supermarket just to be thorough, but didn't get a positive response there. It was like a madhouse on Saturday mornings. If the gentleman had paid cash, they probably wouldn't have remembered him. No matter, Evan thought. He had no reason to believe that the Thomases hadn't carried out the rest of their Saturday morning routine, since they were at the post office when Grantley Smith was poking around at the mine.

So what now? He drove back across the estuary in the direction of Blenau Ffestiniog. The next step was to see if his friend Constable Meirion Morgan had returned and to discuss his suspicions about Robert James. If Meirion had James's fingerprints on file, they could be checked with Forensics against the prints in

the Land Rover. Maybe he was getting somewhere at
last.

It had started to snow again as he drove into Blenau,
soft flakes that drifted across his windscreen. The sky
above was yellowish and heavy with the promise of
more to come. Evan was disappointed to find the police
station closed and a note on the door reading: "Gone
to lunch. Back around 2." So Meirion obviously hadn't
returned from court yet. Evan wasn't sure how much
longer he should hang around. He went to a phone box
at the end of the High Street and left a message on the
station's answering machine, saying he was in the area
and hoped to see Meirion.

Evan wasn't very good at answering machines. He
could never seem to think of what he wanted to say in
the time allotted. He was in the middle of stammering
his way through the message when he glanced out of
the call box and realized that he was looking directly
at the entrance to the mine. "Hold on a minute," he
said to the answering machine. He was almost sure he
had seen movement over there—a figure darting out of
sight between slag heaps as if someone didn't want to
be seen heading toward the old back entrance.

The message clicked itself off and he hung up hurriedly, running across the street to the place where the
movement had been. He slowed and moved cautiously
as he came to the first of the slag heaps. No sense in
walking into what might be a deliberate ambush. But
there was no sign of anybody. He must have imagined
it, he decided. Maybe he had just caught the movement
of blowing snow, or snow falling from a bramble
branch. But he went on a few yards, down the path that
led to the back entrance, stepping cautiously among
snowy brambles. Every now and then he paused to listen, but there was only that heightened silence that
comes with snow. He looked down at the path for footprints but the earlier rain had turned the path into a
series of puddles.

He had reached the entrance to the passageway. No clear footprints here either, but there were some small clods of snow that could possibly have come from a boot. He stood in the semi-darkness, watching and listening. Nothing. Too much imagination, he told himself.

He was about to turn back when a sudden wind sprang up, shaking snow from branches with a soft pattering. And from behind him came a sudden, horrible, creaking groaning sound. He spun around, his heart thumping. The rotten wooden doorpost had come away from the wall and the door swung free in the wind.

TWENTY-SIX

EVAN HESITATED FOR a moment, then ran back to his car. Lucky he always kept a good torch in the glove compartment, and a spare battery, too. It had come in useful before, as a potential weapon as well as a light source. He might need both now. He grabbed it and ran back to the mine entrance. Cautiously, he pushed the door open, looked around, and stepped into the passageway. The door swung shut behind him, leaving him in darkness. He switched on the torch and started hesitantly down the steps, trying to move silently, pausing often to listen for sounds ahead of him.

Down and down he went. The blood was singing in his head and his heart was pounding so violently that he felt its sound must be echoing from the rock walls around him. He could feel cold sweat running down between his shoulder blades. Only the torch felt solid and reassuring in his hand.

How many steps had there been? It seemed like thousands, going down and down. His legs were like jelly. He felt as if he was part of a nightmare. He had almost given up and turned back when the floor flat-

tened out and he stood, muscles quivering, on the floor
of the first chamber. He put the torch into his jacket
and waited, hoping to see a glimmer of light or hear
the crunch of a foot on the loose slate to betray another
presence down there. He waited what seemed an eter-
nity, but couldn't have been more than five minutes,
before he decided to move on.

He thought he could remember the way. The first
part had been pretty straightforward, the passages wide
and square. He passed into the second chamber, then
at last he came into the great cavern where the pictures
had been stored. He entered cautiously, shielding his
light again, but nothing moved and there was no other
light. He began to think that the other figure had been
all in his imagination. So the door had finally broken
free. It had been rotting for years and the police inves-
tigators could have finished off the process. Anyway,
he decided, if someone had tried to lure him into the
mine to kill him, they had had plenty of opportunity
already.

He felt himself relax slightly. Actually, he was rather
proud of himself for having made it this far. He realized that his biggest fear had been of the mine itself,
of all that rock over his head and the total darkness
around him, not of a potential killer lurking in wait.
Well, he had come down the steps and he had reached
the biggest cavern, and even though it was bad, it was
nothing he couldn't handle. He started to breathe more
easily.

Now that he was down here, he shouldn't waste the
opportunity. Grantley Smith came down here alone for
a reason. He must have thought he was onto something
pretty big—big enough to make him change the focus
of his film. Either he had found what he was looking
for and had it taken from him when he was killed, or
he hadn't found what he was looking for, but was getting too close for someone's comfort.

Evan moved around the cavern wall, trying to remember which passage they had taken when they discovered Grantley's body. This time, it wasn't too hard. Enough booted police feet had tramped through recently and there was even a length of incident tape dropped on the floor. He crouched over and entered the tunnel. This one wasn't as easy to handle. The low ceiling, brushing against his hair, gave him the constant feeling that someone was right behind him, and made him feel very vulnerable. If someone jumped him here, he'd have a hard time defending himself.

The passage twisted and turned until his torch lit up the black waters of the pool where Grantley Smith had lain. He must have been killed here, because there were no signs of a body having been dragged—which must mean that Grantley was surprised in his search in this area. Evan looked around. Something could have been hidden in the water, but why, when there were piles of loose slate cuttings in almost every corner. Myriad places to hide anything as small as a painting. Carefully, he put the torch down on a rock to light up the area and patted the spare battery in his pocket for reassurance. Then he started to dig through the nearest pile. It was wet and muddy. Any painting hidden here would have been ruined long ago.

Then he came to a long, narrow alcove, half filled with rocks. It was drier here, but it would take time to move these larger pieces of slate. He lifted them aside, one or two at a time. There was a symmetry about them that made him feel they were more than randomly stacked. As he worked, the pile of rocks grew in the passage and diminished in the narrow cave. But still his torch failed to pick out anything like paper or wood from a crate—only more and more gray rock. Then he lifted a particularly large, flat piece of slate and stood looking down at something that made him go cold all over. It was a bone.

Evan dropped to his knees and picked it up. A thin bone, about eighteen inches long. Had animals ever wandered into the mine? he wondered. He knew that sometimes there were sink holes into which sheep disappeared. But he was now standing many stories underground. Anything that got in here would have had to come down all those steps. Too big for a dog. A pit pony, maybe. They had used pit ponies down the coal mines. He wasn't sure if they'd been used in the slate mines, too. But if this was a pony's leg bone, then a nearby hoof would confirm it.

He scrabbled at the rock again, lifting another big piece and seeing the torchlight shining on something beneath it. Not a hoof, but the decayed greenish leather of a woman's shoe with a peek toe and a square, high heel.

She was right, as usual. It was a brilliant idea. I'd been panicking for nothing. But for some reason my legs were trembling as I went down the steps into the mine. I'd been up and down those steps hundreds of times. I couldn't understand why my legs felt like jelly now. The torch seemed to have no strength at all. Down and down I went and this voice in my head was whispering that I was going down to hell. I tried to shut it off, but it wouldn't go away.

At last I made it to the sheds and stood there, panting as if I'd run a long race. Steady boy, I told myself. All you have to do is open up the shed, find the fake picture, and drop it into a pool for a while. The wet wrappings should make sure that it's moldy and rotten by the time they get the paintings out. I was in the middle of prying the board off the back of the shed when I got the uncanny feeling that someone was watching me. I could feel the prickle at the back of my neck. I spun around and nearly died on the spot. A white figure was standing in the shadows behind me. I swung my torch onto it and Ginger's laugh echoed around the huge space as if twenty people were laughing at me.

"Your face, Trefor," she exclaimed. "You should see your face!"

"What are you doing down here? You nearly scared me to death!"

"If you want to know, I followed you down because I wanted to make sure you weren't going to go soft on me at the last minute and put the real painting back. But you aren't, are you?"

"I said I'd go through with your idea and I will," I said. "Now you're here you can help me by holding the torch." I handed it to her. The wooden board came away easily enough and she followed me inside the shed.

"Ooh, look at all this," she exclaimed. "I bet every one of these is worth a few thousand quid. Pity I didn't bring my shopping bag."

"You're not to touch anything!" My voice was harsh with fright.

"Don't worry. I'm not stupid. One picture is all I need to get me where I want to go." She stood right behind me. "Is this it?"

I nodded and handed it to her. "There's a pool of water over by the wall. We can lie it in that to make sure it's good and soaked."

We crossed the cavern and dropped the package into the pool. It floated until I held it under. The water was icy cold. I kept holding it under until no more bubbles came up. I jumped a mile as there was a splash right beside me and icy water hit me.

"What on earth are you doing?" I demanded. ·

Ginger was squatting beside me now. "I'm making it look authentic. You can't just have one picture getting wet. If water came in, then several pictures would get wet, wouldn't they?"

The enormity of what she was doing hit me. I scrambled to my feet and yanked her up too. She had a pile of packages beside her. One was already floating in the pool. I reached for it and dragged it out. "Those are priceless treasures. I'm not going to let you damage them."

"Oh, don't be so stuffy. They're just boring old things that nobody likes these days anyway." She reached for one of the pictures. *"You have to make it believable, Tref. We'll just chuck in a couple more then, all right?"*

"No!" I grabbed her arm and pulled her away from the pool. The picture clattered to the floor and slid into the water. *"Now look what you've done!"* I shouted. I must have shaken her and she lost her footing, falling against me. That's when I felt something—the hard, rounded curve of her stomach.

"What's that?" I demanded.

"Nothing."

"Yes it is." I knew. My married sister had had a baby the year before. I'd felt her stomach once. *"Ginger, you're going to have a baby!"* I felt a great surge of manly pride. *"Why didn't you tell me, you dope?"*

"I couldn't, could I? Not with you slaving away down that mine. I was going to before you joined up. I was just trying to find the right moment."

I put my arms around her. *"We'll get married before I go."*

"All right," she said.

I started laughing. *"Let me look at you!"* She laughed and tried to pull away. But something else was beginning to register. I hadn't touched her since Christmas. That was all of seven, eight months ago, and she wasn't that big. My sister was enormous by the time the kid was born.

The laughter had died away.

"It's not mine, is it?" I asked her quietly.

"What do you mean? Of course it's yours." She was still trying to pull away from me. I was still gripping her wrist.

Pieces of a jigsaw were falling into place. *"It's his,"* I said, and my voice was harsh again, like the way I spoke when I came back parched from the heat of the coal face. *"That Johnny bloke I saw you with. I heard you talking to that girl in the laundry room. You said he'd do the right thing. That's what you meant, wasn't it? You and that Johnny bloke."*

She was looking at me defiantly now. *"I suppose you*

had to know sometime," she said. "He's going to take me back to America with him. He lives in California, Tref. I'd be right there, close to Hollywood. Just what I dreamed of."

"And me?" I demanded. "What about me? You were fooling around behind my back when I was slaving away down that hellhole."

"You shouldn't have gone away and left me alone," she said.

"As if I had a choice."

"Yes, you did have a choice. Everyone has choices. You could have refused to go down that coal mine. They'd have had to have found you another job if you'd made enough fuss. Other men did."

This had never occurred to me before and I was angry that she had known all along and not told me. "You weren't going to tell me, were you? You were just going to go away with him and never tell me." Then I realized something else. "And you were going to take the picture and bugger off to America and let me get caught. Let me and my family go to jail!"

"No, I wasn't. Honest. I was going to write." Her voice was tight and scared now.

"Don't lie to me anymore!" I was yelling now. The whole cavern was echoing with angry sound. "You're a filthy little tart. I bet you slept with all those blokes. You were probably laughing at me behind my back. Poor stupid Trefor Thomas who doesn't know any better than working down a mine. He's only a boy. A stupid village boy." Without warning I started crying. "Well, I won't let you go."

"You can't stop me."

My hands came around her throat. "You're not going away. Not to him. I won't let you." I was shaking her like a rag doll. Tears were streaming down my cheeks. I kept on shaking until there was no more life in her.

I found a nice quiet spot where it was always high and

dry. I arranged her nicely too, with her yellow hair around her face and her arms crossed across her chest. She looked like she was sleeping. Then I buried her under a pile of slate.

TWENTY-SEVEN

"YOU'VE FOUND HER then," said a voice in the darkness behind Evan.

Evan reached for the torch, but he wasn't quick enough. The other man grabbed it first and shone it into Evan's face. "I knew it would only be a matter of time," he said. "When you came back this morning, I knew you were onto me."

Evan was trying to place the voice and put a face to the shadow beyond the light. In his shock it had taken him a moment to realize that the man was speaking Welsh, not English.

"Robert?" he asked.

"What are you talking about? Who's Robert?"

The light was shining directly into Evan's eyes, blinding him. The figure beyond the light was part of the blackness, no recognizable shape.

"He knew, didn't he?" the voice went on excitedly. "That Englishman. I could see it right away. He knew. That's why he came to see me."

Tudur Thomas then. It had to be. But how?

"But you were down in Porthmadog, at the post office," Evan heard himself say. "They remembered you."

There was a cackling laugh that echoed from the rock walls. "Not as bright as I thought you were. Still, it doesn't matter now. You've found her. That's all that matters."

Evan blinked in the blinding torchlight. Not Tudur Thomas. Trefor. It had never occurred to him until now that it could be the old man. Now he saw how stupid he had been to have ignored Trefor Thomas as a suspect. Just because his son treated him as an invalid didn't mean that he was physically incapacitated. His own son had said it was his mind that was going. And his body was strong from fifty years down a mine. Evan stared down at the shoe, trying to make sense of what he was seeing.

"Wait a minute," he said. "Your girlfriend—Ginger, wasn't it? She didn't run off with an American, did she?"

"She was going to," Trefor Thomas said. "She'd been seeing him behind my back. She was going to run off with him and leave me. I couldn't let her do that."

"So you brought her down here and killed her," Evan said.

It all came back to the most basic of reasons again. He had told Bronwen that ordinary people only killed from the most primitive of human emotions. He should have known all along. The National Gallery didn't seem to think they had mislaid any paintings. It had nothing to do with stolen pictures or clever schemes— just a boy and a girl and the despair of losing someone he loved.

"I didn't mean to kill her," Trefor Thomas said in a broken voice. "I didn't know how to stop her from going. I was just so angry and upset, I didn't know what I was doing. Before I knew it, she was lying there, dead, at my feet. So I buried her. I knew I'd be found out one day. That young English chap, he was onto me, wasn't he? Why else would he have come back?"

"You saw Grantley Smith on Saturday morning? But I thought . . ."

"It was his bad luck that I didn't feel like going with Tudur to Porthmadog on Saturday. Usually I go with him, you know. I like the outing. But that morning I just didn't feel up to it. So I stayed behind. And that young chap came to the door and started asking me a lot of questions. I saw then that he knew. So I told him about the back entrance to the mine. He was quite excited. I followed him down, just to see where he went and what he did. When it looked like he was getting too close to her, I killed him."

He paused. Water dripped into the pool with a clear *plop* and the sound echoed unnaturally loud.

Trefor Thomas sighed and the sigh echoed, too. "It wasn't hard at all, really. He didn't even put up much of a struggle. Neither did she . . . my Ginger." His voice cracked with emotion. "It's easier to kill after the first time. And by the third time, it's no trouble at all."

He waved the torch tantalizingly in Evan's face.

"You wouldn't find me easy to kill," Evan said. "You managed to take Grantley Smith by surprise. I'm a big bloke, and I'm trained, too. I don't think you'd manage to get your hands around my throat. No, you missed your chance, Trefor. You should have hit me over the head on the way down."

"I don't need to fight with you, Constable," Trefor Thomas said easily. "I reckon I know these passages like the back of my hand. I worked down here long enough, didn't I? I'll just switch out the light and go back to the surface. You'd never find your way back in a million years. And they'll probably never think of looking for you down here."

"Don't talk daft, Trefor," Evan said, although he had started to sweat at the thought of being abandoned in darkness. "You think I can't keep up with you? You think I can't take the torch from you if I want to?"

"You can try if you like."

"Come on, Trefor." Evan softened his voice. "Haven't you been suffering long enough? Own up and get it off your chest. They won't put you in prison now. Your son will tell them that you're old and sick. They'll put you somewhere where you're safe."

"The mental home, you mean? I heard him talking on the phone. That's what he plans to do, you know—put me in some kind of home. But they'd put me in prison, all right, when they found out what I'd done. And I'm not leaving my home."

Without warning, the light went out. Evan had been dazzled by the light in his eyes. Now he was left with phantom lights flashing in front of him and the sound of feet scrunching in the passage ahead. He ran after the sound, trying desperately to catch up with the old man. It could be a trap, he knew. All the old man had to do was get far enough ahead, wait until Evan came past, and then jump him or strike him from behind.

He must be moving fast and quietly. Evan's own footsteps masked any sound. He stopped for a second, his heart pounding. Silence, except for the eerie drip of water, somewhere to his left. Surely the old man couldn't have got away so quickly? Was he waiting for Evan to come past? Step by step he moved forward, imagining a figure poised with a large rock in his hands around every next bend in the tunnel. Surely it hadn't been as long as this, had it? Had he taken a wrong turn already? Sweat was running down his face, stinging at his eyes.

Then he heard it—a faint crunching of gravel ahead. He moved toward it, holding his breath, willing each footstep to make no sound. He could hear the old man's breathing now, almost sense the warmth of his presence. Evan took a chance and hurled himself forward. His large frame cannoned into the old man and they went crashing to the floor together. Trefor grunted as he hit the rock, then lay still. Evan felt for a pulse. The man was still breathing. The next step was to find the torch. He groped around, but the passage had already widened into the cavern. It could have rolled anywhere and he was reluctant to leave the old man. He started working out in a methodical circle, keeping one foot against the old man's body. If he couldn't find the torch, then there was no hope for either of them.

Suddenly, he stiffened. He was sure that he'd heard something—the scrunch of a footstep, maybe? Yes. Someone was coming. Help was on the way. Constable Morgan must have seen his car and realized where he had gone.

"Over here," he called. "In the big cavern."

A faint glow of light appeared, getting brighter and brighter. Someone came out into the cavern and torchlight strafed the walls.

"Over here," Evan called again. "I've got Trefor Thomas. I need help with him."

"Is that right?" a voice demanded, and Tudur Thomas stood over Evan, his torch shining down on him. "You've got my dad there, is it? What happened to him?"

"He fell and hit his head," Evan said. He changed position so that he could get up quickly if needed. He wasn't sure if he was facing an ally or adversary. Just how much did Tudur Thomas know? Surely old Trefor couldn't have thrown Grantley Smith's body into that pool alone. And Mrs. Williams had said he would do anything for his father. Did that include killing?

"What's he doing down here?" Tudur asked, shining the light onto Trefor's face.

"He followed me."

"Did he try to kill you?"

"You know about Grantley Smith then?" Evan braced himself. Tudur Thomas was a big chap, about his own size, and he was holding a large torch in his hand.

"Yes, I know," Tudur said. "I got home and found

he wasn't there, so I came looking for him. He'd come down here before, you know. There was something down here he must have been searching for. . . ."

"His girlfriend," Evan said. "The one who was supposed to have gone to America. He buried her down here. I found her just now."

"So that's it, is it?" Tudur sighed. "He's been rambling on a lot lately—since that bloody English bloke showed up. He kept talking about Ginger. So that was her, was it? I half guessed. Then I followed him down here and found he'd killed Smith. That's when I knew I had to get him put away quickly."

"But you helped him?"

"I helped him with the body, yes. I didn't want him to go to prison, did I? He's my dad. And I took the keys and drove that bloke's Land Rover away so that nobody would think of looking here for him. But you did look here. You're too bloody smart, you know that?"

Evan could almost sense Tudur weighing up what he was going to do next. He was already an accessory to one murder. . . .

"Your dad needs help," Evan said. "If you want him to live, we should get him to a hospital as quickly as possible."

"Maybe it would be better if he died now. Maybe it would be better if I left you both down here."

"You don't really believe that," Evan said. "You'd never leave him to die slowly in a mine."

Tudur sighed again. "No, you're right. I couldn't. I've already got enough on my conscience. I don't want anything more. I'll stay with him while you go and call the ambulance."

When Evan returned with the ambulance crew, he wasn't entirely surprised to find that Trefor Thomas had died.

TWENTY-EIGHT

"YOU HAVE THE luck of the devil," Sergeant Watkins greeted Evan later that afternoon as he finished making his report to D.I. Hughes. "Or else you're psychic."

"Just lucky, Sarge," Evan said. "I was in Blenau, following up on Robert James, when I thought I saw someone going down the mine. I followed him."

"Bloody silly thing to do, considering."

"Yes, it was. I realized that right away."

"And it turned out to be nothing to do with an art theft, did it? Just another little human drama, like most murders. I'm only surprised that none of this came out before. How did he manage to keep it secret for so long?"

"She left letters, apparently. He must have forged her handwriting and sent letters to her folks. It was wartime—not that easy to trace people. She'd talked about running away to America so much that nobody was surprised."

"Poor old sod," Watkins said. "What a life, eh? All those years of waiting to be found out."

Evan nodded. "He was so sure that Grantley Smith

was onto him—but of course he wasn't."

Watkins clapped him on the back. "Coming to the cafeteria for a cup of tea then?"

"I'm supposed to be driving Edward Ferrers back to Llanfair," Evan said.

"A few more minutes won't hurt him. He owes you a favor, anyway. If you hadn't stumbled on the real killer, I don't reckon he'd have got off in a hurry." He glanced around, then moved closer to Evan. "I've got some interesting news for you as well."

They walked together down the hallway.

"About Howard Bauer?" Evan asked.

Watkins grinned. "Yeah. We had a little talk this morning and he confessed to everything."

"Confessed?" Evan pushed open the swing doors and was met by the aroma of meat pie and greens, lingering from lunchtime.

"Yeah. It appears that Grantley Smith had been blackmailing him. He'd paid out quite a bit and then Grantley suggested that he lend his name to this film he wanted to shoot. Thought it would help him take that step to the big time. So of course Howard agreed in the hopes of getting Grantley Smith off his back."

"Lucky you didn't find that out earlier, or he'd have been our prime suspect and I'd never have gone up to Blenau," Evan said. "No wonder he seized his chance when he thought he could get rid of Grantley."

"Seized his chance?"

"The train," Evan said. "I thought you said he confessed to everything."

Watkins's eyes opened wider. "Howard pushed him out of the train?"

"Nothing so crass. He just made sure the lock didn't close properly. Grantley did the rest by leaning out." He took a cup of tea, paid, and moved to an empty table. Watkins followed.

"You didn't mention that to us."

"I was going to. It wasn't really relevant to this case,

though. I pretty much decided that Howard wasn't strong enough to kill with his bare hands. So why had Grantley Smith been blackmailing him—love connection?"

Watkins smiled again, then took a long slurp of tea. "That Oscar-winning documentary—you know, about war in Africa? It was a fake."

Evan looked up from his own teacup. "Bauer faked the documentary?"

Watkins nodded. "He went to Africa, but he never went near a war zone. He got tribesmen to reenact dramatic scenes. They loved playing at war, of course. Then he cut in real shots taken from newscasts."

"How about that!" Evan laughed. "But how did Grantley Smith find out?"

"Grantley Smith was his intern, remember? It was Howard's bad luck that Grantley Smith had studied anthropology at Cambridge. He had specialized in Africa. So he looked at photos and recognized that they weren't the tribe they were supposed to be. After that he did more snooping and he realized that the whole thing had been staged. Well, Howard's reputation would have been ruined if the truth had come out, so he paid Grantley to keep quiet."

"Is the truth going to come out now, do you think?"

"It's none of our business, is it? It's nothing to do with this murder case."

"Howard stole the photo of himself with the Africans," Evan said. "And Edward stole a photo of himself with Grantley."

"Grantley Smith obviously liked having a hold over other people," Watkins said. "He liked to live dangerously. Like you, boyo. Just make sure you don't end up like him."

"I don't intend to. Just do my job, go out climbing at weekends. That's about it."

"Sounds like a boring life to me. It's about time you settled down and learned the real meaning of life."

"Raising a family, you mean?"

"No, I mean mending leaking washing machines, putting up wallpaper, mowing the lawn."

Evan chuckled. "I expect I'll get around to it eventually, if I find the right girl, that is."

As he was speaking, the doors opened again and Glynis came in. Her eyes lit up when she saw Evan. "I've heard all about it—you were the one who tracked down the real killer. Brilliant! You must tell me how you do it. I've got so much to learn if I'm ever going to be any good at this job."

"What do you mean, he tracked down the killer?" Watkins demanded. "It was pure luck that he stumbled on him. He said so himself. The man's just born lucky, that's all."

"That's not such a bad thing, is it?" Glynis gave Evan a winning smile. "And I think you're being too modest again. You must tell me all about it."

Watkins got to his feet. "I think I'll leave you to it."

Evan got up as well. "No, it's all right, Sarge. I have to be going, too. I promised to drive Edward Ferrers back to his hotel. Boy, was he relieved to hear he was off the hook. He almost cried." He looked down at Glynis. "Sorry, I have to be dashing off."

"Some other time then." She gave him her dazzling smile again.

"Oh, absolutely. Cheerio then."

He walked to the door with Watkins. When they were outside, Watkins nudged him in the ribs. "See, I told you she fancies you. Like I said, luck of the devil."

Half an hour later Evan drove a very subdued Edward Ferrers back up the pass to Llanfair. Neither man spoke. Evan really didn't want to talk to Edward and Edward was still too stunned by his release to talk much. So even Sergeant Watkins thought that he had solved the case purely by luck this time. Oh well, he wasn't so far wrong, was he? Evan had sensed he was getting close. He had been heading in the right direction, but it had been pure luck that Trefor Thomas had been left unattended long enough to have followed him. And luck that he had stumbled on Ginger's remains. That would never have crossed his mind in a million years. He was so caught up in his stolen picture. So he supposed it had been luck, after all. It didn't matter much. He wouldn't be likely to get any credit for it. In fact, D.I. Hughes would probably be annoyed that he'd poked his nose in again. So, no nearer to a promotion.

They drove through the village and Evan dropped off a very grateful Edward Ferrers at the Inn.

"I can't thank you enough, Constable," he said. "You've literally saved my life. If there's anything I can do in return . . ."

Stay away from Bronwen, Evan wanted to say, but didn't.

"Just doing my job." Funny how the old standbys always came out so easily. "So, what's going to happen with the plane now?"

"Oh, I intend to finish what I started," Edward said. "We're very close now. Another good day should do it. I'll get the crew up there tomorrow if it's fine. See you in the morning then."

He waved and walked into the Inn, not looking at all like a man who has just stepped out of the condemned cell. Evan went back to the police station and wrote up a full account of the day. Suddenly he felt very tired. All the time he had been down the mine, the adrenaline had been flowing. Now the shock was setting in. A large brandy at the Dragon was one option, but then he'd have to deal with nosy villagers who had heard rumors of what happened and wanted all the juicy details. And he didn't feel like talking. He felt like being alone.

He locked up and took the path up onto the hill, not even aware where he was going, just enjoying the wind in his face and the strength returning to his leg muscles. Suddenly, he found himself approaching the burned cottage—the one he had dreamed of restoring. He stood there, staring at it. He didn't know why he had thought it might be possible to rebuild it. It was a hopeless, blackened shell. Rebuilding would mean starting from scratch. And was there any point if there was no Bronwen to share it with? He understood what Trefor Thomas had been through. He knew how angry and powerless it felt to realize that the one you loved was slipping away and you couldn't do anything about it.

"So, do you reckon it's doable?" The soft voice spoke beside him, making his heart almost leap out of his chest. Bronwen's cheeks were very pink from the climb and her usually neat hair was blowing across her face.

"I've been looking everywhere for you." She was panting from the climb. "Edward came and told me. You're incredible, Evan. I can't thank you enough."

The platitudes about just doing his job had somehow deserted him. There were so many things he wanted to say but couldn't.

"So what happens now?" he asked.

"He says he's determined to finish raising his plane and then they'll go, I suppose."

"And you?"

"Me?" She looked surprised. "Life will go back to normal, I suppose." Her eyes narrowed. "Wait a second. You didn't think . . . ?"

"You told me you still loved him."

"Well, I do—like a mother hen loves its chicks. But you didn't ever think that I might go back to him, did you?"

"I didn't know what to think."

"Evan, he told me he was gay and walked out on me. Hardly a promising basis for wanting to continue a relationship. And if you really want to know"—she looked down and dug her toe into the nearest clod of

earth—"it wasn't too hot before that. This was a man
who spent his evenings making model planes. There
were fourteen different World War Two fighter planes
in my bedroom, Evan. Hardly an atmosphere that
breeds passion—that breeds anything, for that matter.
I do want to have children someday, you know." She
looked up abruptly, her gaze challenging.

"You seemed so at ease with those people," he said
accusingly. "I felt as if I didn't know you. You were
all speaking the same language and I wasn't even on
the same planet."

"Cambridge was fun, but I'm quite content here
now, thank you very much. People grow up, don't
they? Except people like Grantley. They don't." She
shivered. "So, what do you think about the cottage? Do
you really think you can build it up again?"

"It would take a lot of work," he said. "I don't know
if it's worth it. It's inconvenient and a long way out of
the village."

"But a wonderful view, isn't it? The whole world
spread out at your feet. Think of waking up in the
mornings and looking out at that."

Evan nodded. Llanfair lay slumbering in a wintry
haze below them. The road wound down the pass to a
distant hint of ocean. Across the valley the mountains
rose to the snow-crested peak of Snowdon.

"And too far for anyone to come looking for you on
your days off," Bronwen continued, "or for my parents
to come pestering me, for that matter."

"Bronwen, are you suggesting—"

"It had crossed my mind. I don't know why. You've
never even told me you love me yet."

"I do love you," he said.

"I love you too."

He took her into his arms and went to kiss her.

"Evan," she protested. "We're in full view of the
whole village up here."

"As if they don't know everything already." His eyes

were laughing into hers. "They know what time I go to your house and what time I leave, and probably what goes on in between."

"You're right." She wrapped her arms around his neck. "In which case I'm already a loose woman and it doesn't matter if you kiss me in public, does it?"

"Not at all," he said, and proceeded to do so.

"So you'd seriously consider coming to live up here— if I get it fixed up?" he asked as they walked down the mountain together.

She pushed her hair back from her face. "Someday maybe, but not until you've had a chance to fend for yourself. Mrs. Williams has completely spoiled you." Then, when she saw the disappointment in his face, she took his hand. "Come on, you can start now. I'll cook you supper and then you can do the washing up!"

She started to run, dragging him down the mountain like a small child running with a large kite trailing behind it.

Next morning, Evan was back at the site beside the lake. It was a gray, moist day with the promise of rain. Mist hung over the surface of the water so that the diving rig loomed like a large black monster, out in the lake.

"It should be coming up any moment now!" Edward exclaimed. "They've secured the collar and now they're inflating it."

A tense group of onlookers waited at the lakeshore. Howard had the camera rolling. The two divers appeared at the surface with thumbs-up signs. Bubbles came up, then, like the Kraken waking, a large shape rose. A wing broke the surface, rising like the dorsal fin of a huge whale, then the cockpit bobbed into view. There was a collective gasp, and the group broke into spontaneous applause.

"We've done it!" Edward ran around hugging anybody who couldn't get out of the way. "Bloody good, chaps. Brilliant work."

They watched one of the divers swim out with the winch cable to tow it in to shore. Then Sandie shouted, "What's that?"

They peered through the mist.

"What is it?" Howard muttered.

A white arm was rising through the water, brandishing a sword.

"It's the Lady of the Lake," one of the camera crew exclaimed. "Bloody hell, it's the Lady of the Lake!"

A white face followed the gleaming arm to the surface—a white face with dripping red hair around it. Evan had rushed to the edge of the water.

"Betsy!" Evan yelled. "Get out of there this instant."

"You don't have to tell me that," Betsy shouted back. "It's freezing in here. I can hardly move my arms." She started gasping for breath. "Help! I don't think I can make it. I'm drowning. Save me!"

Evan peeled off his jacket to dive in after her, but the divers were already on their way to her. Betsy managed to make it as far as the plane and hauled herself onto the inflated collar until the first of the divers reached her. Then she allowed herself to be towed to the shore.

Evan ran to help her out. "Of all the stupid things!" he yelled. "You want a good spanking, Betsy Edwards!"

She looked up at him with a shy smile as someone wrapped a towel around her. "I wouldn't mind, if you were volunteering."

A shout came from the lake. "Watch out. It's going!"

"I can't hold it. Get away!"

Edward let out an anguished cry as the plane gave a convulsive jerk, the collar came loose, and before anybody could react, the old bomber had slipped silently into the depths again.

"What have you done?" Edward's despair echoed

across the lake. "It's gone. We've lost it. We'll never get it back now!"

"I don't think it's that bad," the winch operator said, trying to calm the distraught man. "We have the line attached. They only have to get the collar around it again."

"But that will take days!" Edward lamented.

"Let it lie, Edward," Howard said softly. "Like that old German guy said, this is a grave. Nothing good comes of trying to wake the dead."

"Did I do that?" Betsy turned to look back at the lake with eyes as big as saucers. "I didn't mean any harm, honestly."

"You probably had nothing to do with it," Evan said, although it did occur to him that she might have helped dislodge the collar when she grabbed onto it. "A plane like that's a tricky thing."

"I'm really sorry. It was stupid of me. I know that now." Betsy stumbled beside Evan, shivering in his overcoat. "But I didn't mean any harm, honestly."

"I know," Evan said. "You just wanted to be in a movie. People have taken stupid risks before to make that kind of dream come true."

She looked up at him adoringly. "You do understand. You were being such an old killjoy, I thought you'd be really angry with me."

"I'd have been really angry if you'd drowned yourself," Evan said.

She looked up at him hopefully. "Would you, Evan *bach*? Would you really?"

"Of course I would. Of all the stupid things to do, Betsy—swimming in a lake in the middle of winter. You must want this very badly."

"Ooh, I do. I didn't realize before how much I wanted to be famous."

"Then go about it the proper way," Evan said. "If you really want to be an actress, save up to take classes.

That way you'll know if you've got any talent or not."

"Talent?" Betsy demanded, no longer submissive and shivering. "I've noticed you appreciating my talents before now, Evan Evans. Judging by the looks you men give me in the Dragon, I'd say I'd got a lot of what it takes!"

Then she strutted ahead of him along the trail back to the village.

As they drew level with the two chapels, they saw a sign on the door of Capel Beulah: "Children's Christmas Pageant. Rehearsal today."

Suddenly a loud shriek echoed from Capel Beulah. The door burst open and Mrs. Powell-Jones came flying out, pursued by a large and angry sheep. Delighted children ran to the playground fence and cheered as Mrs. Powell-Jones and the sheep disappeared down the road.

I wanted to get rid of that painting, but I wasn't going down that mine again, ever. So I left it on the wall at home. If they found it, they found it. I was going to fight. I didn't expect to live anyway.

But I did live. I was sent to the Far East and I found more hell waiting for me there. I was captured by Japs and spent a year in prison camp. Oh, yes, of all the hells I've been in, this one came closest to the real thing. I still can't talk about it, even now. Most of my mates died, but I didn't. Then I saw that it was God's little joke. He wanted me to stay alive and relive what I had done again and again.

At the end of the war, I came back home and went back down the mine. You might wonder how I could do that. Well, jobs were hard to find after the war and the place where Ginger was buried was in old workings that we didn't go near anymore.

A year or so later, I even got married because everyone pushed me into it. It didn't seem like such a bad idea at the time—every healthy chap needs someone to share his bed with, and to take care of him, too. She was a nice enough girl, quiet, not bad-looking. I thought maybe I might feel something for her one day, but I never did. She must have sensed that, because she got pneumonia one winter and she didn't bother to recover. She left me to bring up our little boy. I tried to be a good father to him, but I never could feel much for him either.

Everyone thought it was because of the war experience and the prison camp that I was such a changed person. But it wasn't. My heart had died in 1942. And I never painted again.

The painting? Well, it's still hanging on my wall. When I die, my son will probably throw it out with all the rest of my stuff. He'll never know the truth, because nobody is ever going to get this tape. Now that I'm done, it's going in the fire—up in smoke with all my dreams, my love, my life.

Pick up all four Constable Evans adventures by Rhys Bowen

Evan Above	0-425-16642-2	$5.99
Evan Help Us	0-425-17261-9	$5.99
Evanly Choirs	0-425-17613-4	$5.99
Evan and Elle	0-425-17888-9	$5.99